MAISIE & THE MUSIC HALL WARRIORS

by Neil Patrick

MAISIE AND THE MUSIC HALL WARRIORS
First published by Touching Tales 2018

© Neil Patrick

THANKS TO...
Judith Bowers, author of Glasgow's Lost Theatre, the fascinating story of Glasgow Britannia Panopticon, the oldest surviving music hall in the world; and to Sharon Reid (book design).

Publisher address: 484 Oundle Road, Peterborough, UK PE2 7DF

ISBN 978-0-9576083-9-9

Also by Neil Patrick...
The Healing Hut (ISBN 978-0-9576083-0-6)
Just Dying To Tell (ISBN 978-0-9576083-2-0)
Putting Down The Poison (ISBN 978-0-9576083-4-4)

Neil Patrick has asserted his right to be identified as the author of this book. All rights reserved. No part of this publication may be reproduced, stored in, or introduced into, a retrieval system, or transmitted in any form or by any means (electronic, mechanical, photocopying, recording or otherwise), except by a reviewer who may quote brief passages in a review, without the prior written permission of the copyright owner. Any person who does any unauthorised act in relation to this publication may be liable to criminal prosecution and civil claims for damages.

1

Max Pyle slumped down next to his wife on the front bench of the top deck of the horse-bus. He sighed contentedly and drank in the cold air.

It had gone well. Gertie had kept her nerve. It was going to be all right.

Max lay his fiddle case across his knees, looked up, and to his surprise saw stars winking in the black velvet canopy of the sky; for once there was no grey veil overlaying the East End.

He was glad to be out in the biting air after the smoky mugginess of the hall and the furious pace of the act, happy to wait for the driver's return. It felt good simply to sit there bathed in gas light, easing down with Gertie and Tom and Maisie.

Gertie was impatient, looking this way and that for the driver returning from his quick rum snifter, or his mug of tea.

Beneath the family perched on their horse-bus benches the crowds were still spilling from the Astoria. Dark figures drew coats around themselves, expelling foggy breath, rubbing their hands together, chattering excitedly about the show.

He knew it would look odd on such an arctic night but Max took off his hat and used it as a fan. The horses, held at the halter by an unkempt boy, were steaming, and – he noticed with amusement – so was his forehead.

The intoxication of performing was always slow to ebb out of Max's system. He felt as if he was emerging from a raging fever into lukewarm normality. A leisurely bus ride along the Mile End Road with the wind round his ears would be just the ticket.

Gertie was silent, stoical. Tonight had been a test after the lay-off. On one knee lay her squeeze box and, upended on the other, a side drum. In the valley between her knees was a tiny, quivering dog.

Max allowed Gertie her reticence, or, rather, was chary of challenging it. With exhaustion came tetchiness, he knew that, and he was in too good a mood to have it spoiled. But she was a worry.

When the family last worked, months ago now, in Hoxton, he'd noticed that while Tom and Maisie skittered around on stage like mayflies, Gertie had looked ponderous. She seemed even more heavy-footed tonight. Rustiness, he supposed, and the weight of the years.

Anyone who knew about the business would concede that Musical Mayhem was a punishing act. People had no idea, but Max would tell any punter prepared to listen that frankly, half way through the routine you wondered whether you might croak before it finished.

You started leaking sweat and your throat was parched but you had to keep the music as crisp as a cracker, until the very last note. On top of that, you had to smile like a bally Cheshire cat, with your chest going in and out like a concertina, and seeing a red haze in front of your eyes.

He'd seen the haze tonight all right but the main worry had been Gertie – Maisie had whispered to him as they got off that her mother looked unsteady on her trotters.

He didn't want to dwell on it, and he certainly wouldn't mention it to Gertie, but frankly she had been puffing from the start, and even lost her way for a bar or two on the squeezebox. Sweaty fingers, perhaps.

Max thought of the family in terms of his fiddle. You needed all four strings to get the tune you wanted. When he looked at the state of Gertie he saw testing times ahead. He knew now that he had been right to give up on the dashing across town doing extra turns. Two a day at the Astoria was going to be more than enough, thank you very much, what with all the carting of instruments.

Musical Mayhem was the sort of act that offered no scope for a passenger. That said, the audience had given them thunders tonight, reminding Max of the vim they invested in what they did.

The sopping shirt beneath his greatcoat testified to the sheer graft.

He reckoned that only barrel-jumping acts matched the exertion they put in. Jumpers and, maybe, the tumblers, and the strongman turns, like the Droitwich chap who went on second tonight, billed as Atlas of The Empire, getting people to hang, actually hang, from his outstretched arms. It had looked to Max as if the veins on his forehead were going to burst.

Max had also been reminded tonight of the relief he always felt when they finished the turn. What bliss to roll off the stage and collapse into the wings! Tonight, at the end, he'd felt his ticker going like the clappers and he gasped like a trout on a riverbank.

Some old-timer – he couldn't recall who – had said to him years ago: 'They pay for you to entertain them, Max, but they love to see you suffer too.'

As to all the hurtling around, with the family looking as if they were all off their chumps, people didn't realise that it was all calculated; every move worked out with metronome precision. Organised chaos, was the way Max described it, always adding: 'Very organised – and not chaotic at all.'

There was not much time to rest after you'd got your breath back, or the chance for a pint of beer. The instruments had to be gathered, checked and packed.

Max had always insisted on the family toting everything they needed. At the start he had thought of Musical Mayhem as being nomadic, primed to go wherever there was a gap on a bill. But things had changed. Now he was daunted by the prospect of long journeys, unfamiliar digs, all the trailing around.

The bus driver arrived, slapping his gauntlets together, and pulling his cap onto his brow. The bus eased away from the hubbub and soon they could only hear the clatter of hooves and the creaking of the bus chassis.

Maisie and Tom were silent; strange, after such an exciting night. Very strange. Max confessed himself stumped.

The horse bus had passed the silhouetted landmarks of the

Model Lodging House and the cemetery, so the Pyles began to gather their instruments and prepare to traipse through rows of terrace houses to the rooms above Haim Cohen's fish shop.

When they reached the rooms, Gertie revived the fire and disappeared; Max knew that this would be to get out of her corsets. Tom fetched the toasting fork and two slices of bread he had hacked from a loaf. Maisie sat on the horsehair sofa having brought her journal and a pencil from under her bed, but had then decided to slide away to the cramped privacy of her room.

The mood was heavy, considering today's good showing. Max had noticed that hardly a word had been exchanged since they left the Astoria. Something was brewing; he felt it in his water.

He settled in the low chair and when Tom kneeled on the sparse pegged rug in front of him, with a plate and the toasting fork, Max rubbed his hands together, feigned a shiver and said: 'Come on young Thomas, let the dog see the rabbit!'

Once, Tom would have responded warmly and wittily but he just smiled weakly and moved back.

Not like Tom to be mopish. Not like Maisie to slope off without saying goodnight.

A shame. Gertie had got in a few slices of ham and some Madeira cake for a little bit of a beano to celebrate earning again. But from the look of it, supper would be a solitary affair.

My journal

January 13
We are back! Loud cheers at the Astoria.
Razzle did his stuff, earning his rissole. Pa on cloud nine, of course.
Tom and I glad to be earning – and how nice to see little Eli again, less so the fawning Cecil who, as we came off, picked me out for praise, ignoring Ma and Pa and Tom. 'Bravo, Maisie, they loved you,' he said in that oily way he has.

Tonight's triumph allows me to start my 1907 entries on a high note (they say better late than never!). Actually, doing our act tonight gave me no great satisfaction. Tom and I agreed that something has changed. I think that the 'something' is US.

I confess on this first page that I am filled with guilt. I cannot bring myself to tell father that one day soon I will no longer be the sweet little girl behind the tuba.

Tom is being slippery too. His heart is not in the act.

He has bold plans but like me stops short of being truthful. There is so v. much we could do to actually IMPROVE this world instead of just AMUSING people. As Tom says, the slumbering bear is waking. The poor are hammering on our door and now we must listen.

Perhaps in years to come I will read this journal and blush but I will have a record of how I navigated my way through momentous times.

When father talks of his city childhood and mother tells tales of growing up in Crail, I am reminded that life rushes by like scenery observed from a train window.

People disappear; look how poor Uncle Wilf in Glasgow lost Aunty Morag.

I am already vague about what I did just a little while ago when I was eleven and twelve. I want nothing of my life to be lost. The journal will be for my children.

Best moment today? It was after we came off, watching Les Filles de la Bicyclette doing their daring loops in their red outfits that cling to their legs like an extra skin. Thrillingly dangerous!

Tom v. impressed. I teased him because when we talked to the riders he was as red as their costumes!

PS What a topping feeling, sitting here, mere YARDS from my family, writing things I could never share!!! But as mother says, I'm a chatterbox so I know that now I have started my pencil is going to run away with me!

FOOTNOTE: It's true that my attempt to make an entry every single day in last year's journal failed miserably but this year, now I have started, it will NOT happen again – I have new resolve!

2

It could so easily have been the perfect day for Max Pyle, carrying with him the euphoric glow from the previous night's triumphant return to the halls. But in his experience, whenever things went well there was a price to pay.

He'd often say, after life had been kind and then inflicted the inevitable corrective blow, that he hadn't shot an albatross, so far as he could remember, and although he was no saint, he could claim to be a good father and a faithful husband – so wasn't he allowed a little unbroken run of contentment once in a while?

The answer, evidently, was no. For a year or more, life had been – in a phrase his mother had always used when perplexed by life's capriciousness – as queer as Dick's hatband.

First there was Maisie's illness, a couple of months back, and the fierce battle that night with Gertie over whether the girl would be well enough to go on at the Foresters ("What are you thinking of, Max? Look, man – the poor lassie's got a strawberry tongue! Going on could kill her!').

The sickness turned out to be scarlet fever, confirming Gertie's diagnosis and Max still felt deeply ashamed that in his eagerness to fulfil the contract he had been blind to Maisie's suffering.

Then, worst of all, came Gertie's collywobbles – some sort of panic that had her running off the stage at the Clapham Grand. Yes, that was the worst – Gertie's jitters, and the act turning into a shambles.

Max's credo held that performance was just one half of being a music hall act; reliability was what kept you on the bills. Word of non-appearances spread like the summer runs.

He marvelled at the fact that Mayhem were back on a bill, any bill, things had looked so dire. It had helped to have a cast-iron reputation – all those years of being good old Max, a man who would never let you down, had paid off when Cecil was looking to fill a gap at the Astoria.

With every 'up' over the past few months being countered by a 'down,' he was not surprised that today's promising start had petered out into wretchedness.

By midday, with the family in tow, he had left the photography studio whistling, his head full of plans. By early afternoon he was down in the privy, reading the letter that would put the kibosh on everything.

There was some consolation; the second appearance at the Astoria was in front of an even bigger and even more approving house.

Yes, there were still little faults – Gertie trailing a bit, the dropped piccolo. But it was a cracking good turn. Cecil had even muttered that Musical Mayhem were turning out to be crowd-pullers; he used the grudging tone that ensured acts didn't become fully aware of their true commercial value.

But now, spoiling it all, was this blessed note from Wilf – and some simmering discontent or other in the family. And here he was, out in the cold in more ways than one – perched on top of the stationary horse bus that might as well have been a hearse, judging by the faces of the three doleful statues up there with him.

He would find the reason for the long faces but he would have to dig. He edged nearer to Gertie and remarked that it had been another good night.

'Tiring. But, yes,' she said. 'They liked it.' There was no warmth in her tone.

'No more jitters? That feeling that you had to get off sharpish?'

'I held it in. I got through it.'

'You did well then Gert. Just nerves. You'll get into it again now we've got a run.' She did not reply.

In repose, Gertie's face tended to fall into a melancholic expression. Her brother Wilf had always teased her about it – 'Cheer up sis! You've got a face like a torn baffie!' he would say.

Some Scottish terms she and Wilf exchanged left Max feeling excluded. It irritated him to not know what a baffie was, and to have to be told by Gertie that it was a slipper – and he didn't care for the way Wilf pronounced 'torn,' as if singling out the 'r' for special treatment.

Max glanced at Tom and Maisie, side-by-side on the bench behind. They were silent. Their knees were covered with instrument cases, and they stared forward, eyelids fluttering, being pelted by the sleet.

They hadn't uttered a dickybird since coming off stage.

They'd changed. Lately, their minds had been taken over by blasted politics. It was like a disease. They talked like revolutionaries and most of it was juvenile bosh. Could that be what had knocked the smiles off their faces, too much politics? Max asked himself.

Max ventured a word, shouting over his shoulder above the hubbub of the street: 'I think we can safely say we left them wanting more tonight, Tom.'

He waited in vain for a response.

'Can't beat word of mouth,' Max said, persevering. 'Better than a town crier. They'll all go off and talk about us after tonight. There'll be an even bigger house tomorrow.'

Silence.

'And what about this, you two? Eli tells me the Comet man was in tonight. The critic. He said the geezer was laughing all the way through.'

Max waited for a reply but Tom remained stubbornly silent, turning away to look at nothing in particular. Max persisted. 'We must have been really good because even Cecil gave us a compliment!'

Tom said flatly: 'And quite right, Pa. Cecil should be chipper. The place was heaving, thanks to us. Imagine how much went into that cashbox of his...'

He thrust his chin out and raised his voice – 'Compliments are cheap, Pa. Especially when they come from Cecil.'

Here we go again, Max said to himself. Same old theme: the bosses bleeding the little man dry. How long would it take Tom to grasp that this is the way the world works?

When Max turned over his shoulder to listen, he had noticed that Maisie was looking into her big brother's face with undisguised admiration. Icy globules sparkled on Tom's brow and his downy moustache. Poor lad, he had no idea how awkwardly in-between he looked with his grown man's trappings, or how pathetic he sounded with his revolutionary talk.

Tom said testily: 'If we are bringing in the extra custom, father, they should be doing the decent thing and upping the fee.'

For a moment Max was thrown by Tom's anger but then he snapped back: 'Yes, and pigs might fly.'

He was about to remind Tom that filling the hall was actually the family's job, what they were being paid to do, but feared where it might lead. He hesitated. Gertie hated fall-outs of any sort.

The sleet was lashing down obliquely, and stiffening into big, wet snowflakes. Max, who had now come out of his customary after-show fever, felt dampness on his shoulders. There was still no sign of the driver.

Tom leaned forward so his father would hear what he had to say over the hubbub around and below them. Two snow-topped flat caps came together, almost touching.

'You've had to take it for years father,' Tom said, without rancour. 'And I know it was all for us. But they won't get away with it for much longer. Eli tells me that that there's some sabre rattling in the big London halls. Fighting talk.'

Max disapproved of Tom's pleasure in hearing the rumbles of discontent. He turned again and caught Tom beaming and rubbing his hands together –'In fact I hear that there's the cheering prospect of a proper dust-up...'

'Cheering?' Max replied, incredulously, glaring at his son. 'Cheering?'

For a moment he was rendered speechless.

'I'm not bally well cheered by it. You think this union warmongering is a good thing, Tom? You actually want a strike?'

Tom didn't reply and looked down. Max wondered whether he had taken some wind out of Tom's sails.

'I'll tell you what, young man: Two days with an empty belly and you'd be on your knees licking the polish off Cecil's boots to get back on a bill....'

'Please, Max!' Gertie cut in. 'Let's just get home! You know how falling out upsets me.'

Max regretted being sharp with Tom. He had not talked to his son like that since, well...he had never talked to his son like that. He pulled his coat round him as if to comfort himself but it did nothing to ease the apprehension he felt about the future.

At last, the horse-bus driver, a stiff-legged snowman, arrived. He gulped down what was left in his steaming mug then, wheezing and whistling through his teeth, brushed snow from his seat, and swathed his lower half in blankets, overlaying them with a mackintosh cover. He clicked his tongue and the bus pulled away past the home-going stragglers.

Max could see from the top of the bus, under the lobby lights, Cecil and little, limping Eli the stagehand, checking the frontage ready to bolt up the Astoria for the night.

Razzle lay doggo under the hem of Gertie's coat. She distractedly scratched the back of his ears, and stared forward intently, as if to bring home closer, quicker.

Max knew better than to bother Gertie now. Over many years he had learned when to talk, and when to hold his tongue. When Gertie had a certain face on, even venturing a question was like running a stick along a cage at London Zoo; you'd get a snarl or a raking claw. He called it her 'Scotch side.'

The last remnant of the joy he had felt as he left the Astoria had melted away into the night. Now all that was left was a niggle about the letter from Wilf. It had come second post, and he'd not had chance to share with the family; he did not want to distress Gertie before the show.

The letter was written in Wilf's madcap style but hidden in the breeziness lay a stark truth: Wilf had been sacked again. He had been savaged by a particularly merciless house in Glasgow. Whelks had been thrown by a pack of rowdy boys. The letter said he would like to come down to stay and test the London music hall scene, the smaller halls. Was that all right?

Max knew what Gertie's answer would be – but also how Tom and Maisie might resent this new incursion into the scant privacy afforded by the digs.

The Pyles had what they could afford: One room, with a coal-burning range set in the longer wall, and three poky rooms leading off, plus a bathless bathroom, in reality a curtained-off area containing a large sink and, stacked alongside it, boxes of Mr Cohen's matzo meal. It all made for an unnatural intimacy. Wilf's lanky form and boisterous way would push things from the barely tolerable to the unbearable.

Max sensed that Maisie and Tom put up with, rather than enjoyed, Uncle Wilf's company now they were older. But he knew they each had a store of goodwill for him from childhood, and, lately, growing admiration for Wilf's contempt for convention. There was something reckless about the man, a trait that appealed to what Max saw as their growing tendency to anarchy.

When Tom and Maisie were children, Uncle Wilf was a story book figure; madly exciting because he had the dust of Africa on his boots, and owned a pith helmet, one that showed signs of active service (he had stained it with tea, he told the children, to make himself a less obvious target). He had a bagful of riveting Zulu mementos, and the yarns to go with them. He would wave the Zulu club round and tell them: 'The Zulus made it from the root of a tree so it was especially hard.' He described the bravery of the Zulu nation, and the contempt that was heaped upon cowards.

'If you ran away from battle, the chief would not just call you a cowardy, cowardy custard. It would be this!' and he would bring down the club within inches of Tom's head, and they would laugh together.

The children regarded Wilf as a hero but he was a lionheart without valour. In sporting terms, he had 'retired hurt.' He had not been rendered an invalid gloriously, by a jabbing assegai. Wilf was discharged because, on one scorching morning in camp, miles from the nearest Zulu, the ends of two of his toes had been flattened by the wheel of a horse-drawn wagon bringing a barrel of brandy to beleaguered troops gathered around the mess tent.

Wilf blamed a 'donkey-walloper' (the infantryman's scornful name for members of the cavalry), who had let the cart swerve into the over-excited, red-coated contingent.

A mundane end to a military career, but in Wilf's irrepressible way he made a larky tale out of it, cheerfully claiming that on his tour of duty he had spent almost as much time repelling marauding flies round his foot as he had tackling Zulus.

'Trust your Wilf to be the one to get his daisy roots under a bally wheel!' Max had said on hearing about the accident, infuriating the ever-loyal Gertie. He refrained from drawing attention to the sweet irony of such a mishap befalling a soldier of the 24th Regiment of Foot.

Gertie had pressed her face into Max's and hissed: 'Tell me, Max. Have you any feeling for brave people who go out into a living hell in the name of the country to defend us all?

Max's answer had been 'For some,' an honest answer but one he left unsaid. From what he had seen of soldiers, including some military musicians who had lately been sniffing round the halls for work on the side, most were ne'r-do-wells seeking a few bob, a bed, and bully beef rations – riff-raff happy to be herded together by stuffed shirts with posh names.

Max was far from pleased about everything the Musicians' Union did but he was right behind them when they wrote to the King asking him to stop foreign incomers stealing work. He would have asked His Highness to order servicemen to stop scrounging work as well.

Of course there were real military heroes, but as for Gertie's talk of defence of the realm, and Wilf's valiant role in it, from what he had read, the realm was doing very nicely, thank-you, ruling the roost throughout the world. And, anyway, if the 24th of Foot hadn't been over there in the first place, Wilf's toes would be as right as rain.

My journal

January 14

A day to forget. An awful to-do with father over a report in the Comet. I ran off and beat my pillow. Have hurried to bed now, to show him I'm still furious.

Our silly argument started when I made some comment about the students at Oxford trying to put Emmeline P off her stride by letting a mouse free when she was in the middle of her speech. Far from squealing for help from some man, she gathered it up and petted it.

Father simply can't understand that sometimes I am deeply touched by things like this, and the spirit of the movement.

Bless him, he finds it hard to budge from a position once he's comfortably settled in it. But to give him credit, he really is most caring and industrious. He's the selfless one with his hand over his bowl, declining his share of strawberries when they are dished up.

He is self-reliant and believes that the failure of others, the thousands of them starving on his doorstep, is the result of idleness rather than illness, or bad luck, or ignorance. And he thinks that I'm like Razzle and can be silenced with a pat on the head and a bit of rissole.

Dismounting from my high horse, I have to say that tonight's show was top class, only marred by Cecil's over-familiarity as we left.

I caught Eli's eye as Cecil tried to help me with the tuba, touching my waist, and his face mirrored the fury that I felt. Cecil's brother Artie is just as repellent but is at least silent, mooning around like a morose bulldog.

PS The latest of my cuttings from the Comet is a gem. It is a reply to the editor, who had asked in print: 'What are women coming to?' Today a suffragette replied in a readers' letter: 'Sir, you ask what women are coming to. The answer is: Their senses.'

Clarence Dubois regarded himself as the luckiest man alive. Each working day was pure pleasure. Life had treated him kindly, and so had the Comet. But then, he had built a loyal following from readers over the years, thereby enriching his employers.

Clarence had a routine. He slept long and deep, and followed a frugal breakfast with a gentle walk into town, and a saunter down Maiden Lane where he would settle in his favourite seat in a nook at Rules restaurant.

There he would sip a chota peg (two fingers of gin, thimbleful of lime, one cube of ice) and, opening the leather-bound menu, would gird himself for the most taxing phase in his daily ritual – choosing what to eat.

In the world of London critics, Clarence was the best known and most influential.

He had found that writing for a living was like taking money under false pretences. It was not work. Adjectives tumbled into his mind like ripe peaches falling on to grass, and he had a telling metaphor for every occasion. He could make or break a career with careless ease but he did tend to equivocate when he had a napkin tucked under his chin.

So, today would it be the partridge, or the venison? Or, for a change, some fish? ('Two beautiful turbot have just been delivered, Mr Dubois. Chef is preparing them now...'). No, this is not a fishy day, Clarence said to himself decisively, and then reconsidered before deciding, finally, that this numbing weather called for suety fuel.

But could he do justice to a main course as he would want to follow it, as always, with something heavy and jammy? His suppressed craving took command and Clarence heard himself saying: 'The steak and kidney pudding, Roland. Oh, and six oysters to start.' And then: 'I trust the roly poly is on today?'

An hour later, rendered drowsy by the food and the claret, he paid, then folded up the receipt and tucked it into his waistcoat pocket for presentation later to the Comet Expenses Department. And then, as he always did, he bent forward and tilted his arms up, as if preparing to fly, while a solicitous member of staff dressed him for his perambulations around the wintry West End.

There, he would take in a matinee, retire to a café for cake and tea, and jot down notes for his review, timing his exit for the start of the evening performance in another theatre.

Tonight it was to be Peter Pan at the Lyric – not really his sort of show. The production would be frippery, all lights and expensive scenery, and Peter would be hauled into the air by some inelegant system of wires to the wonderment of children and the easily impressed. He had seen it all before. Many times.

He couldn't complain because last night he had been treated to a jolly evening of great variety. The venue was less salubrious but then, when writing his extra weekly corner featuring music halls, he would often find himself in noisy and dingy theatres; in some the smoke was so thick you could barely make out who was on stage.

What Clarence felt but couldn't say – certainly not in print – was that he'd swop all the glitter and plush velvet of the best London theatres for a good, honest music hall.

He liked the rawness, the colour and the novelty. He even liked the smells. There was something authentic about the life in the halls.

Leaving the Lyric, his worst fears about the show confirmed,

Clarence called at the British Beefsteak Bar for a quick supper of chump chops before taking a horse cab to the Comet offices where he would dash off an anodyne, thousand-word review of Peter Pan.

While he worked away at his desk in a corner of the reporters' room, a young messenger arrived at his side with the galley proof of his music hall review.

He proof-read it then sat wondering whether he had been carried away last night, and had been rather too generous in his praise of the family act, Musical Mayhem.

As a test he asked himself: 'Did they stand out from others on the bill? Did I laugh to bursting and marvel at their talent and their musicianship?' The answer in each case was: Yes.

What reassured him further that they were deserving of his accolade was his memory of how that shy young girl came on and immediately won the audience's sympathy, before pulling that tiny dog out of the tuba. What a showstopper!

Clarence initialed the proof and called for the boy to take it away, back to the sub-editors.

ROUND THE HALLS

The Astoria, Mile End Road

We have no idea where Max Pyle, the veteran musical maestro, has been hiding of late but the Astoria has lured him back to the boards where he is delighting full houses with the help of his multi-instrumental brood.

There can hardly be a more arresting, and charming, opening gambit than the entry Max's Musical Mayhem have devised. Max's daughter, a tiny figure, appears carrying a tuba that is almost as big as she is. She blows, and at first feigns perplexity at the unmusical row she is making. Then she makes a discovery.

Your correspondent will not spoil the pleasure of those

planning a night at the Astoria by revealing what comes next but suffice it to say that a diminutive canine figures strongly.

From that moment, the Pyle family invade the stage and go at it full pelt, weaving in and out to a breathtaking medley, in what is a veritable choreographic kaleidoscope, throwing instruments to one another while weaving a musical tapestry. A fleeting glimpse of mock ballet is transformed in a second to furious clog dancing which, in my humble view, surpasses that of the Surtees Brothers and other Tyneside exponents.

Of course, the routine benefits greatly from Max Pyle's musicianship and his comedic imagination that led your correspondent some years ago to claim that here was a man who could make a stuffed bird laugh.

Veterans of the halls will surely recall his solo performances with just a fiddle and a hangdog face (that he used to great effect in settling down the crowds!). This is an artiste who for several years treated us to ingenious skylarking with a violin. After some pizzicato poultry sounds would come a memorable finale, a moment when, with great solemnity, Max Pyle would pull a few hairs from his bow and, cupping his ear to call for quiet, and with his fiddle clamped down by his chin, would hold each end of the hair and proceed to play Bach's Air on a G String.

So here we have Mr Pyle, formerly a master of drollery, back in London in a new guise and with the bonus of added talent at his elbow.

It is clear that the entire Pyle family brims with musical talent, and it is richly ironic that musical mayhem of the calibre on offer at the Astoria is the very reverse of that descriptive title. This so-called 'mayhem' is as precise as a clock movement, and the music a masterly mix that hurtles ahead so fast the audience is left in its wake. - CD

Three years before their return to the stage, there had been an

especially propitious moment in the life of the Pyles. It was when Max had come up with the idea that was now keeping a roof (albeit someone else's roof) over their heads.

Tonight, as the family left the Astoria for the third time with hurrahs still ringing in their ears, Max congratulated himself on having seized the opportunity and to have believed that the Pyles could become a professional turn that would keep the bailiffs at arm's length.

Necessity had been the mother of Max's invention. He had been failing to achieve enough bookings as a solo act to pay the rent, even when he made 'the dash' – scurrying from hall to hall doing spots.

After a life on the road, he had wanted to plant roots but in limiting his geographical range he was appearing at halls where his fiddle-playing and patter had been heard many times. He had been performing himself out of a job.

The family act emerged as the sweetest of solutions. Maisie had reached 13 and was soon to be free of school. Tom was unhappy and rebellious in his job, his first, at an insurance office. Gertie, who had stopped performing when pregnant with Tom, had time now the children were not reliant on her. All three had natural musical talent.

Max had been schooled in music by his father, a 'proper' musician, a formal man who would never have approved of Max's decline into providing music for the masses – nor forgiven him for sloughing off his middle-class pedigree.

Max felt it his duty to teach his children music, and had ensured that the lessons were taxing but also fun. Within months Tom was competent on trumpet, and cornet. Maisie learned to play everything she picked up. Gertie, back then, had been more than adequate on the squeezebox and, in the words of brother Wilf, had a voice as sweet as heather honey.

Out in the cold, on top of a horse-bus, and once more waiting for the driver, Max re-traced the journey the family had made.

Pride warmed him a little in recollection.

He had a clearly drawn blueprint from the start – 'Something amusing with Maisie and the tuba to open. Then polished multi-instrumental playing with harum-scarum action – bursts of dancing, a pratfall or two... a family having a musical beano together.'

In the end they settled on the name Max's Musical Mayhem and over months, Max began to acquire instruments on his travels – a piccolo from a drunken, deserting matelot outside a pub in Greenwich; castanets bought in South Shields from a hard-up dancer; Gertie's leaky squeezebox, now patched with a scrap of glove leather, from a bric-a-brac shop in Petticoat Lane.

The tuba had involved Max in a crisis of conscience. He had glimpsed it through a doorway in the back of a pawnbroker's in Edmonton but decided not to buy it because he felt sorry for the nameless person, perhaps a brother musician, who would be hoping to redeem it.

Two weeks later, flush with funds from a week's work at the Balham Duchess, Max stood outside and saw that the tuba was still there. He had held back for five minutes and then went in and asked the price, before haggling because there were dents in the bell. The fortune he paid, 6s 6d, had been returned countless times; the tuba became the Musical Mayhem trademark.

Max could see the horse-bus driver now, under the theatre canopy, clutching his mug and talking to another driver, then waving to the boy holding the horse to show he was about to return. Shuffling, dark-coated spectres spilled from the bar rooms of The Mitre and the Golden Hind.

Max was struggling unsuccessfully to clear his mind of Wilf and his impending visit. He was sure that one consequence of Wilf's presence would be that his already deteriorating relationship with Gertie would worsen. Now they were working, he had hoped to apply a little soft soap, make up for his recent grumpiness that had come from the worry of being without work, and being kettled up together.

Gertie was right. He had been irritable during the lay-off ('Crabbit, and downright nasty!' she said). He had missed the closeness they had enjoyed when things were going well.

Now, at least, the immediate money worries had eased; they would be secure for a while. This was a relief but in a way also troubling; having an income again somehow brought into focus the precariousness of life in the halls.

Once more tonight he noticed Cecil beaming, wringing his sweaty little paws over his cash box, in raptures about the way the show had gone down. Now, after the lay-off, Max felt a new contempt for him.

The fee wasn't good, almost insultingly stingy. But there was a bonus – they were just a bus-ride from the rooms, and not in some dubious digs above a pub in Hartlepool, or trudging round like drowned rats trying to find beds in Manchester.

Max had known Cecil for years, since he first took over the Astoria. He had arrived green as grass after running public houses. He was cocky from the start, his chubby face betraying none of the insecurity Max knew was lurking beneath the swagger and the bowler (Cecil kept the hat on, inside and out, in wet weather and in dry, as a symbol of his status).

With his quick-fire Cockney delivery, darting black eyes and his furtive restlessness, he seemed perfectly cast as a stage villain. Once he had found his feet, the villainy came out. Poor Eli Sherman, short and round and baby-faced, was his hard-done-by acolyte, limping along in the wake of his master.

Max had been taught a salutary lesson soon after Cecil's arrival. It involved a half-crown in Mayhem's fee. The dull coin was suspiciously heavy and left a dark line when Max drew it across a piece of white muslin. Home made, Max decided at once. Lead mix, boiled up in a saucepan in some scullery in Hackney or Bow, and poured into a cast.

Cecil resisted changing the coin; Max insisted. Five minutes before the family were due on, in the wings, Max asked Cecil for a pukka coin and when Cecil resisted, Max said, in very reasonable tones, unless he replaced it he couldn't possibly do his turn.

'Who'd go on for nothing, Cecil? I'm already 2s 6d out of pocket'

Cecil took back the fake, and sent Eli lurching off to fetch another half-crown.

The matter was never mentioned again and whenever others bemoaned falling victim to Cecil's ways, Max would boast: 'I can always spot it when Cecil tries to work one. It shines like a new florin on a chimney sweep's arse.'

But Max had no illusions. Cecil, and men like him, dealt the cards. Of course it was demeaning having to appear grateful to someone who was so loathed but whatever Tom and some of the young bucks in the business were saying, there was an order in life, things you couldn't kick against. Well, you could kick but nothing would give, and you'd end up with sore toes.

Max's view was that there was consolation enough for the family in simply being good at what they did. Things were the way they had always been. There wasn't going to be a revolution, he was convinced, despite the union posturing of late, and all the unrest everywhere, and Tom's dreaming, and all the beery bluster.

Max thought of a way to sum up the futility of all the recent sound and fury, all the agitation about the state of the halls. And he would let Tom have it next time he climbed on to his soapbox. He would give him a picture to think of. He would say that war with the owners would be like him standing on the parapet of that new Vauxhall Bridge and pissing into the wind. Sure enough it would cause a hooha. But it wouldn't change a bally thing – 'Except,' Max would say, 'that I'd be the one going home with chapped legs.'

Tom had a lot to learn, and one of those things was that it was sometimes better just to buckle down.

Life wasn't like Woolwich Arsenal where there was a man with a whistle to make sure there was fair play. Life was putting sweat and tears into something that set you ahead of others, something people would pay for.

Life was this, here, now – sitting on top of a horse bus in brass-monkey weather hoping that the nice little number at the Astoria would go on for a while, and then lead to a spell of steady earning, at least to see them through rest of the winter.

My journal

January 15

Put out the bunting! I am now five feet tall.

Standing with my back to the edge of the door I placed my ruler flat on top of my head and found that I have edged past the last pencil mark (at four feet eleven and three quarters).

So perhaps I am not doomed to spend my life as "little Maisie," although I cannot expect ever to resemble those ladies sweeping along Oxford Street on giraffe legs.

Nor do I expect to rid myself of the tendency towards redness of the face. A hateful blush overlays my dark complexion and gives me the appearance of a Spaniard. The lemon smuggled into my room is not having the desired effect. Although I look forward to trying some of the lipsticks now on sale in some of the stores I fear red lips will make me look even more like a flamenco dancer.

Mother seems to have twigged that I am not committed to Mayhem. Mr Cohen's daughter Esther has begun training to become a typist and today Ma gently dropped this into the conversation.

Typewriting is becoming a craze. I made it plain that I want to be an originator and not someone who copies things for a living. Mother's face revealed nothing in response.

Today, Dazzle was sick after I did a little training with him. He had bolted the bits of rissole I gave him as reward. I say reward but he had done nothing to deserve it!

Razzle, who was undoubtedly the star of the show tonight, would LIVE in the tuba if I let him but Dazzle flees as soon as he has secured his titbit (maybe, like me, he is turning his back on the entertainment business.)

PS: My belated New Year's Resolution – I will NOT wear a corset.

When the Pyles next appeared, there was barely a spare seat in the Astoria, the crowds having ventured out on the coldest night of the winter.

The loudest applause of the night was for Musical Mayhem but Cecil did his best to deprive them of any kudos they might take from this. He was reticent, lukewarm. He had learned that compliments could quickly turn into bargaining tools.

That night he also revealed a menacing aspect of his character, although only Max seemed to have picked up on the chilling malice that lay behind what others had seen as a misguided practical joke.

Max, Maisie and Tom gathered the instruments, piling them alongside a wall in the entrance of the Astoria, where Gertie was leaning, wearily, waiting to go home.

Max became aware that Cecil's eyes never left Maisie. He was leaning with his elbows on the cash box watching her every move. Razzle was curled up on the table next to the box.

The last few members of the audience, mostly older and infirm, were leaving and Max and Maisie chatted with a knot of them for a few moments, as they passed on their thanks for a turn they had greatly enjoyed.

It was only when the Pyles began to pick up the instruments that they noticed that Razzle was not near the cash box. They looked round the entrance hall and Cecil made a great play of looking under the high seat.

Maisie called but Razzle did not appear, and each member of the family took an area in and around the entrance to search.

Cecil, meanwhile, continued to lean on his cashbox. Max noticed that his expression was especially smug.

After a few minutes, Maisie came in from the street, distressed. 'No sign of him out there. Gone!' she said.

Max noticed that Cecil seemed very focused on Maisie's expression. It seemed to Max that he was studying her descent into anguish, and seemed be timing an intervention.

'Just one place, Maisie, one place we haven't looked,' he said. He walked to his office door and when he opened it Razzle trotted out and ran to Maisie.

'Solved! The case of the disappearing dog!' he said, stooping to stroke Razzle at Maisie's feet. 'Now how did he get in there?"

Max knew the answer. Only Cecil ever went into Cecil's office; it was a rule invoked by an insecure and self-important man.

Later, when they were on the horse-bus, Max said to Gertie: 'That business with Razzle was no joke. It was to show his power. He set it all up. Hid the dog. He wanted our Maisie to be grateful to him.'

'Surely not, Max. It was just his silly idea of a prank. Don't credit him with thinking.'

'He wanted attention from Maisie, and he wanted to remind us how we are in his power. He enjoyed seeing her getting upset and he couldn't wait to be the one who made it all better.'

'Bosh! You're seeing what isn't there Max.'

Sometimes Gertie's reluctance to confront the obvious infuriated Max. This was one of those occasions.

'All right Gert, here's something to think about. Remember how Maisie put Razzle on Cecil's desk while we got the tackle together?'

'Yes. He was curled up asleep.'

'So can you tell me how a dog that has difficulty getting down a doorstep, lowered himself from a table top five feet high and then got into an office used by only one person, all within the space of a minute?'

Gertie was silent. Then she said hurriedly, as if she had not heard: 'It's time we were getting up. We're at nearly at the stop.'

As the horse-bus dropped the Pyles off, they found themselves slipping on ice formed after the daytime thaw.

On the quarter-mile walk home through streets, measured out by pools of light from the street lamps, each family member carried musical instruments, and, with them, small hopes that eased the most tiresome stage of the journey.

Tom's wish was that there would be embers in the fireplace, heat enough to redden a shovelful of coal so that he could get out the toasting fork and go to bed with the edge taken off his hunger.

He was famished all the time nowadays. If Ma had an egg left in her food cupboard, he might fry it. Then he remembered that he had noticed earlier that there were tracks made in the solidified fat where a mouse had skittered across the pan.

He also hoped that when they finally reached the rooms, father wouldn't linger round the fire. When Pa dallied, he tended to drone on. He'd been especially gassy lately, Tom had noticed, and his talking had begun to feel like a tether.

Maisie walked with her arms encircling the tuba.

Her hope was for some solitary thinking time before bed, and that she would not be too tired to continue writing her journal. It was so easy not to bother. She was exhausted and tonight her resolution to write an account every day would be tested. She would have to think it as a ship's log that had to be filled in, on pain of punishment.

And Gertie? She hoped that nothing would stop her getting off her feet and into bed as soon as possible. But of course there would be things to do, the routine things.

She would fill the big kettle for mugs of Bovril, a consoling nightcap when the rooms were so cold that you could see your breath. She had bought a new jar, with other groceries, on the strength of the family earning again.

When emptying her wicker basket, she had noticed that there was a new drawing and motto on the label: 'The Two Infallible

Powers – The Pope and Bovril' and immediately thought about her father, who would have thrown the jar off Crail harbour wall.

After making the drinks, she would fill the big kettle again and, in turn, the stoneware hot water bottles for Tom and Maisie. This act of solicitude was redolent of their childhood, and a reminder of the needs they had outgrown.

And then, finally, there would be the joy of shedding her corsets, and easing out of her boots.

'I'm fair puckled,' she sighed to herself, as she walked. Doing the turn had drained her.

She feared Max would want to talk before he became unwound enough for bed, so she planned to get into her night gown immediately, put her head down on the bolster and feign sleep, willing herself to dream of something soothing after the agitation of the night. This retreat into the past had become a nightly ritual.

She would be a girl again, living in the cottage in Crail, overlooking the sea. She would summon up a panorama from long ago: Players emerging from Crail Golf Hotel, and stepping on to a length of undulating fine green tweed, stick-like figures bathed in the late-evening sunlight, their shadows twice as long as their bodies.

She would watch them, as she once did from the window, with their clubs and bags, stopping and starting, pausing to weigh up a shot, then swinging and stooping.

As she sat at the window, the smell of smoked haddie would drift in from the scullery, and on the windowsill there would be a jam jar filled with wilting harebells. It really had been very much like that, her childhood by the sea, a taste of heaven before the black clouds came over and they had to move to Glasgow.

- *Mother, why are we havin' tae go away?*

- *We have tae, that's all, Gertie. But wait till ye see Glasgow, and the People's Palace and the Kelvingrove Park! Jeez! Just think, all they ice cream shops! They trams!*

- But will I no see Isobel again? Or Nan? Or Miss McNairn?

- Sure Gertie! We'll come back some day. Dinnae sniffle. Look. Here's a promise. We'll go doon the watter! We'll get on a boat called the King Edward and sail oot and away frae the city, to Dunoon and Rothesey, and we'll send them all a postcard wi' a picture on...

- But mammy, could we no get the boat man tae just sail us back tae Crail?

As Gertie walked the last yards on aching feet she was preoccupied with one more wish – that whatever had been bubbling away within the family would show itself so it could be tackled, and to get along with Max like she used to.

He had always been a selfless husband and doting father, and she knew he was also unhappy about their growing remoteness, and puzzled by whatever was brewing with the children.

It was clear to Gertie that he had been troubled especially by Maisie's quite sudden mutation into an opinionated and spirited woman. He was perplexed by Tom's anger, and the boy's fiery questioning of beliefs he held dear.

She understood. She felt what mothers feel, regret that their children have to grow up, and the painful things that happened as they did. But they really did have to grow up, and Max could not halt what was happening.

If she were being honest, she would have liked to preserve them – not like butterflies pinned to a bit of cork, but preserved nonetheless; living, breathing and laughing, in a place like Crail – the Crail of her dreams, where the clock hands didn't move and calendars were turned to the wall.

Max was sitting alone enjoying hearing the coal spit and splutter. The embers turned carmine and then very slowly to orange. When sleep finally overtook him, there was just grey ash.

Max woke suddenly, feeling the cold. He pulled together the heavy, velvety curtains and saw icy tracery on the inside of the window. The clock showed half past two. Stretching and yawning, he took Wilf's letter from his waistcoat pocket and read it again.

It was addressed to him and not his sister; a cunning touch, Max decided. Wilf knew that Gertie would take Wilf in without hesitation but he might be seen as a stumbling block and so Wilf had addressed it directly 'To Max Pyle', challenging him to say no, in opposition to Gertie.

It was such a jolly note considering Wilf's undeniable run of bad luck; army service cut short, bereavement, collapse of livelihood. But it was odds-on that he was still undaunted, laughing at life. Max had to give it to him, Wilf was a brick – or was he just plain potty? Could people be clever and stupid at the same time? Max knew he would never get to the bottom of this pickle of a man.

Lighting a candle, Max went down to brave the paralysing cold of the lavatory in the yard. Then he crept, shivering, into the bedroom, and tentatively edged towards Gertie's warm bulk and was asleep immediately.

In his dream an elderly doctor sporting a droopy moustache and wearing pince-nez was pinching the floppy limbs of a woman spread-eagled on his examination couch.

Max recognised her as the contortionist Juanita, The Boneless Woman from Brazil, the turn mentioned in Wilf's letter from Glasgow. With an irony that Wilf had found hilarious, she had lost her spot on the bill at The Queen's having broken her leg, falling out of The Sarry Heid in Gallowgate after downing several bottles of Fowler's Wee Heavy.

Juanita was a woman Max despised, doing the sort of act he abhorred. Her origins lay a long way from Brazil, in Tring in fact. Her name was Blanche and not Juanita, and was far from being boneless, as the fracture proved; in fact she was known to have used her bones to good effect in a couple of manager's offices.

He had seen her working, been on a bill with her. To his mind, she had no ability, except to slither about to light classics, and in doing so took the bread from the mouths of talented folk.

In his dream, the doctor was turning from the prostrate woman saying gravely: 'I am so sorry, miss. I would dearly like to mend your leg but, curiously, you appear to have no bones...'

Max was woken by his own laughter.

An elbow dug into his ribs.

'Max! For the love of god, settle down!'

My journal

January 16

Tonight Razzle caused a commotion by going missing just as we were about to catch the horse-bus. I was beside myself after we'd searched around the entrance of the Astoria. Then Cecil had a brainwave: Could he be in the office?

Oh, the relief when he found him!

Father seems to think that it was some kind of cruel jape by Cecil but I cannot believe that even he would be quite so heartless.

A stunning crit in the Comet! It has been clipped out and propped against the clock on the mantelpiece. It makes me wonder whether I should be staying with what I'm good at after all, and not indulging in my grand plan to win women's suffrage and fight for the relief of poverty.

But, no! I must not have my head turned, and today I learned why.

Taking a short cut back to Mile End Road I found myself passing the entrance to an alley between dilapidated dwellings.

Along this passage, a dozen filthy children with sour, old faces were busy wielding axes, making kindling for sale. Others were sitting on stone steps, and one group was huddled round a fire made from rubbish. Not ONE child was dressed against this polar weather. Not one.

It was the sight of a girl of perhaps six years that stays with me, and convinces me that to stay in the music hall would be to fritter away my life.

Her threadbare coat trailed to her ankles and beneath the hem she wore a single shoe. There was something about that solitary shoe, and the girl's pitiful acceptance that one over-large, tattered shoe was a good deal better than no shoes at all, that brought me near to tears as I went in search of a tram.

A similar scene can be encountered any day of the week here in the East End, just one corner of the biggest city in the world, the richest city the world has ever known, and the seat of an Empire of a size that defies belief.

Max carried Wilf's letter with him, and next day, after the show, on the horse-bus, he was tempted to share it with Gertie but decided he would leave it until they got back to the rooms. This was not the place for landing such a thunderbolt, and anyway there was the clamour of cars, the racket from the motor-buses, and the clatter of horses' hoofs, to contend with.

He knew that Gertie would be upset and make a bit of a scene if there was any resistance to putting Wilf up, and Max needed to have his say.

When he did, he would ask her to remember what happened last time, and also when they had digs in Hackney. Of course, Gertie would have conveniently wiped from her mind the conflict that summer when the tide went out on Wilf's work on Yarmouth sands and, marooned once more, he came to stay for a couple of days that extended into weeks.

The family routine went to pot. He and Gertie were at each other like terriers in a sack. And when Tom and Maisie weren't bickering they were noisily debating topics Wilf had planted in their heads. 'Uncle Wilf says...' was a familiar cry.

Despite all this, Gertie had been sad to see her brother go when eventually he found work and left for Paisley, reviving his long-abandoned ventriloquism act.

That morning, when at long last the guard's whistle echoed

round the station roof, and the big, greasy engine wheels turned and Wilf disappeared north in a cloud of steam, Max felt as if a particularly fractious poltergeist had been exorcised.

He remembered that he had been elated at getting Gertie back, to talk as they used to talk, without Wilf wading in. He knew there would be more meat to go round, fewer of those sodden cloutie dumplins Wilf adored. He had looked forward to having more time at the sink, and shorter waits at the top of the stairs for the privy. He would reclaim his razor and have immediate access to his newspaper.

He would no longer be greeted, as he left his bedroom, by a streak of pump water in long johns, either coughing his heart up, studying his toe stumps, or playing a blasted reveille on his cornet.

And what a relief it had been to be spared the daily irritation of Gertie and Wilf lapsing into broad Scots, of them chortling conspiratorially over their mickles and muckles, their goonies and their dinna kens.

It had left him feeling excluded. He was sure that Wilf, who had, like many other Scottish artistes, 'gone English'– diluted his dialect over the years to be comprehensible to a countrywide audience – deliberately had been piling on what Max called 'the haggis-bashing stuff.'

It was Wilf's way of parading his special bond with Gertie, he was sure. When Wilf was around, Gertie used phrases she had hardly uttered in all their years of marriage, and her return to her native tongue became almost comically exaggerated as Wilf's departure date grew closer.

On that red-letter day, when Wilf was leaving for Scotland, Gertie had noticed that his collar was besmirched by soot.

'Wilf! Yon's as black as the Earl o' Hell's weskit!' she had protested, fetching a clean collar from Max's drawer. Max hadn't cared for the sly smile that Wilf gave by way of a thank-you.

Through tears Gertie had prattled on about him having once been just a peely-wally bairn who had been dildered aboot by their faither. Max couldn't recall a single peely-wally or a dilder having passed Gertie's lips before.

He had no difficulty in predicting what Gertie's reaction to the letter would be tonight when, at last, they reached the rooms. In fact, he'd bet a guinea on what she'd say...

'The poor man will still be grieving for Morag... he's been so unlucky with his work... we can't turn him away.... His toes...he has nobody.'

Max allowed for all that as best he could. But his personal well of sympathy had been dry, bone dry, for some time. What Max perceived was that Wilf was at it again, pulling Gertie's strings, wheedling his way in. And, of course, once more promising yet another new start.

'I'm already at work on a bit of business, totally different, that will tip the punters off their seats,' he wrote. 'If I don't freeze to death on the train, I can use those eight hours to get it ship-shape and we can look for a slot in London.'

We? We? Max was especially needled by the presumptuousness of the postscript: 'Don't worry too much about sleeping quarters or food, etc. A bowl of workhouse skilly will do for me! Might even bring you some of the whelks they threw at me (ho, ho!).

PPS: Reference rent. Be assured I will be in a position soon to settle up when Morag's affairs are sorted out.'

Rent?

When Max had first read that word, down in the privy just before they had left for the Astoria, his heart plummeted. Wilf was really setting his stall out. You don't offer rent for a couple of overnighters.

Max shook the snow out of his collar. Fresh flakes landed on his eyelids. He was finding it difficult now to see ahead, in more ways than one.

They were rounding the corner into Nelson Terrace and on the breeze was the distinctive whiff of Haim Cohen's fish shop. It was a smell that even when the shop was closed somehow snaked into the atmosphere and found its way into each of the rented rooms.

Max said that it was down to the fact that Mr Cohen fried in olive oil. It was olive oil, so that the fish he sold would be kosher, and because the fish done this way tasted nice cold when eaten next day on the Sabbath. Gertie doubted this; surely olive oil was just for bunged-up ears?

Max would normally have been nicely relaxed back at the rooms once he had settled at the fire with his Bovril, unbuttoned his waistcoat and taken his boots off. But tonight the unease he had felt on the ride home lingered and wouldn't let him be.

The news of Wilf's return was bad enough. But at the back of Max's mind there was another irritant.

After the show, Eli had slipped the news that now more and more halls were being taken over by syndicates of owners, there was a bit of a squeeze starting, speculation about new rules concerning where artistes could and couldn't work, rumours about extra, unpaid matinees.

There was even talk about retaliation if the owners didn't cough up for them. Troubling. But then, Max asked himself, when had things been any different? And as to rebelling, did anyone really believe that a bunch of singers, and wire walkers and fire breathers could unite to bring the owners to heel?

He sat back, eyes shut, thinking, blowing pipe smoke out through his nose. The moisture inside the pipe bowl bubbled from time to time and occasionally Max would shake the stem of the pipe at the fire, sending a spurt of spit hissing into the flames.

He sipped from the mug Gertie had brought, and mulled matters over. The musicians' union was certainly getting stronger and pushier but then people everywhere seemed to be rolling up their sleeves and putting their daddles up for a scrap.

Nowadays there was a Karl Marx in every London back room bar, with disciples practically draped around their feet. You couldn't say good morning to Tom at the moment without him coming back at you with an earful about what Keir Hardie thinks.

He had overheard Tom telling Maisie that he'd been envious of one of his friends who had been drinking in Clerkenwell and heard some Russian spouting passionately about the need for a violent uprising.

When Max had tutted in disgust, Tom had teasingly challenged his father to say what he thought of this Russian's assertion that one man with a gun was all that was needed to control a hundred men without one, and that ends justified means.

Max had stammered and grown angry under Tom's steady gaze, and had felt humiliated. Tom was not only tenacious; he was almost rabid in his pursuit of truth. Increasingly, Max, who had his views tidily packaged, was found wanting in justifying them, or persuading Tom of the merit of them.

Max would concede, a little reluctantly, that although unions could be a force for good they ought to understand how far they could go. He had to acknowledge that some would see him as an enemy of advancement but that was the way he was.

Harking back, he remembered that his deeply conservative father had talked approvingly about the East End match girls' strike that shamed their bosses and captivated half the nation, and had shown grudging admiration for those who fought for the Docker's Tanner.

He could understand that. But you had to pick your fights. In Max's view there was no chance of winning against the new breed of music hall owners. They would just soak up the punishment. It wouldn't be a fair fight. The men running the biggest halls in London were invincible now, the Stolls, the Mosses and the Thorntons, and your Adney Paynes. They could brazen it out.

If artistes were daft enough to strike, the bosses would simply bring in amateurs and retired acts, and try to intimidate proper performers by threats. Some artistes would buckle – in fact Max knew many who would decide on the spot to put bread and cheese before principles.

You could hardly look to the big stars for support, and expect them to sacrifice fat fees. So the cause was lost before the bell for the first round. In Max's opinion, the union might as well try whipping one of Sanger's elephants into shape with an ostrich feather.

There was something the agitators hadn't realised – and he was sad to say he counted Tom as an agitator now he was dabbling in dangerous ideas. It was that work in the halls was not like machine-minding, or stitching suits, or the sort of job where the day's work could be accounted for in a clerk's ledger. It was a fickle business.

Sometimes you were in, sometimes out. On a stage you had maybe 4,000 bosses judging you, and a manager eyeing you from the wings.

It was like life, precarious, and you have your rich and your poor. You've got your stars being paid a king's ransom for singing a clutch of popular songs, and America offering them even greater riches. And if you have a songwriter's knack of getting a 'catch' into a song, so that everyone was whistling it, life was featherbedded, butter-over-bacon.

But for the most part, the business is packed with small fry. Little individuals, stage hands like Eli, and pit orchestra players, and in London alone, hundreds of artistes giving their talent in exchange for a modest living.

Max tried to consolidate the message he had for Tom: We're all disposable, and when all's said and done, except for the big names, we're all having to dance to the dots on the score the owners hand you.

It was the natural order of things, so it didn't surprise him that the bosses were looking for a few more drops of blood from the same stone. They had been bullying people in exactly the same way all those years ago at the match factory, and in the docks, so not much had changed.

He was not in the least surprised to hear no mention from the owners of extra spondulicks in return for extra work. He summoned up one of his favourite sayings: 'What do you expect from pigs but grunt?'

My journal

January 17

Ghastly news!!! Uncle Wilf is coming to lodge with us again!

Just before bed, I came up from the privy and father was holding a letter under the light for mother to read. He looked as if he was learning of the death of someone dear. Yet mother was wearing an angelic smile.

Tom was in his room with his books, and they called to him, and mother told us that Uncle Wilf was going through a sticky time once again...needed a roof over his head ... had been unlucky with his work... had no one but us...was still suffering with his chest and what was left of his toes.

We nodded dutifully. Tom sighed when he heard the news and mother scolded him.

To be fair, Uncle Wilf HAS been dealt many blows and comes through gamely. He keeps smiling that glistening smile, the product of his horrid arnica nut paste and some foul powder he buys.

(Alas, arnica was not the answer for poor Aunt Morag who had all her teeth extracted as a twenty-first birthday present and wore her false ones for the first time on her wedding day).

I am blessed with good teeth but am still trying to find a remedy for my thermometer for a face. In hot and cold, my cheeks are still becoming unpleasantly red. Egg and borax works but the dreaded redness always returns, instantly on these wintry days.

Talking of my face reminds me of a painful moment involving Uncle Wilf.

He had given me a book of poetry for my birthday, a celebration that was spoiled for me by the eruption of a truly mountainous spot on my chin.

While I tried to hide it (and my embarrassment), dear Uncle Wilf went round the house absent-mindedly singing The Simple Pimple, the old George Robey song!

Of course, it was not meant but unintended cruelty is just as painful as cruelty inflicted with pleasure.

To welcome back her prodigal brother, mother is procuring a fatted calf – brisket, actually – Mr Cohen and his kosher oven allowing. Father has a face longer than his fiddle. A telegram is expected.

PS: Something MUST be done soon about my boot. The hole has grown and tonight the piece of playing card I had put in merely served to soak up freezing water. But we are back working at last, so very soon I will ask father to please SAVE MY SOLE!

6

On the fourth night at the Astoria, drawing a full house, Musical Mayhem had been pressed by prolonged applause into giving an encore. Afterwards, Cecil had joined Max at the side of the stage and told him that he might see his way to giving the family another week's work, and another £1 on the fee.

Max had tried to appear nonchalant but was jubilant. He told the family the good news on the bus. They made approving noises but Tom spoiled the moment for Max by wondering aloud what percentage the £1 represented of the increased Astoria profit for the week.

When the Pyles reached the rooms they clumped up noisily, arms grasping instruments. Max felt his way into the main room, held a match to the mantles of the wall lights, moved the Comet from his chair to the floor, and sat down.

He shook coal from the scuttle on to the mound of ashes in the fireplace and sparks rose. Things felt better if you got in front of a fire.

It was good to have Razzle, reunited with Dazzle, dozing at his feet. Max sometimes envied the dogs their life of privilege. Occasionally he would nip them by the side of their mouths, and put on the sort of voice generally used to talk to babies, look into their eyes and tell them how lucky they were to be a cut above their peers, rat-catchers in northern mills.

The coal was beginning to crackle. Max picked up the Comet and began to re-read what he had read that morning, biding his time. He hoped that the young ones would stay up with him a while at the end of what had been a special night. It would be good, talking. Easing down. Making plans to build on tonight's business.

Tom came up from the privy but instead of poking around at the table for a scratch supper shouted goodnight from behind the half-open door of his room. Max heard Maisie go downstairs and a few minutes later come up again.

'Goodnight Father,' she called brightly (too brightly, he judged) from her room. No peck on the cheek. No word about the encore, or the increased fee.

He wondered whether she was still smarting from the morning, when they had fallen out over a report in the Comet. She had praised the solidarity of suffragettes who were reported to have turned away the dinner offered by jailers, in response to one of their number having been treated badly.

Max had taken issue.

'They want punishing, not pampering. I'd have been straight John Bull with them. I'd have said: "Please yourselves, ladies. Starve if you want for as long as you want. All the more for the those who are hungry."'

Maisie had fiercely argued the suffrage cause, her cheeks reddening, and as Max conceded to himself later, she had out-manoeuvred him.

He had countered with a point about what he called mollycoddling by the authorities – 'If they go looking for trouble they shouldn't be surprised when they find it,' he said, and immediately regretted having sounded so pompous.

Maisie almost choked with exasperation.

'But Pa, you must admire the self-sacrifice these women are making. Imagine: They are going to jail for an ideal, a principle. These women are saying they will risk their lives for a cause. That can't be too difficult for someone to appreciate, surely?'

'And that someone is me?' he demanded, giving Maisie a hostile stare that he knew would quieten her.

Unlike some children in music hall families, Maisie and Tom had been educated wherever they found themselves, tutored, usually, when earnings were good. Max was intent on giving them the sort of start his father had given him. He had always stimulated them, tried to teach them about the world. Now he felt that they were throwing it back in his face. Of course Wilf hadn't helped by putting his oar in, and giving things a stir over the years.

Maisie looked defiant, standing her ground, glaring at her father.

'Get back in the knife box Miss Sharpe!' he shouted, and Maisie ran to her room.

She stopped at the door, and, her voice quaking with outrage, shouted: 'That's exactly the sort of patronising suppression we're fighting!'

'We're fighting, Maisie?' Max protested. 'We're fighting. And since when did you enlist in the Pankhurst army, young lady?'

Max had regretted his words immediately and would have said so but Maisie had slammed the door on him. Now he wanted to put things right. More than that; impossibly, he wanted to have back the Maisie of old, the mild and pliant Maisie, not this Joan of bally Arc.

But this was life, he mused, rubbing a plug of tobacco between his hands until it was a nest of strands. You have children. They become part of you, almost the biggest part. And then you lose them, in a way – or rather they lose their reliance on you.

A point comes later where things are reversed, and you need them.

People set out thinking that their children belong to them. But children belong to themselves.

Max could see that Tom and Maisie were asserting that now. It was natural and he knew he had to get used to it. He just hoped they'd be less damned cocksure about it.

Max took deep, slow breaths to ease the agitation in his chest. He sought comfort in the flickering of the fire. Then suddenly he remembered next day's appointment with the photographer and began to visualise how they might pose.

The postcard photographs would go some way to spreading the word, he had no doubt, but Max had no illusions; the stuff about a picture being worth a thousand words was way off the mark. Musical Mayhem had to be seen and heard. No mere photograph – static, soundless, black and white – could begin to do them justice.

He thought of it as an almost magical mix. Maisie made her comic entry with Razzle. Then there was ten minutes or so of rip-roaring action with snatches of a dozen tunes, visually funny stuff (like the cod ballet). Then Tom and Maisie would start clogging like fury to the fiddle.

Finally there was a spoonful of schmaltz from Razzle. He'd come back on in his ribbons to Max's wobbly tear-jerker played on the saw, and he'd look out at the audience with his head held high, like a blessed Emperor, taking the applause on behalf of them all.

Sometimes the little beggar dragged the tambourine with him, or just happened to bite the bulb of his car horn at the finish. When he did, it always got absolute thunders. They adored Maisie but they went absolutely mad over Razzle!

The routine had taken them many hours of practice ('People don't know the half of it,' Max would say). They'd walked through the moves in the back yard behind the rooms, anywhere where there was space. They had even commandeered Victoria Park last summer when Sunday strollers, out in their finery and drawn by the sound of the fiddle, congealed into an audience.

Thinking of that open-air rehearsal for a moment, Max again regretted not having stuck to his guns when Gertie stopped him passing round his cap. After all, they were hard up, and most folks out promenading wouldn't think twice about giving a penny to a hurdy-gurdy man, or an organ grinder. So why not send the cap round for what was, more or less, an open-air concert?

Maisie and Tom had seemed oblivious of the facts of the family's hardship in the summer but he was sure that they must have picked up the worry that hung, like Haim's fishy smells, over the rooms. They would learn in time about the insecurity of this way of life, Max knew. At the moment their heads were full of what might be.

But, fair play to them, they'd been tip-top tonight, the pair of them, with their quick brains and young lungs. They could sleepwalk through the routine. Conversely Max had just learned that, from now on, he really needed to work at keeping the creaky knees going, and rewriting the moves on his brain.

The layoff had taken its toll, reminded him of his age. He would also need to keep a protective eye on Gertie. He feared that one night she might have another attack of the wobbles and put the mockers on everything.

My journal

January 18

Today started terribly. Father began goading about suffrage. I had promised myself that I would not take the bait but he was SO stony hearted about a sick suffragette languishing in jail, saying 'they' should have granted her wish to be a bally martyr if she refused medical treatment.

I had my say, and managed to stem my bitter tears until I reached my room. Razzle, dear mite, followed me and looked at me with pitying eyes.

I'm aware I sometimes come over as a saucebox but father is showing the very same instinct as the authorities. Suffragettes are not just LED out of meetings, they are now being THROWN out, assaulted for their impertinence in daring to speak up.

Tom gallantly tried to defend my right to have strong opinions.

When father said he never thought that he would see the day when his children turned into anarchists, Tom was so very plucky, looking him full in the face, saying some suffragettes were as brave as war heroes.

At this, father turned sarcastic asking whether Tom included those 'fearless' ladies who this week had wrapped a note of demands round a potato and, with no thought for life or limb, had pluckily thrown it at Winston Churchill's window before bravely running off.

Actually, the window didn't even break but the mention of the report certainly broke the tension between Tom and father! They began to laugh.

Finally, Tom said in a kindly way: 'You must see it Pa! It really is no good any more rearranging the apples. The cart has to be turned over.'

Mother, who was at the sink, and had been silent throughout, shouted to them to stop quarrelling, as she was getting a headache. I notice that her bottle of Dr Jenner's tonic is almost empty.

Best thing today was when we managed to steal a moment before we went home to see Les Filles once more. They were on after us. They have added to the slope a large metal loop and tonight two of the girls got a rattling speed up and rode UPSIDE DOWN, to gasps from the audience! Guillaume, the leader, noticed me at the stage side and smiled and nodded. He has a kindly face and an intent look.

The art of bicycle riding has progressed greatly since the fad came in. When I was six and, with mother, watching legions of women gliding around Battersea Park in the fog, cycling seemed so sedate. The riders moved in and out of the mist like swans on the Thames.

Now, scorching is fashionable among the more daring riders, and it seems it is not unknown for young women to go downhill 'coasting' with their feet up! I will be THAT sort of cyclist!

PS Tom said that he'd heard that the other day Emmeline P put down a troublesome bully in a most delicious way. When, eventually, the heckler called out: 'Emmy – don't you wish you were a man?' she replied: 'Don't you wish YOU were?'

I must try to find equally lethal rejoinders to stop father in his tracks.

7

Wilf had never been a drinker but he delighted in the convivial atmosphere of a busy bar. He simply looked and listened, savouring the snatches of whispered intrigue, the drollery, and the tales told indiscreetly once liquor had loosened tongues.

Over many years, unwinding after doing his act, he had enjoyed beer-house patter in many Scottish towns and had often felt humbled because in his view some comic exchanges, especially in Glasgow bars, outshone professional music hall routines.

He admired the spontaneous wisecracks and, cold sober, had been moved by closing-time songs that drew tears from hard men, rendered maudlin by halves of heavy and whisky chasers.

Many times he had returned home late at night from some Glasgow suburb and, using his flair for impersonation and exaggeration, served Morag titbits he'd gathered, scraps of conversation and morsels of scandal, along with her supper.

– Hey, Hughie! Did ya see yon one-legged tap dancer at the Scotia?
– No. By the time I got in, he'd hopped off hame!

'I so wish I'd been there!' Morag always said, knowing that going anywhere would soon to be out of the question. He was aggrieved on her behalf that her illness had robbed her so cruelly of the convivial life she had once known.

When Wilf made his claim that the man in the street was as capable as any music hall artiste of making people laugh, modestly he included his own, variously failing, acts.

It was true that his vent routine had tottered along nicely for a few years, and he'd had some reasonable seasons in beach shows at Rothesay. But he had no illusions about the more original comedy ventures that followed. They had been received, first with mortifying silence – in his view worse than any sound on earth – and then by angry rumblings from all parts of the house.

There was an irony there: He knew that at the very moment he was being vilified on stage by a merciless audience, in some pub down the road an anonymous shipyard fettler would be raising the roof with an unrehearsed jibe...

Did ya see Big Tam's sister? She's even bigger than him! She's got an earse like a bag o' washin.'

Aye. A real munter. But I widnae say that to Tam, not if ye wantae keep that wee pointy nose of yours nice and pointy!

Puir lassie. She canna help being sae ugly. But at least she could stay in the hoose...

Wilf had found that his kinsmen, of all audiences, knew what they wanted for their money. On the worst of nights over the years, the obscene gestures from boys in the gallery drew attention to his shortfall, a verdict sometimes confirmed by the arrival of a rotten tomato, or a handful of punched-out metal fragments from a day's riveting in the shipyards, or both, with a few handfuls of horse muck to follow.

Wilf remained objective about the scorn. He accepted that it was richly deserved. Quite simply, he had failed to give people what they wanted for their money. He would have felt like that if he'd paid for a bit of black bun at the bakers and later found they'd put a bannock instead in the wrapping paper.

Once, when he was starting his career, a pack of bawling boys had tried to piss on him while hanging from the gallery rail. He regretted that the musicians had been drenched and not him but he allowed the boys their opinion. They were entitled to a point of view about his material.

He had other routines and so he had decided then to soldier on – and for years he had done just that. It took a long time for him to see that he had been wrong – giving audiences what he thought was good for them, presuming that they appreciated subtlety. He had continued to lose work but could never quite rid himself of the urge to offer something more nourishing than candyfloss.

'Too clever by half,' Max had once said, when, a couple of years before, Wilf had talked his brother-in-law through a new routine.

Max had been right, just as he had been when he had urged caution over what turned out to be a refreshed but doomed version of Wilf's old ventriloquism act.

Seeking novelty, Wilf had smeared himself with charcoal, donned his old black wig and dressed as a Kaffir tribesman. The doll on his knee was a monocle-wearing aristocrat who, in an upper-crust accent, answered the Kaffir's naïve questions about England and the English. The act, heavy on satire, generated feeble laughter in pockets of the halls, but mainly mute indifference.

Max had regarded the new material as Wilf 'having a dig' and urged him to 'stop trying to get people to think about things like morals.'

Naïve as he could be, long ago Wilf had grasped the fact that people are hypocrites. He was intrigued by this, how some were solemnly protective of the institution of marriage, at the same time relishing a song about adultery put over with a saucy wink and a double entendre.

You were never, ever sure of your ground. Wilf had found that you could give them a searing shaft of satire and some of them looked up at you like stunned cattle. What was hilarious one night sank without trace on the next. Audiences were as fickle as the Glasgow weather.

On the third night doing the Kaffir-and-the-toff routine, Wilf was shown the door, and his week's booking cancelled.

Morag had been supportive, as always. She relied on Wilf for some everyday tasks but, despite the needs created by her illness, had insisted that he go off to find work in the halls. She bolstered his self-belief. She lauded his originality. With so much change going on in the world she was sure there were fresh, daring things to be done in the halls, and, in her view, her Wilf was the man to do them.

'They'll come round in time,' she would say, stolid in her faithfulness.

Since Morag's death, a period when he really wanted to be

busy to ease the heaviness of his grief, he had found few openings. Then, after a few weeks' searching, Wilf noticed a sign outside the Hippodrome in Gallowgate saying Acts Wanted.

He used his mimicry to good effect in the manager's office, giving a convincing rendering of Will Fyffe's I'm Ninety-four Today but sung in a warbling voice, like a sheep's, and a comical impersonation of Keir Hardie calling for "a wee bit more jeely for our piece."

It was enough to impress Mr McNab, the manager, who guardedly offered a trial week.

But instead of playing safe, Wilf immediately worked on widening his range to include other public figures, some of whom turned out to be unknown to those in the audience who were not in the position to enjoy leisurely breakfasts perusing the Herald for gossip about the cream of Scottish society.

And so Wilf was left with an audience that did not know who was being caricatured, and who were therefore unable to judge whether the impressions were good or bad.

Very quickly, and unanimously, they decided that they must be bad, so far as they could tell.

The only sound as Wilf left the stage, the derision having abated, had been his footsteps. Mr McNab had concurred with the punters, and as a large contralto dressed as a tramp stepped on stage, to loud applause, he had sidled up to Wilf in the wings.

'I can't let you go on again, Wilf. You need to try elsewhere.'

Hearing this, Wilf had felt more sorry for the manager than he had for himself. Poor Mr McNab: What a job, to have to tell a chap that he was a washout!

– Can't fathom it, Mr McNab. From the stage it was like looking down on a graveyard...

– You're right. I've never known a time when none of them clapped. You can expect booing and foot stamping, even near rioting. I've seen pigs' bladders on string bounced on the conductor's head. I've seen horse shit thrown by the ton. But for them to just sit there...it's puzzling.

– Tell me straight, Mr McNab: Where did I go wrong?

– It's not so much you, Wilf. It's the stuff you do. That last bit of business, for instance, the man with the beard and the wee ball, the big belly and that tiny schoolboy's cap... that was tip-top. Tip-top. But Wilf... who were you ragging? Tell me who in the name of God were you were taking off?

– Grace.

– Grace who?

– WG Grace. The great "WG." Everybody knows him. The man who advertises mustard everywhere. The greatest cricketer in the country.

– Which country, Wilf?

– England.

– But we're in Calton, Wilf. Calton in Glasgow. Glasgow in Scotland.

– But there's Scots up the road in Pollockshields playing cricket...a proper cricket club...

– True, maybe a handful, but most of the people in tonight, like every night, are bog-trotting Irishmen. Hurlers and scrappers. Topers, poteen merchants. Chaps who follow the horses, not the cricket scores from England. Now, come with me, laddie. Let's sort out the wee bit of money we owe you...

Mr McNab had turned the key of the drawer in his tall desk in the office off the foyer, and was reaching for his cashbox.

He paused and looked over his spectacles at Wilf, saw a likeable, lanky man with the concave chest, starkly white teeth and weak smile, a bruised no-hoper, and said: 'Have one more night, Wilf. One. Try it again. Keep your Will Fyffe, put some new stuff in, and give it a tickle here and a trim there. And have you a song? You know how the Irish love a good tear-jerker.'

Wilf hurriedly put together a new topical routine to replace the WG Grace segment. He based it on King Edward arriving in Clydebank – wearing the Grace false beard – as a stately foreman checking that the workers building Alexandra, the new royal yacht, were not slacking.

The punters were restless from the start, and he fluffed a caustic line he was convinced would bring applause.

It was then that the first of several warm steamed whelks hit him on the neck and he heard Mr McNab begging from the wings for him to surrender...

Wilf took another tiny sip of ginger ale and thought about the curious contradiction he represented – a teetotaller addicted to pubs. The fact was he did not need strong drink to quicken his imagination, and there was always good company in city pubs.

He began musing, thinking of public houses in terms of watering holes in the bush, like those he'd seen in Africa, and, to distract himself, he looked round the room and began to compose a little soliloquy in his mind...

...Go to this place at sundown, and you will see wearied human beings gathering at the bar's edge, checking who has made it unscathed through another day.

They are parched and heavy-footed and they are reuniting at the day's end, to cool their feet, and drink deep...

Stay quiet and you hear them commune with their own kind.

Lie low and watch from the fringe as kith and kin act out their lives for you...

That was what Wilf especially liked about drinking dens; they were places where you could simply sit and think, dream dreams, talk to yourself within you head. They were refuges, places where rootless individuals could just be.

Take a place like this, Wilf said to himself, putting his ginger ale to his lips. He was a stranger passing through but he could see immediately that The Greetin' Wean was a home from home.

Regulars called to each other across the carpet of sawdust, like family members, every third word a profanity, every laugh louder than it need have been. Hand-shaking. Shoulder-squeezing. Singing snatches of sentimental songs into each other's faces.

All of these are shows of love, endearment in disguise, Wilf decided. How fortunate that havens like this still exist! Each pub was a spit in the eye for the temperance people who wanted the law to ban people even sitting down to drink in case they became too comfortable, and, God forbid, started enjoying themselves. He wiggled his damaged toes and counted his blessings.

Despite the spoilsports, Glasgow was a city of magnificent pubs, watering holes that rivalled churches in their splendour, with stained glass, brass, patterned tiles, the finest hardwood brought from distant shores, and ornate overhangs above the bar.

It had big, echoing pubs, and smart, modern pubs, like the spanking new Tolbooth Bar in Saltmarket. But it also had snug, womb-like pubs like the Greetin' Wean - utilitarian, basic, the enrichment coming in human form.

Pubs like this one were an absolute godsend to the sort of drifter who pays off his landlord, says his goodbyes, gathers his life in a couple of bags, and goes off in search of a bolt-hole where he can wile away time in the warm before taking yet another big step into the unknown.

A drifter like me, in fact, Wilf said to himself, feeling no self-pity. But a new day would be dawning soon. The telegram to Gertie in London had gone off. He had just stoked up with mince and tatties at Granny Black's in Candleriggs, the homely café he had visited at lunchtime before confronting the enemy during his short run at the Hippodrome.

Most important, he still had a bob or two from the policy payout from British Legal. Morag was the realist; he was the dreamer. Her forethought about insurance was allowing him to indulge his creativity for a little while longer, now she had gone.

In the smaller of his two bags he had a plain loaf with the blackest of black crusts, and a bottle of milk, his rations for the day on the train to London and the cab ride to Gertie and Max in the East End. He loved being a nose-bagger; having provisions about him added to the enjoyable sense of rootless self-sufficiency.

The army had taught him long ago how to bear a little hardship. He would freeze in the train carriage, he knew that, but he had pencil and paper, and now at least there were toilets aboard.

He would divert himself with work on the new act. He decided he would appear on bills in London as The Crazed Zulu. That is, if he got on a bill.

At any rate, little outlay was involved. He would use the wig he had worn for the Kaffir act, and in the larger bag at his feet was the assegai spear and knobkerrie, the Zulu club. He had smuggled these home as souvenirs when the injury ended his war service fighting the Zulus.

Each time he looked at the weapons now he was appalled by their murderous capability, and each time he regretted having had to part with the lions tooth necklace he had acquired as part of a cache of secret spoils.

During shipboard bargaining on the way home from Africa, after a night of card playing, he had traded the necklace for a handful of coins that would go towards re-launching himself into civilian life.

He sat back and took another sip of ginger ale. He found himself yawning, and feeling decidedly mellow in the heat of the pub.

It had been a long day, and there was a long night to come. That morning he had limped round the poorer corners of the city, and, in Moncur Street, where traders' carts gathered, had come across a display of metal scraps that included a brazed metal frame with a cup on top, some blacksmith's attempt at a plant pot holder. It resembled a coconut shy and it had suggested to him a refinement to the act he was working on. He spent fivepence on it and stowed it in the bag for the journey to London.

For a man in his perilous position, and with his history, Wilf was surprisingly confident about the future.

He knew he could travel hopefully because as well as the insurance money from Morag's death he had a constant safe haven – with Gertie and Max. They always came up trumps. They had never had to be asked twice. There was always a welcome, even if Max did turn a little pettish from time to time. One day, when Morag's affairs were settled, he would pay them back.

With the long journey to face at first light, Wilf was relieved to have found a seat in a timber-lined nook of the pub; his toes were playing up after all the walking.

The promise offered to the street by the lemony light of the windows, beneath the gold lettering of the signs advertising whisky, was being fulfilled now he was inside, in the warmth.

He had been drawn especially by the painted, swinging sign showing a howling child with his fists in his eyes – a wean, greetin'. It pleased him to see human frailty shining out among the soulless red sandstone frontages of banks and offices.

The thought of a crying infant reminded him that he would soon be enjoying the company of Tom and Maisie. He and Morag had never had children but Wilf had strong paternal feelings. He would never say it in front of Max but he saw himself as a second father to Maisie and Tom.

There had been a strong bond since they were little. This had made Gertie happy but he could tell that Max had been a little put out when, during visits to see Gertie, the children treated him as if he were the Pied Piper.

Suddenly, Max was no longer in demand for his bedtime stories. Wilf found it embarrassing. The children would chant, demanding Wilf's more outrageous tales, and Max would skulk off, wounded.

Wilf could picture how the children's wide eyes opened further and further with every exaggeration, every bit of silly invention. Sometimes they would become red-faced and breathless with laughter. Then there would be a sharp word from Gertie, and Max would tut and give Wilf a glare.

Wilf believed that his arrival used to make for red-letter days; the children would know that there would be board games, horseplay, and lots of bright chatter (they had been ravenous for knowledge).

Tom had always been on the serious side, like his father, and avoided shows of affection but Maisie had been a joy from the start, and free with her fond feelings. He grew excited at the thought of being with them again, and especially hearing Maisie's laugh.

Wilf knew he could loiter here in the pub until the last stragglers were led to the door and the landlord made it plain that he was shutting.

He noticed that his chest had settled a little sitting in the nook, despite the pipe smoke, but he knew the cough would be back as soon as he hit the bitter, acrid night air.

He would wait, and watch, and listen to the craic and then he would take to the streets with his bags and stroll around until dawn.

At first light he would wend his way to St Enoch's. He would pass the sumptuous new station hotel full of cocooned toffs asleep on their goose-feather pillows, or, freshly bathed and perfumed, breakfasting on kidneys and bacon served from chafing dishes.

Then he would find somewhere sheltered to sit, wrap up as best he could, chew on a black crust from the loaf, and wait for the train.

My journal

January 19

What a palaver, trooping off with all the gear and the dogs to the studio!

Father is cock-a-hoop, explaining to Mr Blanchard that he wanted the photograph made into postcards, a dozen of them to start with.

He tells us that for less than one penny per card he can reach all the best halls lying within a bus-ride of the rooms.

We had to go away for an hour so that Mr Blanchard could prepare a rough print of his pictures. Razzle and Dazzle had been restless, so they might have been blurred.

In the end the photograph we chose made us look like the cast of a play in the West End.

Pa had struck a pose with his fiddle just below his chin and his arm outstretched towards us, as if he was saying: 'Presenting...Max's Musical Mayhem!'

For the first time, I was taken by the similarity between Pa and Tom; the swarthy look, the black eyes, the squareness of the shoulders and short legs. They might well have been images of the same man taken at each end of an interval of thirty years.

Mother looks so MATRONLY. She has developed the beginning of a double chin and her upper arms have become fuller. But the picture does not do justice to that rich brown crowning glory, a quality we share, nor the unfading rosy cheeks that Pa always used to refer to as her 'souvenirs of Crail.'

She wears a hat so beautifully. She had on the one with cherries and ribbons that makes her look like a French oil painting but she cannot take a compliment – 'The hat's a nice distraction from the face,' she says.

And me? What could be seen behind the tuba was, as usual, a bit of a mixture.

Hair – good-ish shall we say, tumbling from my mop cap. Eyes – kindly, at least.

But, oh dear, my revolting lips! Much too full, teeth too prominent. I blame the tuba but father says that it was precisely because I was blessed with good lips that I could get a sound out of the thing at a young age.

Mercifully hidden from sight in the picture is my thick waist. But my midriff will wander where it will. No corsets!

Alas, very much in evidence in the photograph were my sturdy milkmaid's calves, swelled by the clog dancing. I am reminded of this affliction every time I button up my boots.

But this talk is vanity. As Ma says, it's not the piecrust that counts so much as what lies beneath.

8

The Pyles were returning home in triumph once more, although no one seeing them looking so joyless and frozen on top of the horse-bus would have believed that they had just thrilled hundreds of people, and brought them applauding to their feet.

The Astoria audience – having again demanded and been given an encore – had begun to spill out onto the icy street, good natured about all the slipping and sliding and glad that they had braved the snow for such a top-notch evening.

Gertie had tucked Razzle deeply into the warm den between her knees. Her expression was as glacial as the weather.

Perhaps soon there would be a telegram from Wilf, and her mood would lift. Max noticed that she had been already been out buying pillows – 'He needs to be up high, for his chest,' she countered when Max fretted about the expense. She had also been pulling blankets from beneath the bed, and buying things he liked to eat.

Max could understand Gertie's pampering – up to a point. Her brother was after all the only living link with her childhood, the co-survivor of the move from Crail, and her family's struggle to adapt to the flintiness of Glasgow. They had been slow to adjust to the smoke and the clanging of steel, the grittiness of the language, the dung-laden roads, the overcrowding.

The Crail business was a mystery but Max knew that something unmentionable had happened. Gertie only ever hinted at something dramatic but the profound import of whatever it was sometimes showed as a change in her face.

Max accepted all this was a perfectly valid reason for her closeness to Wilf. But who remembered old Maxie when the milk of human kindness was doled out?

In the closed cab of the horse bus, below the family, a woman began singing, tipsily and tunelessly, a chorus from that night's show. Under the boxes on Maisie's lap, Razzle's tambourine chinked with every bump.

'Nearly there,' Gertie said flatly, stirring in her seat. They had passed the new Model Lodging House, the black expanse of the cemetery, and had nearly reached Blum's Pawnbrokers with its three balls, a sign that marked the stop the family needed.

Tom and Maisie took the handles of the various instrument cases and got up. Tom clasped the tuba to his chest. Max cradled Razzle with one hand, and held his violin case in another. They tottered on to the spiral bus steps as the cab lurched to a stop.

Max stepped on to the pavement, and a bloated man in a homburg and black frock coat, recognising him and the family, leaned out from beneath the stairs and as the bus moved off, pulled the cigar from his mouth and shouted: 'Fizzing turn tonight, old man! Absolutely topping!'

Max lifted his violin case aloft in acknowledgement. The compliment made him feel warmly sentimental, and less isolated. This chap was a gent, certainly not your typical East Ender, a man of discernment. But then, even in the plainest halls, you'd find rough and smooth. Max always argued that music hall defied class differences.

The working man loved to see 'characters' – the Cockney coster and the emaciated flower girl. And so did the nobs, who also enjoyed acts that were exaggerations of their own type, the idle bounders swanning about with malacca walking sticks and long cigarette holders, especially (for a reason Max had never understood) when the man about town was a woman.

Whatever your station in life, Max guaranteed you could have a very good night at any music hall, including the Astoria, especially if you had a thirst for a pint of Kentish wallop, or a drop of Yorkshire Stingo. Tuppence, that's all, for the beers. As cheap as milk!

And if you were lucky, you might just pop your waistcoat buttons laughing; look how Bessie Thwaite had brought the house down tonight with What Her Rent Book Didn't Show. Max called this sort of song 'human nature set to music.'

He had witnessed so many times the heartening effect of a night out at the halls. You'd see people troop in, some some footsore, some weighed down by the blue devils. They'd hand over their hard-earned florins and three bobs and enter a world of curiosity, wonder, weirdness, laughter and song.

Later they'd teem out refreshed and taking with them pleasure to re-live in their minds, and to share with their workmates next day.

Most artistes took their talent for granted. But occasionally Max found he could step outside the nightly routine, and see just how special they were, not just his family but legions of performers. People who got up on their hind legs in pit towns, seaside resorts, and godforsaken city suburbs, and braved the crowds to show what they could do that others couldn't.

It took courage, especially starting out, or when the natives were restless. You could feel like the quarry at a foxhunt. Some punters had small brains and big mouths. Some wanted to use you as a blotter to soak up all the sourness in their daily lives.

He remembered when Maisie first went on with the tuba, how she trembled, and how – above her fixed stage smile – her eyes brimmed with tears that were caught in the lights.

She had often said since that she would have run off but that her legs had been jelly. She had decided to pretend that she was in a dream and stare up at the the stained glass window above the gallery.

Punters could smell fear, somehow pick it out from the other smells: the smoke, sweat, foul breath, cheap scent, beer. There was a lot of orange-eating going on that night (and some peel-throwing later). The air was heavy with it, the orange peel, and the fear. Maisie hadn't been able to eat an orange since. But, fair play to her, she had brazened it out and received her reward of cheers and foot stamping.

Max believed that his thorough musical training had

somehow inured him against braying louts in the audience. He learned early, from watching nervy performers, that audiences feasted on insecurity, like leeches on blood.

When starting with his solo fiddle act, with a booking up in Liverpool, he had been given advice by a tottery, kilted singer. He was known as Whiskery Jock and was one of many Scottish characters audiences favoured then. Drink had turned his act into a ramble and his face, as purple as heather, into a landscape of cracks and crannies.

Max had watched as he had dried, struck mute a minute into his act. He stood there, resolute in the face of ridicule and only yielded when the manager called him off from the edge of the stage.

As he left, to shouts and whistles, and Max went on, he waved his walking stick to Max and yelled: 'Always stand your ground, laddie! Never yield! Face the buggers down!'

And so Max had decided then that he would never, ever be cowed by an audience. He knew his worth; self-belief came from the sound musical training his father had given him. He knew that this quiet, very correct man, in manner and speech, would have been proud of his professionalism – less so of Max's adoption, over the years, of the local lingo and of becoming 'common.'

Max was painfully aware that if the old man were still around he would have been crestfallen that the little well-brought-up tot, who, in his dress, used to play nursery rhymes on his half-size fiddle for Lily the skivvy, had taken a wrong turn while growing up and somehow ended up more of a Cockney than her.

Of course Max wouldn't use the term 'noble calling' about being in popular entertainment but that's how he thought of it sometimes.

He'd just had a flare-up with Tom whose head was now so far up in the clouds with his politics that he seemed to regard the family act as a trivial diversion for people who should be rioting and seizing the means of production.

'When all's said and done, Pa, we're only a petty sideshow in the scheme of things,' he had remarked. For a moment, Max had wanted to slap some sense into him. Instead he pointed to the dining table set for lunch; bread, cheese, pickled onions, and apples.

'That's what we earned last night. We earned the means to eat, to keep out of the workhouse. Turn your back on it if you like, Tom, and see how it feels when your bellybutton is stuck to your backbone.'

Max was shocked by the vehemence of his delivery. He was relieved that Tom smiled sheepishly, rather than showing hurt. It was as if both of them knew that they were going through a rite that did not endanger their mutual love.

Tom would never accept it but as far as Max was concerned, entertainers did good works in the here and now, more than politicians, and offered more joy and comfort than any religion.

Entertainers gave folks a tune to whistle to. They showed nature defied, and made mouths and eyes widen in wonder – people like those on the bill tonight, the Welsh chap who ate razor blades, and Amazonia, the slip of a girl who lifted an anvil two men had carried on stage.

They gave people magical moments and death-defying stunts to think about, images to replay in their heads as they bent over their ledgers next morning, or slaved at their lathes, or – wreathed in steam – dolly-pegged coppers full of long johns and petticoats, knowing rain was on the way.

Max had been furious about the letter in the Comet that week. A clergyman had written that music hall acts seemed to be based entirely on two or three people standing around on stage doing 'nothing very special'.

The vicar had lamented the prevalence of smut, the proximity of strong drink (despite 'laudable civic efforts towards enforcing sobriety'), and 'salacious encounters' befouling even further what he called a damned demi-monde.

Next day, Ormiston Chant, the busybody who had already brought about the closure of one hall, was in the newspaper saying she was quite disgusted over the appalling new living statuary acts arriving in the halls. She had almost fainted when she saw a poseuse called La Milo 'as God made her.'

Max fumed as he thought about these enemies of merriment. The meanness of their spirit was to be seen each night in the person of the protesting clergyman outside the Astoria, the man with the bloodless cheeks, grey face fungus and greasy dog collar.

One night, Max vowed, he would tell this killjoy that he'd got his bearings wrong when he made the sign he waved at people. Never mind This Way To The Pit Of Hell; it should say: This Way To A Bally Good Time.

Max always said a night at a music hall would do more good to a glum body than a quart of some quack's sarsaparilla. More than any sermon. More than a bucket of French fizz.

He didn't think it excessive to claim that, for some, it was the only reminder that behind the blackest clouds the sun always shone.

He just hoped that Tom and Maisie had the gumption to appreciate their...well, yes dammit, it was a calling of sorts.

Once more they were homeward bound, rounding the corner into Nelson Terrace, following the now-familiar whiff of Mr Cohen's fish shop.

Gertie didn't mind it, partly because she had grown fond of Mr Cohen. She liked his foreignness and his huge, watery black eyes, like a spaniel's, and his soft voice. She liked his shiny pate, resembling a brown hen's egg, but especially she valued his thoughtfulness.

How many landlords would think of making their tenants feel secure? Mr Cohen was approachable and kind, something

Max (to her annoyance) was reluctant to concede.

She didn't care for Max's disdain for foreigners, and she suspected that his spikiness with Mr Cohen was because, as an Englishman, he resented paying rent to not only to an immigrant but to a Jew.

They were home. Max eased open the front door beneath Haim's peeling, painted slogan 'We cook the Jewish way,' and the nailed-on cardboard postscript: 'Ask if you want fish in matzo meal'.

At his shoulder, Gertie looked hard at the floor as the door was opening hoping that there would be a telegram from Scotland.

My journal

January 20

Heavy snow again today. Arrived home wet and cold. Ma, in a fluster, resets the fire for the arrival of Uncle Wilf.

He was going to be treated to a beef joint for supper but in the end mother was too embarrassed to ask if she could use Mr Cohen's oven, in case brisket breached some religious law. So, a pan of pork chops stands ready by the fire for the arrival of His Nibs, around midnight.

Tom and I managed to have a quick chat with the Les Filles de la Bicyclette riders before they went on. Guillaume wrote down his name for me because I didn't know how it was spelled. His surname is Gautier and he explained: 'It means I am a goat keeper!' Then he said, in beautiful English: 'Please, call me William.' I declined – Guillaume is much more exciting!

He is taller than I remembered, quite suntanned, and very calm and attentive. I noticed that when someone speaks, he listens intently, weighing up what they say. He really is interested.

Tom was very opinionated, making a bit of a show I think. I sensed that one of the young lady riders turned his head (Yvette, who has lips like crushed strawberries and who smells of violets and perspiration).

Les Filles have costumes that are as daring as their riding. This had not escaped Tom's attention and he asked a curious question on the way home – 'How on earth do you imagine they get undressed, Maisie? Their clothes are as tight as sausage skins.' I said that I could not help in that delicate matter. I believe he will find the answer in his imagination (!)

When I watched Les Filles scorching around the stage, I concluded that the bicycle is THE most devilishly delightful thing ever invented. I am absolutely ACHING to learn to ride one! There are such beautiful cycling clothes to be had now (alas, only for those with a full purse).

Of course, dear old Pa would not approve of our entente cordiale with the bicyclists. He resents foreign acts taking work in the London halls.

He's with those who wrote to the King about it. But oddly, he has no objection to Harry Lauder, Marie Lloyd, Vesta Tilley etc, etc touring America. He's happy for his old friend Little Tich popping over for work in Europe where he'll be moaning to them, instead of father, about the terrible state of his feet.

By the way, father told us something we never knew: Little Tich has ten fingers and two thumbs. Tom said – rather churlishly I thought – that this would be an advantage when he was counting his money.

Come to think of it, father is guarded about all those who are not true Londoners, let alone British. He supports the protesters who want to turn foreigners away at the ports.

Mr Cohen has not yet fulfilled his promise to have a door fitted at the top of the stairs to cut off the cold striking up, and father puts that down to meanness – 'Jewish equals shrewish,' is one of his sayings.

Mr Cohen takes father's curiosity all in good part. He said very matter-of-factly 'You know, Max, some round here automatically reach for the Keating's bug powder as soon as they see a kippah on someone's head.' Father didn't reply.

Then Mr Cohen said something to the effect that, as father knew well, many silly people revile music hall people for no rational reason – 'So, Max, you and I are just different breeds of underdog.' Ouch!

I think father took the point and was further humbled when Tom said that we all ought to remember that Great Britain is a mongrel nation.

Pa looked on amazed as Tom pronounced, rather grandly: 'You know, Mr Cohen, this particular gentile is ashamed to see newly-arrived Jews in the East End walking in the centre of the road, trying to stay invisible, fearing we locals will have our progress impeded. I apologise on their behalf if Londoners make your people feel unwelcome.'

I'm sure Tom will go far, propelled by his principles. Re my own future, of course I continue to feel v. guilty. I cannot bear to tell father, while he is so encouraged, that this time next year I will no longer be part of Musical Mayhem.

Tom might be off even sooner. He is sworn to help Keir Hardie to dethrone the Brute-god Mammon (whatever, or whoever, that is!). So poor old Pa is going to be left with two pairs of empty clogs, two little dogs, and no act. It is a prospect that makes me want to cry for him.

PS Now 12 15 am: No sign of Uncle Wilf, and so I will escape and hibernate beneath my eiderdown while mother hovers, wringing her hands. She has just written a note that says 'Key in C,' and pierced an egg with a needle to use the white as glue to stick it on the front door.

Father, intrigued, asked what the note meant, thinking it was some sort of musical reference.

'Key in cludgie. He'll understand,' mother said. Evidently, cludgie's a Scottish expression for the privy.

Poor father's head sank in weary resignation and he has now trudged off to bed.

9

'Max, wake up!'

Gertie sprang upright in the dark, making the bedsprings tinkle and sing. Max reached out with both arms and pulled her to him but she pushed him away. She sniffled into her hands.

'Something's happened to Wilf. I know it.'

'Gert. You're crying! ...'

'Something's happened to him on the train. I feel it in my water.'

'Shush! It'll be bad weather. A hold-up. Fog.'

Max felt for the top of the bedside table and then fumbled for the box of matches and then for his pocket watch.

'Is it nearly morning?'

'Just after two. Settle, Gert. Relax.'

'Something's wrong. I know it. How I hate blessed trains! Deathtraps.'

Max knew it would be pointless trying to placate Gertie. She would have already pictured Wilf lifeless in the wreckage of a carriage. She was getting worse over travel; all part of the business with her nerves, he supposed.

Nowadays, she routinely expected disaster on any journey. She clung to Shanks's Pony and her beloved Thomas Tilling horse buses, the few that remained. To her mind, any other way of getting about was inviting injury or death.

It was a terrible nuisance for them when they were working but Max knew that trying to persuade her that the tram was quicker, and that the motor-buses and the new Tube trains were a boon, was a lost cause.

Gertie had always had a nervous side. He had been forced to take back to Maynard's the gas iron he had bought her on her birthday. It was a gift to make her life easier and it was a stretch at 1s 3d but she looked at it as if it was a ticking bomb, and carried on heating the flat-iron in the fire and spitting on it to test the temperature, judging the heat by the sound of the sizzle.

'Look,' Max said. 'There's often bits of problems with trains. You know that. Engine trouble. Cattle on the line. He'll be as right as rain.'

Gertie was not convinced. 'Tell that to Dot Stephens,' she said.

'Dot? But that was a freak, Gert. One in a million.'

They had last met Dot at the Grand Benevolent Show staged by a dozen of her fellow artistes to raise the £200 needed for the some medical apparatus for her legs to enable her to keep performing as Sunshine Sue. Max had done his old comic fiddle routine to show support.

'You saw her, Max. A shadow of the jolly old Dot we knew. And all the poor woman did was take the Glasgow train. Same line as Wilf's on.'

The incident was often mentioned now by Gertie as a reason for sticking to horse power, although she kept assorted chilling instances of accidents handy for quoting. They included mishaps even involving her trusted horse-drawn cabs, because no means of travel was safe nowadays.

Why only the week before, a horse pulling a cab had fallen sideways on to a young clerk walking alongside, trying to cross the road; a hoof lodged in a tramline. She pictured the man, a smart gentleman in a tweed suit, striding out one minute, then flat on his back in manure with the flank of the horse trapping his feet. She had put her hands over her eyes but was still trembling when she reached the rooms.

For Gertie, living hell was the daily maelstrom of cars, smoky motor-buses, rattling trams, bicycles, carts, perambulators, people and horses. At least that young Mr Churchill had grasped the nettle, demanding that the council order some London buses off the roads so people could hear themselves think.

She turned again to Max in her despair and her growing anxiety over Wilf.

'Do you realise, Max, that when that horse keeled over it could have been Maisie or Tom under it?'

'But the business with Dot, Gert, nothing like that's going to happen to Wilf! Come on gal, how many women get up to open a train window because the carriage is stuffy and end up with their feet chopped off?'

She didn't bother to answer, or to mention the sickening

business of all those lodgers dying in their sleep in Glasgow, trapped in their wooden cubicles, when she'd been up seeing Morag, and the smell and the smoke that hit them even before her and Wilf had reached Watson Street and witnessed the absolute horror of it. They had called it a model lodging house and it was owned by a city councillor but it turned out to be a deadly tinderbox.

For Gertie, calamities were everyday events, so frequent she'd had to beg Max not to read out reports of them from the Comet. He seemed oblivious.

But what about the two dozen poor devils last year who died in that Salisbury train? Or the ten killed on that Brighton trip, or the thirty perfectly innocent people who died in that Liverpool tram? It was all right Max talking about freak accidents;

Some of them were so unimaginable. What was it in the Comet only the other week...?

'Brave firemen perish in warehouse inferno. Electrocuted through their steel helmets'

It set her thinking of all the music halls that had been burned down during the time she'd been in the business – more than she could count on the fingers of two hands. And all because there was too great a trust in gas and electricity and new gadgetry.

In the roll call of those who had perished in music hall fires, people known to her and Max, she had been most affected by the death of dear Herbert Wilson, Diabolo The Fire Eater. Imagine! Dear Herbert consumed backstage at the Rialto by the very stuff of his trade, along with two Hungarian tumblers.

She had a soft spot for Herbert, a meek man who was a squeaky mouse off stage (Max believed his feeble voice was a result of all the paraffin he swallowed) but who, in his scarlet outfit, was a real presence on it.

A couple of times since the tragedy Gertie had woken distressed having heard his pitiful cries for help in her sleep. Irony was not a word Gertie would use but the contrariness of

Herbert's end – being killed by fire started by his untended candle falling against a dancer's tutu, and then fuelled by his paraffin supply – struck her forcefully and strengthened her conviction that death lurked everywhere.

Freak disasters? They were as common as sparrows in Spring. For all she knew at this moment Wilf was lying like a discarded marionette in steaming, hissing train wreckage.

But it wasn't just things on wheels. Who'd have predicted that the Thames would catch fire? The Thames! The Comet made out that it was an unforeseen twist of fate, some sort of act of God – no comfort if you were out there in a little boat surrounded by walls of flame being fed by floating oil!

It seemed to Gertie that the powers that be were intent on inviting disaster. While the Thames fire was still raging, just upriver, the windbags in Parliament were talking of a Bill to put a tunnel under the Channel to France. A tunnel!

Anyone used to carrying buckets of water would know that these MPs were insane; just think of the weight of the sea pushing down, and then the weight of all the ships!

No, Gertie could not bring herself to be comforted by the statistical singularity of the Dot Stephens tragedy. For a second she saw in her mind the train door flying open, and Dot being sucked out of the carriage, and continued to brood once more about Wilf, wringing her hands and sighing.

Gertie made her way into the main room and, in the weak light from the dying fire, felt cast down further seeing the sofa and the pillow, plumped up, and expectant, just as she'd left it. Where on earth was he?

She lit the gas lamp and took the telegram from the mantelpiece and re-read it. He had said midnight.

Max led Gertie back to bed and persuaded her to rest for a while; after all, there was nothing they could do. He was sure that quite soon they would hear Wilf's tread on the stairs.

They fell into restless sleep until Gertie sat upright again.

There was the sound of muffled coughing coming from the main room. One of the dogs barked.

'He's here Max! I can see a light under the door.' Max gathered his wits and followed his wife.

They found Wilf in his long johns, on the sofa, with the bed cover round his shoulders and a dinner plate on his knee. The plate was littered with bones and cutlery. He was smiling his ivory smile.

'I take it that the chops were for me, Gert?' he said. She gathered his shoulders and kissed his cheek.

'Wilf! You're safe.'

'Safe as houses. And why not? Lovely grub. A supper fit for a king,' he said, pulling his floppy hair out of his eyes.

'So there was no crash?'

'Crash? No, no crash. Why would we crash?'

While Gertie fussed around him, Wilf described how the train had hit dense fog and then been delayed when the driver requested a check by a wheeltapper in Carlisle – 'Vibration, the guard said, but I think it was from me shivering!'

Gertie sighed blissfully: 'But now, thank God, you're safe at last,'

'Safe? I was always safe, Gert.'

The first chink of daylight fell against the window and, over mugs of tea, Wilf began to spill out his news. Morag's affairs were almost in order; a lawyer's search for two elderly distant relatives had so far yielded no response. It would all be finalised soon.

'And your cough?' Gertie asked.

'No change. I invested two-and-six to see a medical man in Argyle Street in Glasgow and after much chin-scratching he concluded solemnly that I was the owner of an awfie, awfie bad chest. This, he declared, was producing an awfie, awfie bad cough. His prescription was in the finest Latin but at the chemist's it added up to a sixpenny bottle of linctus, twopence worth of tallow as a rub and herbal sweeties. So – for me, awfie, awfie expensive!'

Max and Gertie searched their minds for news that would

interest Wilf, naming those who had died, those who had retired from the halls, those who were prospering.

'Did you hear Frank Coyne has passed?' Gertie said.

'No! The Tiddley At The Fountain man? Oh dear...'

'Came back from his South Africa tour completely barmy. Cut his throat.'

Gertie said: 'Somebody said that Zaeo has just popped them as well.'

'Zaeo?' said Wilf.

'Best trapeze artiste I ever saw,' Max said. 'Talk about courage. Walked a wire thinner than my bootlace, right above you, the full width of the hall with just a little Japanese umbrella for balance. It was Sunderland. I'll never forget the sound that went up when she took that last step off the wire. Four thousand people starting to breath again.'

'Did she ever let it out who she really was?' Wilf asked.

'No,' Max said. 'Kept up the mystery. Even when she was in a court case, her husband refused to give her proper name but everybody in the halls knew she was an orphan called Adelaide from Norwood. I remember her best for the times she got into trouble with the law for showing a bit too much...'

'You would,' said Gertie sniffily.

The subject turned to work, and the domination of hall ownership by syndicates.

Wilf said: 'From what I gather, things are starting to go all hoity-toity. Over the years they've tried to put the mockers on the drinks, and now they're installing plush seats in lines. And I'm told that, down here, the owners expect artistes to tighten their belts to fund it. Typical.'

Wilf could see that Max, defender of the status quo, was uncomfortable. He piled on the agony by describing how Moss Empires was harvesting big profits from the new Glasgow Coliseum.

'Worked it out on the train. They can get 8,000 coming in a

night, in two houses. That's potentially more than 40,000 paying customers in a week. There's a waiting room for punters queuing for the second show. Eglington Street's thronged every night.'

'But remember,' Max countered, 'they've got to pay everybody, the big fees for the stars, and there's the bills for the electric and...'

'My heart bleeds for them, Max. No offence but it's people like you, like us, who'll suffer when the big boys finally take over the whole caboodle.'

Max shook his head wearily. He hated being forced to confront what he knew to be the truth, and hearing it from Wilf was doubly excruciating.

He asked: 'Did the news reach you about plans for a strike? Are they getting agitated up there as well?'

'They seem to be watching and waiting. There's talk of us sending a union donation down because you London boys will be calling the tune.'

'This London boy won't. But Tom's already dying to bite a lump out of the hand that feeds him, and Maisie's hanging on his coat-tails.'

'That's youth for you,' Wilf said. 'Tom sees things with clear, young eyes. But if they're piling on extra shows, and changing conditions, and trying to bind people, they'll have to be stopped some time.'

'But they're not. Not so far, they're not. Not at the Astoria. But come on Wilf, you know in your heart of hearts that there's no future in rebelling. Stoll and Moss and Adney Payne and the rest of them have got it sewn up.'

'Maybe. But what about this idea of ganging up with the stagehands and musicians, and squaring up to the owners, and having it out? I think we have to go for that, or just throw in the towel. I'm all for giving it a few rounds.'

Anger clouded Max's face. 'You are, Wilf. But then you're likely to come into a bit of money soon. We're getting by. Just. We'd be dining at the cat meat cart within a fortnight if the owners found a way of putting on shows without us.'

Gertie said: 'It won't come to that, Max. It'll blow over,' but there was no conviction in her voice, and she did not believe what she said.

Wilf looked at them both earnestly. 'Listen. Don't worry. I want you both to know that if I do get something from the settlement, I'll never see you short.'

'Obliged, Wilf. I know. Good of you,' said Max. 'But you know me and charity. We don't get on.'

Gertie was pleased to hear Max call Wilf by his name, something he rarely did, and to hear a little cordiality in his voice.

She busied herself making more tea to distract from the flutter she felt inside, the sense of impending conflict that was spoiling her pleasure in seeing Wilf again.

10

The mood lifted with the arrival of daylight. Wilf talked of the Scottish halls, and a new and fierce rivalry for custom in Glasgow. The big news was that an energetic and eccentric manager had taken over at the old Britannia and was causing such a stir that he was never out of the newspapers.

'A Yorkshireman. Learned to spiel working with Barnums,' said Wilf, stifling a yawn. 'What a showman! You can practically see the ideas tumbling out of his head. He's called Pickard but he prefers The King of Trongate. The Britannia's now the Panopticon. A bit of a mouthful for the locals. They're calling it The Pots and Pans.'

Gertie relaxed a little as Max and Wilf, two seasoned sweats, returned to talk amicably of new acts and old.

Wilf related bad news about a plate-spinner they both knew (St Vitus Dance had finished him, they said), and tidings of a much-disliked manager in Ayr who had broken a hip falling off the stage and had passed out to the sound of raucous laughter.

'There's some of the old crew still doing the circuit. But the man who's really been pulling the crowds in round Glasgow lately is a dotty pianist with hair like a haystack – The Rollicking Rubenstein. Absolutely off his crumpet! Your sort of mixture, Max; top hole music but with daft knockabout.'

Max pondered over this comparison for a few seconds and, although galled, did not respond. He could do without Wilf's lofty, and inaccurate, assessment of his talent. Daft knockabout?

Looking down, Max noticed that Wilf had one sock off, revealing his angry-looking toe stumps, and immediately reproached himself for being curmudgeonly.

Wilf gathered the bed cover more tightly round himself and said: 'They say that this Pickard's an absolute genius. He's running a sideshow alongside the music hall, with waxworks and curiosities. He'll buy up, or sign up, anything that gets the punters curious – animals, freaks, amusement machines, Siamese twins. He's even got a zoo in the basement.'

Max appeared unimpressed. He liked straight, no-nonsense music hall, and prized it even more now it was threatened by corporate greed, frivolity, and agitation from artistes hell-bent on conflict.

'One of Pickard's people lived near my digs,' Wilf said. 'Elspeth. Bonny lassie. She's The Woman With Half A Body for four hours a day. We'd sometimes meet out at the milk cart in the morning and have a bit of a blether.'

'Half a body! Half a bally body, Wilf! How can people believe in all that bolony?' Max fired off aggressively, as if he was holding Wilf responsible for the trends he disapproved of.

'It's because they want to, Max. Pickard knows that folks want to believe in stuff beyond their ken. Things like the existence of a beautiful woman defying death, taking an eternal sleep. He's happy to provide the woman and the glass case – and let people pay for it.'

'They say fools and their money are soon parted...'

'He's got a Sleeping Princess installed now, up in the statics. Elspeth says that when nature calls she waggles her little finger and they put screens round, telling punters that the staff are worried about her, and they need a private minute to check her pulse.'

Wilf roared with laughter. Dazzle woke with a start. Gertie chuckled. Max remained unamused.

'No. Give me a good singer, any time,' Max said. 'Give me a Florrie Ford, or a Billy Williams, or a real master of magic like Lafayette, who sends folks home wondering how in God's name a man can stand there and produce a turkey out of thin air. Tried many a time to get him to give me a hint about how he does it all but he just winks and smiles. It's like trying to get into an oyster with your fingernails.'

Wilf slurped on his mug of tea and sheepishly broached the matter of his sacking, and the business with the whelks. Just as Gertie was about to sympathise, he began to laugh once more, so much that he started to cough.

'It was mainly horse muck when I first started. You'll have had muck in the early days Max?'

Max's curt 'No, never,' was drowned out as Wilf, flicking back his hair with a forefinger, said: 'There's something wholesome about horse muck. Harmless enough. And I've never really minded rivets. We've all had rivets' (Max shook his head). 'But, you know what, I can't ever remember punters throwing whelks at me.'

He was pensive for a moment then smiled with amusement and said: 'I can tell you, you feel a proper jessie being driven off-stage by shellfish. Much more humbling than horse muck.'

Max said: 'I remember the whelks. But I never copped any. Steamed. Sold them in the street in Glasgow. Like the hot spuds.'

'They must have revived the tradition when they saw I was on the bill!' Wilf said before being overtaken by laughter once more and the absurdity of it all.

Gertie looked across at Wilf, who was convulsed; she was in awe at his ability to rise above humiliation. He caught her compassionate look.

'Could have been worse, Gert,' he said, coughing. 'could have been clappy doos instead of whelks!'

Max was doubly irked, first that Wilf leaned round him, as if he was a mere obstruction, to ensure that Gertie heard this, and that here was another term he did not understand. Wilf caught Max's peeved look and said: 'Giant mussels, Max. Huge. Out of the Clyde. Shells like clappers, like wings. Now they would have come keen...'

Wilf was in full spate now.

'But I suppose it could have been even worse if it had been the Paisley Empire, with that lasso hauling you off, or getting showered with old biscuit tins from the flies! They did it, you know.'

'Don't tell me, I know,' Gertie said. 'My father used to say that the Empire on a Friday night was like being back in the Battle of the Braes...'

'But, you know what Gert?' Wilf said, 'I had the last laugh with the whelks. When they pulled me off, I picked one off my shoulder and ran back on stage and shouted: "Keep throwing these, you lot – I'm opening a stall in The Briggait!" That raised the roof. Shame it was the only laugh I got...'

Gertie did not allow herself to appear entertained by this. To laugh would have made her complicit in the cruelty of it all.

Poor Wilf. How shaming it must have been. She asked herself: Doesn't he feel these things? Why can't he show hurt? Max suppressed a sigh of bemusement. Here was a man who rejoiced in derision, he concluded, confirming a verdict he had come to long ago.

Wilf gathered Razzle and Dazzle to him on the sofa then asked: 'So... what of Musical Mayhem, and the young heathens?'

Max's impulse was to describe how Tom was becoming a

worry, and to plant in Wilf the idea that his early influence might have been responsible for the way the boy was turning out.

He wanted blurt out that Tom was now a real radical, perhaps even an anarchist, always at meetings or lurking in West End pubs where Russians talked of the need for the world to be taken apart and then rebuilt.

He was on the point of explaining that Maisie had begun talking a lot of challenging but harmless tripe, and going all dreamy-eyed about the posh suffrage jailbirds playing at being martyrs but he decided to keep silent. But he knew that to talk about the growing independence of the children might have given Wilf something to be pleased about, rather than troubled by.

'You'll see a big change,' Gertie said. 'Maisie is forever at suffragette meetings and Tom has only to catch a glimpse of somebody on a soapbox and he's there soaking it all up. He's either at the Endowed Library or the Workers' Education Society, or in his room with his nose in a book.'

Wilf beamed. 'Bravo! That's the boy! So it's already dawned on them that our politicians spend a lot of time putting poultices on wooden legs. They're young, restless for change, and good luck to them.' Gertie gathered the tea mugs and chipped in – 'Aye, a proper pair of firebrands, so they are, Wilf. But why not, at their age?'

'Better than them joining the slumbering masses,' Wilf said, and Max wondered: Was that a little dig at me? Does he see me as a slumberer?

Wintry morning light was falling through the window on to Wilf now, giving him the appearance, in Gertie's view, of a field hospital casualty: The pallid face, the long johns, the eiderdown drawn round him, the look of being a long way from home (in his woeful case, having no home).

She went for a saucepan and steeped porridge oats in water and put it on the iron pan-holder on the edge of the fire.

Wilf said: 'Maisie always showed she had backbone. And if I remember aright, even when he was little, Tom had a way of getting to the heart of things. They just want to right a few wrongs.'

They had talked for two hours. It was dawn. They heard Maisie moving about in her room. Gertie pushed the pan holder nearer the fire and began to stir with the porridge spurtle, the one her mother had used back in the Crail days.

Wilf looked up expectantly, eager for Maisie to come from her room, then, growing impatient, went to the door and knocked gently.

'Who is it?' Maisie asked sleepily.

Wilf pinched his nose and announced in a snooty English voice: 'And now, Maisie Pyle, here is Mr Harry Lauder singing personally for you, courtesy of HMV...'

> **'I love a sausage, a bonny, bonny sausage,**
> **I love a sausage for ma tea,**
> **I went tae the lobby, to see my Uncle Bobby,**
> **And the sausage ran after me!'**

'Uncle Wilf! Uncle! Be out in a second...'

Maisie emerged tousle-haired and swathed in the embroidered cotton tea-gown her mother had bought when they chose it from Eaton's Catalogue on her last birthday, just before the family had been forced to stop working.

Wilf kissed her forehead, he held his arms out in admiration of the gown, and they laughed as Maisie told him: 'Nice serenade, Uncle, but after some consideration I think I prefer the original...'

Wilf felt a tap on his shoulder and there was Tom, smiling, sleepy.

Wilf was surprised at the strength of the handshake and the angularity of Tom's shoulders and the black fuzz on his top lip. The new, deep voice was disturbing. He was dark and short and had his father's pugnacious air and he was muscular now, manly. Where had the young Tom gone?

Max watched the reunion from his ladder-back chair. He was

ready for his porridge, then a pipe and then a quiet moment with the Comet.

He thought he might slip away to (was it now to be called the cludgie?) to escape the excitable chatter. But as he rose he saw that Wilf had sprung up, and, with his loping hobble, was blocking his way, beating him, heading downstairs.

My journal

January 21

Wakened by Uncle Wilf's rendition of I Love A Lassie but with comical words. Some things don't change! At least I was spared the cornet.

Although I had slightly dreaded his arrival, I've somehow felt reassured by having Uncle Wilf with us. I admire his unending cheerfulness. I expect the novelty will wear off!

Father is fretting about the prospect of the strike. He hasn't taken kindly to Uncle Wilf's subtle digs, hints that he had always been a bit too keen to doff his cap to the hall owners. Tom is champing at the bit, hoping the strike will start soon. There's a rumour that tomorrow will be The Day.

Uncle Wilf came home from Petticoat Lane where he'd bought a huge Union Jack (only a few holes!). He has also brought home four coconuts. They are for the Zulu act he has come up with. He was madly keen to give us an extract but father was still sulky and said: 'Perhaps tomorrow. We'll have an eternity if the halls close.'

Tom came in at tea-time, all excited, not only because the strike seems unavoidable now but also because he had encountered a famous Woolwich Arsenal player on the tram and had introduced himself and shaken hands, something Tom said he would never forget.

When he told father that this player had been very approachable and kind, father replied huffily: 'And I'd be kindness itself if I was getting nearly four quid a week for kicking a bag of wind about.'

Tom came back with 'And that's precisely why there must be a strike, father. Payment for skill.'

Poor Pa surrendered and sank his head into his Comet.

Uncle Wilf was at the show tonight and glowed with pride in us. Father introduced him to Cecil who hinted that there might be a slot for him to try out his new Zulu act. Tom said afterwards: 'He'll be trying to line up blacklegs to go on instead of us.'

Tom and I are full square behind the union and the Alliance, so father will be excused from deciding; he simply won't have a say in the matter, unless he opposes us and does his solo stuff. But there will be no Musical Mayhem at the Astoria.

'And what about your uncle?' Eli asked. I said that Uncle Wilf was not working at the moment but obviously would also be in full support.

It was then that I had a shock.

Eli said: 'That's odd. I think Cecil has put him on the bill tomorrow to see what he has to offer.'

11

Maisie's fitful, dream-filled sleep was broken by a strange murmuring in the depths of night. The voice was disembodied and the tone doom-laden. A second before she heard the noise she had been holding her aunty's hand. Coming to, Maisie decided that a long-submerged episode from her childhood had resurfaced in her sleep.

She remembered it all now. She had been taken to church by her aunt, and confronted by a wild-eyed evangelical preacher whose sermon had terrified her. She remembered the fine spray of spittle caught in the slanting light. She had squeezed her aunt's hand and then clung to her skirt.

But this voice, and she was sure what she was hearing was real, not remembered, seemed to be from another world. It was unearthly but it was controlled, measured...

Maisie lifted her head a few inches from the pillow. She opened her eyes as if this might help her identify the sound. It was then that she knew it was Uncle Wilf's voice, but without the warmth or his Scottish burr. It was the voice of a performer, declaiming.

Maisie hugged the pillow and waited.

She decided that Wilf must be in the throes of a nightmare. But strangely, she heard the rustle of papers being shuffled.

Wilf had been put up in the only communal room, on the old sofa. He had been deprived of sleep on his journey from Scotland, and when she had said goodnight earlier he was already half-asleep, lying coiled and uncomfortable, his legs – encased in long johns – extending like off-white drainpipes over the edge.

Knowing what Wilf had witnessed in the army, Maisie had always supposed that nightmares would be inevitable. He had seen terrible things close up, the poor man. She had merely heard it all second-hand but the tales of Wilf's Zulu war had tainted her, like spilled blood on white cotton.

Even now, she sometimes heard in her head the last words of Uncle Wilf's dying compatriots. She so wished that he had not afflicted her with such anguishing detail when she had been so young but Uncle Wilf felt no inclination to shy away from truth – and yet she knew he would be appalled if he learned that what he had described affected her so.

'The last words... it's a speech we don't plan, the moment we say exactly what we mean,' he had told her with a resigned chuckle. 'Some went all religious. Some raged. Some just sighed as if life had been one, long hard day...'

She crumpled inside when she first heard how Uncle Wilf's friend from Anstruther, who enlisted with him as 'a scrawny bairn,' had fallen at his feet, mortally wounded by an injured Zulu who sprang from his hiding place behind a bush.

Uncle Wilf had burdened her with a haunting image of this boy defiantly pronouncing the names of his family members, honouring them in a roll call.

She decided that she would lie still and let his bad dream run its course, if indeed he was dreaming.

But then felt she ought to act. It might be sort of delirium. She had heard how some soldiers brought back diseases from Africa, health problems that kept recurring.

The voice, urgent and intimate, began again...

'So come with me, if you dare. Come, meet the noble Zulu...'

Wilf began to cough and then, slightly breathless, resumed the monologue. Maisie lowered her head and lay still, straining to listen...

'...not the picture-book Zulu, not the newspaper correspondent's Zulu, but the superbly trained killing machine.'

There was a long silence and then: 'Listen! Zzzzzz...'

Another pause, then: 'Zzzzzzz...

Silence, again then: 'No, not bees exploring a summery English garden but a violent hive disturbed... Zulus advancing, humming as they come for you...a chilling noise...'

She wanted to satisfy herself that Wilf was not distressed but she was shy of being seen in her nightdress, and fearful of finding that he had indeed become deranged, a fate her father had long predicted for him.

She was frightened but fascinated. Wilf coughed again, gained his breath and dropped his voice until she could barely hear it...

'He was as thin as a sapling. Spindly. Just a poor laddie, separated, stranded. He had lost his assegai in a skirmish but showed no fear of us. He dropped his shield and held out his arms to show his chest and in a voice as calm as a diner asking for someone to pass the salt and pepper, he said: Dubula m'lungu.'

There was a rustling of paper.

'We – that is, Angus and me – didn't know what the laddie was saying and so didn't know what to say in return. It wouldn't have been right, not British, to polish him off without knowing. He said again "Dubula m'lungu" tapping his breastbone.

'Angus said: 'He's pleading for us to kill him, Wilf. I think he's saying "Shoot me, white man."'

Wilf coughed again.

'The boy pointed to my gun, what Zulus called our fighting

sticks of thunder. I feared that if we marched this boy towards our positions we might be attacked and slaughtered.'

There was a long silence before Wilf whispered, almost inaudibly: 'He said it again, louder this time. Dubula m'lunga – shoot me.'

Wilf was quiet again, for seconds, before whispering hoarsely: 'And then, to my eternal shame, I obliged the boy...'

A sudden thump of a door being opened was followed by Gertie crying: 'Wheesht, Wilfie! You're having the night terrors. Stop!'

Maisie slid out of bed and opened the door of her room just enough to see through the crack. There was Wilf, looking jolly, holding his papers and a pencil.

Father was walking cautiously towards him as if he expected him to run amok. Mother was wide-eyed and had her arms round Wilf's shoulders.

'God save us, it sounded so...' She tried to find a word that summed up the ghastliness of what she had heard. 'Well... real,' she said finally. 'All these years and that puddled heid of yours is still full of it. Full. I could have actually been there it was so...real.'

'Real, Gert?' he whispered. 'Music to my ears. That's what I'm after Gert. I want to take people there and rub their noses in it. Let them smell a drop of blood and taste it...'

Max raised a hand, the palm flat, like a warning flag, and said: 'Shush!' This was intense stuff, and it could wait until daytime. But Wilf was insistent.

'Can you see what I'm after, Max? Not just singing, and dancing, and the usual flimflam but an act that actually tells them a bit of truth...takes them into the wars they just read about...'

Maisie watched, absorbed. She found some release from the tension of the moment in the comical sight of her father and Uncle Wilf in their long johns and vests, facing each other as if they were about to dance as part of some rite, or to wrestle. For the first time she noticed Uncle Wilf's ragged toe ends.

She saw Wilf lower his head and look contrite, and lean

towards Max. 'Sorry,' he whispered. 'Didn't mean to wake you, Max, old man. Tried to keep the voice down. The thing is, I couldn't sleep because I'd got this confounded act spinning in my head. I think I'm nearly there with it...'

Max decided not to be drawn.

'Look, Wilf. Why not leave it for now?' He mouthed the words in an exaggerated way to remind Wilf that this was, after all, the middle of the night.

Wilf was about to chip in but Max cut him off.

'Look, this is not healthy, Wilf. We need to calm down,' he said, putting a hand on his shoulder. 'Tell me about it tomorrow and I'll put in my pennyworth.' Max was chilled now and yearning to get back under the eiderdown.

'Yes, best to sleep, now,' Gertie said. 'Try counting sheep,' she added gently.

Wilf chuckled. 'Trouble is, Gert, if I even tried to picture a field it would be full of waving grass, with a river of Zulus flowing through it! It really was like a flood arriving..."

Gertie made a sympathetic sound and shook her head, as if she saw no remedy. She was touched once more by Wilf's lack of self-pity. How could he smile like a carefree child while being haunted? Why did pain seem to make him laugh instead of cry?

Max turned away sleepily, muttering some well-meaning advice about the need for Wilf to 'keep a grip.' But Wilf persisted, keen to spill out his ideas for the new act.

'You'll both absolutely love the climax. A fizzing way to round it all off came to me on the train down. Honestly, Gert, your blood'll run cold...' Gert simply shook her head.

Max put a finger to his lips to remind Wilf of the need for quiet. When he reached his bedroom door, he whispered: 'Whoa! Hold your horses, Wilf! Give us a run-through tomorrow, me and Gert and Tom and Maisie. We'll tell you what we think. Straight John Bull.'

Wilf looked crestfallen. Gertie straightened the blanket on the sofa, punched the plush cushion serving as Wilf's pillow and put a shovelful of coal on the embers of the fire.

'Come on, you've killed enough Zulus for one night, soldier boy. Sleep!' she ordered. Her words were those her mother would have used when Wilf when was a boy.

'Never mind Africa,' she urged. 'Do what I do, when I want to escape. Think back to Crail. In the evening sun.'

Max knew that, with the mention of Crail, at any moment Gertie would lapse into dialect. It was as if the language of her childhood was entangled with her memories.

'Think of mother calling for us tae come in for oor tea. Think of faither coming hame wi' a wee Friday treat. Remember tablet? And soor plums?'

Wilf seemed untouched by Gertie's nostalgia, and as Max retreated through the bedroom door, he called out: 'Max. Promise me something. If you have a listen tomorrow, and I show you the moves and the props, and you think that it'll go down well, will you have a word with the Astoria?'

Max's spirits sank. The brass neck of the man!

'Just tell them I'll slot in at short notice if someone drops off the bill ...?'

How was it that with this man you always ended up regretting having shown goodwill? His jaw locked in fury.

As he headed for the bedroom, Max began an inventory of Wilf's shamelessness... the food and shelter, the odd loan, the endless footling, and horseplay he plagued them with, and the way he had put ideas into Tom's head, and agitated Maisie.

'We'll see how it turns out,' Max said. 'Goodnight now.'

12

Max shut the bedroom door and climbed onto the high, bouncy bed and Gertie joined him. They rolled together, meeting at the sagging centre, then each turned outwards making the springs chime. The silence was punctuated by Wilf's coughing coming from beyond their bedroom door.

First Gertie then Max gave a tug to win more of the eiderdown. After a few moments, Gertie was asleep, letting out her breath rhythmically through flabby lips, like the flatulent escape of air from the bladder of a football. Max was still very much awake, and still seething.

He prided himself on being a patient man but enough was enough. Things had to be said. He turned towards Gertie and released his outrage into her ear.

'You know what, Gertie...' he began.

'I'm asleep, Max! Or was!' she protested.

'Your Wilf really does take the bally biscuit. Did you hear him? Pushing me into going cap-in-hand to Cecil to put over on him some untried act, dreamed up by someone who is clearly going balmy on the crumpet. And with a bally strike in the offing...'

Gertie's head spun round to face her husband.

'Stop that nasty talk at once!' she hissed.

He heard a familiar little break in her voice; it was a vocal oddity denoting injury. She could invoke it when she was defending the indefensible and wanting to appear badly treated.

'Sorry, Gert,' said Max but then became defiant. 'Sorry. But the bloke's off his onion. He's cracked! And I'll tell you this for nothing – he'll be the end of us. He's bally well almost taken over. When he's around, Tom hangs on his words, Maisie near wets her drawers over his jokes and you pamper him at every turn...'

'Stop this at once!' Gertie ordered, staring at him, although neither could see the other in the dark.

Using once more the note of pathos, she brought Max to heel.

'Just think. You just think...' she started, and then waited, to ensure that Max did just that.

'Put yourself in the shoes of that poor man, who, if you hadn't noticed, is not in the best of health. Who has fought and suffered for his country. Who has sacrificed three of his toes, well, toe ends.'

'Two. Two toe ends.'

'Two, then. Who has lost his beloved wife. Who has struggled to find an act he can live off and, along the way, been pelted with whelks and God knows what else. Do you wonder that he's ended up a bit strange?'

Max lay and silently soaked up the punishment.

'All we are doing is giving shelter to my only living relative...'

'But Gert, your husband and children are still alive...we're here.'

'...a poor man with a bad chest and a limp, and a mind full of bloodshed and horrors that we can't imagine. Tell me, kind sir, while my brother was facing all that carnage where were you? Where were you, Maximilian Pyle?'

Gertie paused again to create a silence that she dared Max to fill.

'I'll tell you where, Max. Fiddling. Playing in the pit at The Paragon and then enjoying a bellyful of beer and a pipe. And if I know men, no doubt talking smutty about the women in the business.'

She moved her head even closer to his ear so he could get the full effect of her contempt.

'Either that, or you were on stage playing the musical clown at the Victoria, lapping up the applause, while our Wilf was a world away from home, outside his tent, facing discharge, sweating like a pig in the sun and trying to keep the flies off his toe stumps.'

Gertie had said her piece. She gave the eiderdown a pull strong enough to leave Max's backside uncovered. He did not have enough fight left in him to respond and the cold slowly and inexorably numbed his rear end. He lay in silence.

Eventually, Gertie made the involuntary snuffle that announced her descent into sleep. But he wouldn't sleep, he knew, because there was something else to be said; it had to be voiced if he really was a man and not a mouse.

'While we're at it, I suppose you'll want me to smoke outside like last time? Well, I think that it's a bit of a devil if a man can't enjoy a pipeful of pigtail in his own home. At his own hearth...'

Gertie was awake and fired up in seconds.

'But it's not your own home, or your own hearth, Max. It's Haim's, Mr Cohen's. We haven't got a home, remember?'

She delivered this as though she wanted him to know that he had failed her but she regretted it immediately. Her anger fell away. What had happened between them to make her talk this way?

She had alarmed herself. How could she turn on this constant provider, protector, this soul-mate? What was going wrong with their marriage? Max was a good man, a good father.

The hard edge in her voice was replaced by softer tones. It was not easy, even for her, to have Wilf staying, but there was a thing called family duty.

'Asking you to go outside with your pipe today was to ease his cough. Max. Have you not a thimbleful of sympathy for Wilf's state of health? He's clemming. You can hear it; his chest's packing up, never mind his head. Do you want to see him off? Do you?'

'Of course not, Gert. Course not,' said Max. He knew that Gertie would relish the surrender in his voice, and the fact that she knew she had won. Again.

'Now try to get to sleep,' she said, the sharp edge returning. 'And no fidgeting about because I've ...just... about... had enough.'

You've had enough, Max thought. You've had enough?

He knew it would be a long time before his anger cooled enough for him to sleep, and he was right. As Gertie fell to slobbery snoring he gave the eiderdown a gentle tug and won enough of it to cover his bottom but it took him an hour of restlessness before he fell headlong into unconsciousness.

<hr />

Although seven hours had passed, Max felt that he had only just fallen asleep when he was woken abruptly by the sound of a cornet.

He wondered whether the Salvation Army band was playing

in the street. Silly – they were never out in darkness. It dawned on him that it was Wilf greeting the new day with a reveille, no doubt to annoy Maisie. The music stopped and was replaced by some sort of incantation.

Gertie sat up in bed and Wilf, squinting, could see that she was smiling. Evidently last night's thunder had cleared the air; today she was pure sunshine.

'Listen Max...listen to him. Remember that bit of nonsense...?' she said, cocking an ear. She started to join in with the words....'

'...*mistress of all mistresses, get out of your barnacle and put on your squibs and crackers, for a white-faced simminy has got a spark of hot cockalorum on its tail...*

She tilted her head. 'Can you hear, Max? Wilf always used to recite that to Maisie when he came to stay. She'll love hearing him saying it again, even though she's nearly a woman. Remember it?'

'Yes, unfortunately. And I remember the cornet. They're no more pleasing this time around.' Gertie was far too happy to chide him.

When all was quiet again, Max decided to go off to wash and shave, only to find Wilf at the sink, using Max's City Gent Patent Safety Razor.

Wilf was bright-eyed and chirpy. He winked a good morning, and, through a cloud of foam, said that he hoped Max wouldn't mind 'you know, sharing your tackle.'

He did not seem to notice that Max did not reply, nor did he appear to feel any guilt as Max delved in the bottom of the cabinet and brought out the old cut-throat razor. He had abandoned this when Gertie bought him the City Gent, at a time when money was easier.

Max looked on with contempt at the long, bent figure at the mirror and reviled his floppy cowlick and his tired underwear; this beanpole with a nose like the parish pick-axe, this interloper, this leech.

'Topping razor, Maxie. Lovely clean cut.'

Max had an urge to put his thumbs round the freshly shaved throat of his brother-in-law but took the less dramatic option of simply chuntering as he trooped off to find yesterday's Comet.

He tore squares the size of a postage stamp from the margin and had them ready for the inevitable nicks that would come when he finally got to the sink to shave with the cut-throat. It was back to the old routine. Spit and newspaper always stopped the bleeding.

As he returned to the sink, he saw that Gertie had brought from the cupboard a string of sausages for breakfast and was arranging them in a pan beside the fire. They would be Houtmann's best.

He started to walk towards the stairs on his way down to the privy, but Wilf – his immaculately smooth, pallid cheeks, flanking the toothy smile – limped past, beat him to it. It seemed to Max that Wilf had a knack of always being in the wrong place at the wrong time.

As he finished shaving, Maisie emerged from the bedroom, a blanket hanging from her shoulders, her hair resembling dried hay, her eyes barely open. At that moment, she was a child again in Max's eyes.

'Morning, father,' she said huskily.

Max saw that she was in low spirits. He gave her a sympathetic smile and laid his hand on her arm in a gesture of understanding. She turned a thumb in the direction of the stairs and hunched her shoulders as if to ask: 'What can we do about Uncle Wilf?'

He put his arm round her. They were fellow victims. He was about to try to reassure her that the situation really was temporary when Gertie, kneeling at the fire, shouted over the sound of the sizzling and spitting from the pan: 'Maisie, do me a kindness, love. Trip down to Uncle Wilf and say that his breakfast is nearly ready. Tell him it's his favourite – pork links.'

Max tutted to himself. Pork links? What's wrong with 'sausages'? Gertie must be doing it for devilment...

Maisie went off sulkily. Uncle Wilf was being treated like royalty. She saw it as an unholy alliance, him and mother, with no one else counting. A tender feeling of protectiveness for her father flooded through her.

Max, his neck decorated with three patches of bloodied newspaper, turned away from the mirror and scowled towards Gertie who blithely ignored his wrath.

His breakfast is nearly ready. His breakfast?

The words were ashes in his mouth, a mouth that had not been favoured with the peppery delight of a Houtmann's World Exhibition Gold Medal Sausage in many a month.

As he took the steps down to the privy, he cherished a hope that when he returned there would be at least a couple left for the master of the house.

My journal

January 22

The strike will start tomorrow. After we returned from a quite hot-tempered union meeting, another debate started, involving the family.

Father finally accepted that, as Tom and I are determined to come out, he must strike too but he did so with bad grace, warning us that it would be the end of our act and of his career.

Mother was in tears but didn't come down on either side. She is paralysed by her love for us all.

Before we gathered round the table, Tom (knowing that Cecil had pencilled in Uncle Wilf to do his Zulu turn tomorrow night) came into my room and said that he intended to go out there and confront him.

Tom sat at the table and said: 'Uncle Wilf, I don't suppose we need to ask you whether you're ready for the barricades? A bit of picketing?'

He would help, of course, he said. He was one hundred per cent for the strike. Then he said: 'But not tomorrow. I'm doing a spot at the Astoria. Trying the act out.'

All eyes turned to him. Father was dumbstruck, as we were.

Pa glowered and said that he had expected Wilf to be in the vanguard. He asked what had happened to the rabble-rouser of the family.

Uncle Wilf was very calm. He said that he wanted us all to trust him and that 'it' was not what it seemed.

Tom was red with rage. I saw him clench his fists, and when Uncle Wilf tried to explain more fully, Tom cut him, and stormed out. As his bedroom door slammed we heard him say 'Blackleg!'

It was all so alarming but I can smile now about what happened next.

We had planned to listen as Uncle Wilf went through the new act but because he was about to betray us, we denied him the privilege.

Undaunted, Uncle unpacked his gear and proceeded to rehearse, having put on his old pith helmet and swathed himself in his flag

He muttered some of his lines then took off the helmet, put charcoal on his face and donned the black wig.

So there he was, with his lily-white chest, black face and curly wig, and holding his African club and a coconut, apparently talking to himself, when there was a tap on the top stair and Mr Cohen came in carrying a plate of cold fried fish topped by a paper package.

He gave Uncle Wilf the sort of thin smile people reserve for simpletons.

Mr Cohen said: 'Just a bit of fish, Mrs Pyle, and a sliver or two of smoked salmon from my brother in Stepney.'

Then he asked father whether he might have a private word. They went half way down the stairs leading to the privy.

We heard Mr Cohen, dear man, saying that he was aware of the strike, and that father was not to worry about the rent for a month. We were to treat this as a contribution from the Cohens to what he knew would be a just fight.

I would have loved to know what Mr Cohen said to Mrs Cohen about the Pyle family witch doctor when he returned downstairs!

PS There was an advertisement in the Comet today for the most sublime bicycle, illustrated by a young woman scorching down a hill with the wind blowing back the mutton-leg sleeves of her cycle dress.

She was riding ONE-HANDED, using the other to hold on to her hat. The stuff of dreams!

13

There was no cornet reveille to wake Maisie on the first day of the music hall strike, and no nonsensical doggerel being recited outside her bedroom door.

She woke, in daylight, to silence, and was immediately brought down on remembering that Uncle Wilf was in disgrace.

She was over the shock of his decision to appear at the Astoria, and was now convinced that there had to be a reason that did not imply disloyalty to the family.

She could not bear the idea that he was being cut off, and wondered about the consequences for her mother for whom Wilf was irreplaceable.

When Maisie had washed and dressed, she joined her father and Tom at the table. Gertie was stirring the porridge, sitting stiff-backed, rigid with tension. Untypically, Tom, on the other hand, glowed with early-morning energy. The day he had waited for had finally arrived. Father was deep in thought, his hand lying protectively on that morning's Comet.

A burbly cough and splashing from behind the curtain announced that Wilf was washing. He pulled the curtain to one side and called: 'All right if I use the safety razor?'

Max's reply was flat: 'Just for today.'

A pall of silence fell over the table. It was broken only by the chink of spoons against the sides of bowls.

When Wilf emerged from behind the curtain, unsmiling and startlingly pale he offered a stiff 'Good morning.' Gertie answered almost inaudibly, Maisie grudgingly. Max and Tom did not reply.

Max put down his spoon, moved from the table and sank into his chair with his newspaper, and lit his pipe defiantly. Surely Gertie would not expect consideration to be shown to a blackleg, even if the blackleg in question was a treasured brother?

Wilf went about the room laying out, and then gathering, the items he needed for his act and packing them into one of his bags. He stowed away two coconuts and his script and lodged them between the knobkerrie club, the assegai (the blade wrapped in cloth) and the coconut shy. He then slipped his tin of powdered charcoal into his waistcoat pocket.

Wilf declined Gertie's timid invitation to porridge saying he really ought to be setting off for the Astoria. Gertie knew that this would be for a run-through of the new act, to work out things with the musicians, who would be amateurs or non-strikers (she could not bring herself to use the word blackleg, now that Wilf was one).

Tom began scanning The Performer to see if the dispute was being reported. Max was reading the Comet.

He looked up and said: 'My goodness, have a butchers at this, Tom! We're big news. They're calling us The Music Hall Warriors!'

Tom was tickled by the thought, and intrigued that his father said 'we're,' signalling his new willingness to be counted among the strikers. Tom had a theory that, faced with no alternative but to strike, Max would begin to draw on bitterness over past injustices and would find release in the fight.

'So we're warriors?' Max chuckled. 'Some warriors! There's little Eli and his gammy leg. Ma with her swollen ankles. Little miss here, knee high to a grasshopper.' Maisie, taking the top off her breakfast egg, her face deadpan, piped up. 'And don't forget Razzle and Dazzle. What is they say? Let slip the dogs of war!'

Max peered closely at the Comet report. 'It predicts here that tonight a dozen London halls will have to shut. Can't see it myself but time will tell.'

Gertie spun away from her work at the sink, her face reflecting her fear that this strike business would run out of control and consume them.

She was taken aback by Max's sudden, and growing, enthusiasm for the strike but not for long. It dawned on her that he was like a tethered dog that had chewed through the restraining rope and was free, finally, to roam and bite his master. She noted that yesterday once again he had mentioned the dud coin Cecil had once palmed off on them.

Max had, indeed, found the embers of old injustices reigniting within him. Only that morning, in the privy, he had called to mind how Cecil had taken sadistic pleasure in learning that Gertie's funny turn had stopped them working, and had exploited their situation, offering a low fee for them to make a comeback.

Breakfast was over, and Tom began pacing around the table like a boxer calling up reserves of adrenaline – speculating, predicting, exploring tactics the Alliance should look at, ideas he might offer to that morning's meeting.

He reached for the Comet, sat down and devoured the report about the strike, sneering when he read of threats by the proprietors of repercussions.

'Mother, listen to this...

"...and Mr Stoll has sent a message to everyone round the halls saying he doesn't care for strikes." Evidently it upsets him and we must all stop this nonsense at once. Well, too late!'

Gertie scraped away fiercely at the porridge pan, as if she were trying to scrub away her worry.

'Many will heed him, Tom,' she said. 'Fear, you see. He's not a man to cross. Him and Edward Moss, sorry – or Sir Edward, is it? – seem to have got their fingers into every decent variety hall in the country. How can they know what it's like for us?'

Tom scoffed. 'They'll soon see that we're not just misbehaving school children. The arrogance! We'll take the cane away from them, and give them a taste.'

Max winced, then shook his head resignedly. Gertie said: 'I can't see how it's got to this sorry state.'

A moment later Maisie came upstairs from the privy and announced cheerfully: 'We have a visitor.'

Eli followed her, swaying on the stairs, pulling his weak leg behind him. He smiled in his open, child-like way. Gertie led him to the sofa. She noticed for the first time that his hair was greying at the temples. He had the look of an ancient schoolboy.

Wilf had been standing by his bags, with his coat on, ready to leave. He greeted Eli and then walked towards the stairs. Wilf was halfway down when Max came down after him and said grimly: 'We need to go out to the back.'

They stood in the rain, at the privy wall, the tall and slightly stooped Wilf, and the squat, square Max, in his waistcoat, his shirt sleeves rolled up, his collarless shirt undone, the rain disregarded.

'Look, I don't want to upset Gertie,' said Max, 'but I need to know why you're cutting the legs from under us, working for Cecil – giving him a helping hand while we're making a stand?'

Wilf did not answer. His black forelock was flat against his brow, plastered down by the rain. He was hunched. He looked like a gaunt seabird patiently seeing out a squall.

'Wilf – what was it you said to me when you first met Cecil? You said you'd met his sort in the army. A bad egg. All prick and breeches. You said that he was the kind of man people would love to knee in the tallywags.'

'He is exactly that kind of man, Max. I suspect he has no scruples, and I don't care for the way he is with Maisie, the way he looks at her.'

'Right. You loathed him on sight. But suddenly you're happy to help him in his hour of need...?'

Wilf's face hardened a little as he tired of Max's taunts.

'Whoa there! At long last, we're getting a taste of the militant Max!' he said. 'Don't worry, I know that Cecil is only interested in number one. I know he uses people. You should know that too, Max.'

'You're saying that he used me?' Max sounded piqued.

'People are used, Max. It's the way things are. Sometimes, needs must. We have to bend the knee. Doff the cap. But as the great bard said, a man's a man for a' that...'

He gave Max a half-smile of inquiry, cocking his head to see whether he was familiar with the Burns song.

'...the honest man, tho' e'er sae poor, is king o' men for 'a' that.'

Max's took this to be just another wilful display of Scottishness.

'We're all tools in the hands of people who have just a little more power than us, Max. But we have to be clever, and not miss a chance to respond in kind when an opportunity comes up. And there's more than one way to skin a rabbit.'

Max took a moment to fathom what he might mean. Wilf had always been a thinker as well as a clown. He came over as daft at times but he had things weighed up – people, the world, matters that Max struggled to fathom.

'Trust me, Max. I wouldn't work against you and the family. But while you're sitting in judgment on me, ask yourself whether you would be on strike if Tom and Maisie hadn't come out. Come on man, admit it – tonight you would have been up there fiddling like fury for Cecil.'

Max felt as he did when Maisie or Tom argued him into a corner and he was pinned down, the ammunition box empty, the gun jammed. There was nothing he could say.

He turned back and walked towards the door leading to the stairs. Wilf, with his big bag of tricks and his limp-along gait, his raincoat swinging about his legs, hurried through puddles towards the tram stop for the Astoria.

The strike meeting was being held in a dusty hall with a harmonium on the stage, and walls hung with faded grey photographs of the long-dead, and framed certificates turned to a parched brown by the passing of the years. Next to the harmonium was a table around which sat union officials talking intently and comparing notes.

The cacophony of chatter and argument hit Max and Tom as they walked in. All seats had been taken and every few minutes the hall doors swung open and yet more people entered, shaking the rain off their clothes.

Max spotted familiar faces wherever he looked; acts he had worked with over the years, and stagehands he had joked with and teased in theatres throughout London. He could see Eli from the Astoria on the front row of the lines of fold-up chairs.

The chairman, an imposing middle-aged man with the pudgy face of a retired boxer, called the meeting to order, tapping his pencil on a water jug.

'First, I would like to congratulate you on showing readiness to fight against sweated work, and the withdrawal of our right to choose who to work for, and when. You should be proud of yourselves.'

After summarising the grievances that led to the strike, the chairman said: 'Today many of you will feel nervous, afraid even. Well, let me assure you that you have nothing to fear. All we have to do is stick together. Simple.'

He offered an example to illustrate the potent power that came when labour was withdrawn, reading from a newspaper cutting he took from his file.

It described how an orchestral conductor at a concert in America recently took to the rostrum, raised his baton and brought it down to summon up the first chord of a symphony.

'And you know what? There was total silence,' he said, pacing along the edge of the stage.

The chairman had become a comedian after boxing, and before socialism had lured him away from the halls. He had learned how audiences could be manipulated by silences.

'Not a peep. Not a mouse's fart. Not a note,' he said, surveying the captivated faces ranged in ranks before him. 'But there was message in that silence. That silence shouted: Solidarity!'

The chairman let his listeners think about the word for a moment.

'Result? The audience stormed off to demand their money back, and the American musicians' union, having been rebuffed by the management for weeks, sent a message saying: 'We will talk but we will not play. In the meantime, good luck with selling tickets for silent recitals.'

Cheers and laughter rang round the hall. Max noticed that Tom was applauding wildly. There was joy in his face.

'If ever you have doubts, say to yourself: I have skills – that's why they put me on bills. Those skills enrich my employer but I am not a chattel.'

The chairman paused as first one man and then another hurried in to the hall and down the central aisle, and climbed on to the stage to deliver notes.

After a moment's conversation, the chairman said: 'Some most heartening news. Pickets are already turning up at theatres in the West End. The Holborn Empire is closing, and I feel confident that we can expect that a dozen or more will shut tonight'

When cheering and stamping broke out he flapped his hands up and down to request quiet.

'We are also being told that several of our most eminent artistes are showing solidarity with us, and already two have promised that we may use their cars during the dispute. Their financial and moral support will also be forthcoming.'

He paused as a young man arrived and loped down the aisle and whispered something in the chairman's ear and passed him a note.

'I am told that the sun is going down on Adney Payne's Empires at this very moment.' There was wild cheering.

'Halls in Balham...(cheers), Clapham...(cheers) and Croydon...(cheers) are most unlikely to have audiences tonight.'

The chairman tapped again on the water jug and appealed for order and then said: 'Finally, before our brothers outline arrangements I remind you that not everyone will have the courage to do the right thing. Some members will sneak away and help managements to patch together some sort of a bill.' Max and Tom looked at each other in acknowledgement that they had been harbouring one such backslider.

The chairman stooped forward and fixed the room with a penetrating stare, and declared in a malevolent whisper: 'For those people who decide to turn their faces against us, the text for today is: By their deeds shall we know them.'

Max had watched enthralled as the mood in the crowd changed from anxiety to feverish excitement.

'Who'd have believed it?' he shouted, over the hubbub of dozens of fervent conversations.

'Me. I would,' Tom said quietly, fixing his father with a look of mock disapproval and adding: 'Oh ye of little faith...'

14

Wilf had been shot three times on the empty Astoria stage but not once had the sound of the gun going off coincided with his descent to the floorboards.

With the last missed cue came a terrible fear that the young stand-in drummer, whose experience was limited to Orange marches, would turn tonight's dramatic portrayal of war – and Wilf's heartfelt monologue – into hilarious comedy.

The Zulu king's fall was the climax of the act, the shock that would surely bring a gasp from the audience, releasing them from ten minutes of suspense.

Wilf, wearing his black wig and holding aloft the knobkerrie, looked down on the fresh-faced, ginger-haired youth, and his military side drum, with a mixture of pity and impatience.

The boy had mastered the required rumbling on the bass drum that Wilf requested to set the mood as he took his place on what would be a darkened stage but producing the gunshot sound was beyond him.

'Don't be nervous, son,' said Wilf. 'Look, when we do it tonight, I'll lift my heel – look! – and you give me a rimshot; hit the edge of the drum at the very moment I lower it, so I'm shot, and then I'll go down.'

Wilf was breathing heavily from the effort of it all. 'Let's try it just once more,' he said, moving the coconut shy to one side to clear space for his next fall. 'Watch the heel.'

He then went slowly and balletically through the action of clubbing the coconut, without hitting it, and, as planned – turning stage right – put on an exaggerated expression of surprise, as if sensing danger.

He raised his heel and heard the crack of the rimshot, the word 'Sorry sir!' and another after he lowered it by which time he was falling forward on to all fours.

Wilf was devastated. What a shame if this, the flowering of a lifetime's work, turned into a shambles that was more chaotic than any of the many that had gone before.

Yet you could not blame the boy, whose face was now redder than his hair. He was just trying to earn a couple of bob and, as a fellow blackleg, Wilf knew he had no right to criticise.

When Wilf had arrived, Artie – in his loud-check suit one size too small for his muscle-bound physique – led him to Cecil, who was at the cash desk listing artists on a blackboard that was serving as a bill.

Cecil looked relieved, and shook Wilf's hand ingratiatingly, apologising, saying that things were in a muddle but pledging that in the best of old traditions the show would go on.

'I take it, Wilf, that Max has fallen in with the rabble-rousers?' Wilf did not reply. He had a good idea what was coming.

'You must tell him when you see him that we won't need him or the family in the future.'

He announced this matter-of-factly, adding with a touch of cordiality: 'This doesn't apply to you of course, if things go well tonight. You know, even if Max's young lad was hell-bent on striking, and he bullied Maisie into it, it needn't have stopped Max coming on with his fiddle act. Now the Pyles have burned their bridges. Full stop.'

He pointed to Wilf's name half way down the bill, which

contained several smudged deletions and additions.

'Is this all right?' Cecil asked.

NIGHTMARE IN ZULULAND
A hero relives the terror of Rorke's Drift

'Haven't used your name, Wilf. Best not to, not in this climate. Grudges, reprisals. You know, after the trouble ends.'

'But Cecil, I wasn't a hero, and I wasn't at Rorke's Drift. I was at Isandlwana. A disaster. We lost 1,000 men. And I lost two toe ends.'

'Come on, Wilf, how are they to know?' Cecil replied.

Wilf knew that he was talking to deaf ears but he said, anyway: 'Actually, this isn't really about heroes; it's about those who ...well, it's entertainment but there's a serious message.'

'Bunkum man! Bosh!' Cecil said, slapping Wilf on the back. 'Give 'em English heroes and you can't go wrong!'

Cecil introduced Wilf to a tousle-haired pianist – who wore a crumpled dinner jacket with stains on the shiny lapels, and who smelled of gin – and then to the young drummer. An elderly gentleman holding a clarinet and an emaciated girl with a violin arrived and settled near the piano.

A small, bald man with a stoop was on the stage in front of a fold-down table. He had placed wine glasses in a row and was pouring water into them in measured amounts.

From time to time he would call to the pianist: 'An E please' ...'Tell me, does this F sound a teeny bit sharp?' and then pour away, or add, water from a jug.

When, finally, the bald man began to play Two Lovely Black Eyes by striking the glasses with tiny hammers, Wilf took a seat on the front row of the hall where two or three small groups had formed, waiting to perform for Cecil's approval.

He took the opportunity of surveying the Astoria in full daylight, taking in its faded glory.

This was a high hall with central skylights. The plaster walls around the balcony were covered in a raised design, based on interweaving vines and bunches of grapes. The fruit and the leaves had lost almost all their colour. He could just make out that swags of fruit and flowers across the top of the stage had originally been gilded but were now caked with a tarry coating created by cigar smoke and humid air.

Wilf unpacked his bag in an aisle and moved his equipment to the wings of the stage where three genteel, well-rounded ladies in identical kimonos were helping each other to apply black lines to give their eyes an Oriental slant.

He heard one say girlishly: 'So very exciting! What a step up from our G and S evenings in dear old Staines!'

When the man with his tray of wine glasses came off, to overdone applause from Cecil ('You'll do very nicely, Ben!'), the matronly ladies took centre stage.

One called out to the pianist. Her voice was the warble Wilf had heard used by a old comic who would come on as a geriatric dowager duchess– 'Please remember – allegretto grazioso!'

After several attempts, the Three Little Maids From School finally chanced on approximate timing and harmony, only for the pianist to lose the rhythm and finally clunk to a stop.

Cecil emerged from the depths of the hall, pushed back his bowler and shouted, irritably: 'I'm sorry ladies, you're just not carrying. It's too big a big hall. We're losing you half way back. Perhaps another time...?' The trio trooped off dejectedly.

When the last of the auditions was complete, Cecil approached Wilf and assured him that from the sketchy version of the Zulu act he had seen, he believed it would hold the crowd, unusual as it was. Not every act had to be light-hearted, he said. They would love the bloodthirsty bit – especially the climax when the chief was shot dead, and the coconut was smashed.

Wilf did not need reassuring. This act was what it all had been leading up to; the years before had been an apprenticeship.

As he left the Astoria for some food before the performance, he met Eli coming in to start work. Cecil's brother Artie was lurking in the foyer and when Eli spoke it was in a near-whisper: 'I've come from the meeting. Halls are shutting all over the place. I feel terrible about it, being here, but there's mother...'

Wilf took Eli's shoulders in his hands and said: 'Don't feel guilty. We each have to do what's right for us. They might call us blacklegs but things aren't always black and white. Mostly things are grey.'

Eli's face showed that he had not understood.

Taking a seat in the window of a pie shop, Wilf found that he had no appetite. He was troubled by the rift with Max and the children, and anxious about the things that could go wrong with the act; the drummer missing the prompt, or that he would start coughing when he was lying dead. It would take only one mishap to sabotage the dramatic power of the piece.

He loved a laugh, and had always tried to treat life as if it were a lark, while waiting for fate's boxing glove to land another haymaker. But tonight was not a laughing matter. It was a test of something special he had created from somewhere deep inside. It had to be right, even if it was for one night only.

While he toyed with his pie, a few hundred yards away the South London Music Hall was staging makeshift entertainment, despite the strike. Of necessity, it was a basic – simply elephants occupying, then leaving, the stage, followed by scenic pictures projected onto a screen. The images were met with silence.

The audience felt they had been short-changed. When they grew restive, the manager – mopping his brow with a large handkerchief – went on stage and announced: 'You've seen the elephants, and you've seen the pictures. Now which would you like to have again – the elephants or the pictures?' The answer came in a torrent of booing.

Meanwhile, the resolve of the manager at the Holborn Empire to put on some sort of show at any cost was weakened somewhat when only one musician (a drummer) turned up.

Undaunted, he brought in a pianist to play a selection from The Belle of New York. This was followed by a young girl singing 'Goodbye.' The audience responded in kind before storming out, and even the promise of the projected image of The Alps Seen Through A Telescope was not enough to stem the exodus.

Wilf buttoned up his coat, leaving most of his pie. Unusually, he had pre-show nerves. It was not just worry over drummer. It was the thought of Max and Tom and Maisie out there in the cold pleading with artists not to work. The word that kept coming into his head was: Blackleg.

My journal

January 23

I was so upset this morning about Uncle Wilf, and the strike, that I decided to escape.

Knowing that mother would spend the day in a lather while father and Tom were out at the union meeting, I set off on an adventure, exploring bits of London that I had not visited.

I armed myself with a new map that shows all the stations they have just united under the title 'Underground.' It is a miracle of logic – even I could understand it! Later, I found timetables for the Omnibus Company whose vehicles have now been painted a glorious red.

I found two of the cycle shops on my list but did not have the energy to wend my way to Blackfriars where I know there is thriving indoor cycle school. A treat deferred.

In the end I had to sit on a wall for a rest, and eat the sandwiches mother had prepared. (Sorry, Mr Cohen, but you can keep your slimy smoked salmon. Only my acute hunger enabled me to get the stuff down!).

How I appreciated being back in the warm after my tiring day of meandering, and it was a pleasure to hear from father that the strike is already causing grief to the owners.

It was good to see that a common cause has drawn father and Tom together. Great excitement and chatter between them over the stew tonight!

It is almost 11 o'clock now and there is no sign of Uncle Wilf. Mother says, with a quiver of her bottom lip, that as Wilf will be uncomfortable with us when he returns from the Astoria, she expects him to stay out late (hence another Key in C note).

I believe he will leave us tomorrow, as things are so difficult.

I told Tom that I simply cannot wait to hear whether the Zulu act was a success. Tom said he didn't care and made a sour quip about Uncle Wilf not having to use charcoal on his legs (ie that he was already a blackleg).

Cruel, I thought, and told him so. For me, Uncle Wilf is still my uncle and it is my duty to try to understand why he acted as he did.

15

Wilf was up and shaving before anyone else had stirred. Gertie was woken by the rattle of the lid of the boiling kettle on the trivet of the range, and muffled coughing.

Max was snoring beside her. She eased out of bed so as not to disturb him and crept into the main room where Wilf was filling the teapot.

He was dressed, and the eiderdown was folded beside the pillow on the sofa. His two bags lay alongside.

Gertie looked up into her brother's face and said: 'Wilf – you're not away? Surely not. There's no need. We'll all talk.'

Wilf's smile showed appreciation of his sister's concern. 'No bother, Gert. Things won't be right, so I'm off back to Glasgow.'

'No, Wilf. Stay. I'll talk to Max.'

'I chose my path and knew what to expect. Anyway, I should be getting back to see how that lawyer's getting on with Morag's affairs. He should know more by now.'

Gertie poured tea and then said gently: 'How did it go? The act.'

'Even better than planned. Perfect. The coconut shattered a

treat. I even died at the right time,' he said happily.

Gertie looked puzzled but then all her life she had found Wilf as baffling as he was endearing.

'But the rest of the bill was a farce. Terrible music, terrible acts. The punters were hopping mad but, you know what, Gert, they gave me a hearing and absolute thunders when I'd finished.'

Wilf could see Gertie's eyes brimming. At last, she said to herself, some joy for Wilf after all those years in the wilderness – the taunts, the heckles, the iniquity of the whelks.

'No need to upset yourself, Gertie. Come on now. Look, there's a train mid-morning and I'll be on it. But I need a favour. If anyone comes here asking about me, tell them I went off to do the vent act in Darlington.'

'You're going to Darlington?'

'No. I'm going to Glasgow.'

She held her hands to her mouth.

'Wilf. You're in trouble. What have you done?'

'Nothing bad, Gert. Actually, something good.'

Gertie tilted her head at a sound from the bedroom. Max was stirring.

Wilf picked up his bags and she led him down to the foot of the stairs so that she could say goodbye properly, away from Max.

They sat on the stairs and Wilf said: 'Today I feel better than I have in months so, as your auld faither would have said, dinna fesh, lassie!' He looked into Gertie's face and said earnestly: 'But I'll be feshed over you, Gert. You're not right. You're scared all the time.'

'Not all the time. It's only nerves.'

'All the time. It is all the time. And when I get what's coming from Morag's money I'm going to pay a doctor to look inside that head of yours. There's a whole department now up in Stobhill Hospital looking into... well, damaged feelings I suppose, the hurt life can leave us with. Injuries nobody can see.'

Gertie said nothing.

'Tell me. What is it, Gert? Is it Max? Or the young ones?'

Again she did not answer and in the silence between them they heard water being poured into the sink, and footsteps above.

At last, Wilf said: 'I think something big happened around the time we moved from Crail. And I think that now something sets you off, lets loose what's locked in your head. You know, Gert, I saw you change that time you came up to help me with Morag.'

Gertie found Wilf's insight disturbing. He was right about the trip to help with Morag.

She remembered her terror on the train but there was also the harrowing scene they came across next morning, out walking near Gallowgate.

'Wilf, do you remember the big fire. That big lodging house in Watson Street?'

'Who could forget it...'

He looked expectantly at Gertie, wondering what anguish the sights and sounds of that day had inflicted on his sister, and said: 'What stays with me is the sight of the blind man coming out, and the cripple on the roof. And did you see the one-legged man who was helped out and was so grateful to have been saved.'

Gertie shook her head. 'Poor Irishmen who'd come over to earn a crust. Simple, blameless chaps.'

Wilf said: 'Did I ever tell you that someone had gone round shouting "Fire" but nobody went out because they'd had stuff pinched from their rooms before when there'd been false alarms...?'

'Poor devils. It really got to me, hearing the tales. People jumping, crawling out. And just think Wilf – all of that horror happened just a few steps from the hall where I won that tea caddy in the singing contest when I was wee.'

Wilf laid his hand on top of Gertie's head, and said: 'One day we'll find a doctor who can flush your demons out. And that's a promise. You're carrying too much painful stuff in there!'

He stood up and after a few moments, during which he

appeared to be girding himself to say something important, confessed softly: 'You know Gert, I'm not jumping on your bandwagon but I think I've been carrying a ghost about with me.'

Gertie looked up with a start. Wilf was not given to self-confession.

'But people would never know,' she said. 'You're so full of it, Wilf, the life and soul.'

'Don't be fooled. And don't think I'm feeling sorry for myself but for years I've had this strange feeling of not being totally in charge of...well, me, myself.

Gertie asked in a whisper: 'But why didn't you let on, Wilf?'

Wilf looked away, and became pensive, as if regretting having let his guard down. Then, suddenly, he said: 'Did you know I killed a Zulu boy?'

'No, but if you did, that was your job, Wilf. You did your duty.'

Gertie remembered the chilling monologue she had heard Wilf practising in the night.

'Duty? It was me, Gert, a human being, who shot him, and never mind about it being my duty. The lad was not killed by the 24th Foot, he was killed by my finger squeezing the trigger.'

'You can't blame yourself. I won't allow it. You'd been sent to kill. Trained for it. Paid to do it.'

'It's no excuse but you know, Gert, Zulu fighting was merciless, and not only towards us, the enemy. You might end up a dead Zulu if you came away with a wound in your back. Clubbing round the head, then an agonising death, sometimes with a spear stuck up into you from below; that's what cowards got.

'So when this boy begged me to kill him, it wasn't only courage, he was just following training. Just as I was when I killed him. But there's a difference, Gert.'

Wilf looked at his sister with an intensity that, she knew, would lead to some vital revelation.

'Zulus don't fear death as much as us because they know that their spirit will move on. Maybe it was my guilt playing tricks but after the murder – because that's what it was – for a long time I felt that the boy's spirit has been in me.'

'Dear God.'

'But don't worry Gert. He's gone! I feel different inside. Maybe it was doing the performance last night.'

Wilf's grin returned. Gertie got up and he clasped her to him, then picked up his bags.

He paused outside the privy door and said: 'About the strike, Gert. Try to explain to Max that although I went to work, it was for my benefit, not Cyril's. I used him, and his hall, and his audience, to find out if the Zulu turn worked. When I'd done that I managed to damage him and his takings.'

'Damage?"

'Well, let's say that last night I did more for the union cause than Max, or the children, or any union picket. And I'll be most surprised if Cecil managed to get his bowler hat on this morning.'

Gertie stood open-mouthed, puzzled and fearful.

He kissed his sister's cheek, walked off and, turning, shouted over his shoulder: 'And don't forget, Gert. I'm in Darlington!

'So he's gone,' Max said, putting on his jacket to go for his copy of the Comet. 'And you've been having a blubber.'

'Yes. And why not?'

'He felt ashamed of going on last night I suppose...?'

'Actually, no Max. He sounded proud. And I'm proud of him.'

Max sneered. He was desperately curious to know how Wilf's act had been received but chose not to ask. In the event, minutes later, Eli arrived and gave him every detail.

His head appeared at the top of the stairs and he tapped with his knuckles on the top one, out of politeness. He looked furtive.

'Is Wilf about, Mrs Pyle?'

'No, he's away to catch a train.' Hurriedly she remembered Wilf's request and added: 'Darlington. He's got a short run there with the vent act.'

'Thank God he's got away. I think they'll be coming for him

today. The bluebottles. Cecil wants him charged.'

'Oh no,' Gertie said wearily. 'What next...?'

Max decided to delay for his newspaper. Maisie appeared at the door of her bedroom and, wrapping a shawl round her shoulders, came out and greeted Eli, then, feeling the tension in the air, went off to wake Tom.

'So, come on, what's he done, Eli?' Gertie asked, bracing herself for the reply.

Eli wore the expression of a child being forced to own up.

'I suppose he told you about the show and the act and how they loved it? They raised the roof for him.'

'Yes. Eli, but he was a bit mysterious about what else had gone on...so tell me, what happened?'

Maisie and Tom sat down at the table. Eli who clasped his hands together and began to talk very quickly.

'I was in the wings waiting to put a table on stage for a man with musical wine glasses. The place was as quiet as a church when Wilf was on. They listened to every word. It stopped all the heckling of the rubbish that we'd just had. But then the business with Cecil started...'

'What business?' Max asked eagerly. 'Tell us, Eli,' Gert said. Tom and Maisie were listening intently.

'Did Wilf tell you he was going to make a speech?'

Gert shook her head. 'No but go on...'

'Anyway, after he'd done his bit, and they'd stopped clapping, he took his wig off and said to the audience that if they valued nights at the music hall they'd better stop coming for a while. He said that he was begging them to keep away from the Astoria until the strike was over, and to support artistes who were being treated badly, people like him and his family, acts like you lot, Musical Mayhem.'

Tom said: 'And Cecil just let him stand up there and say all this?'

'He'd got it out before Cecil could do anything. But when Wilf started gathering his stuff, and people whistled and clapped,

Cecil yelled from the side "Get off my stage!" Then he shouted to me "Eli, fetch Artie!"'

Eli described how he knew that Artie would be at the theatre entrance, because there was a picketing party with posters outside.

'I made myself scarce for a minute,' Eli said. 'I was going to come back and pretend to Cecil that I couldn't find Artie, and when I did come back I saw that Cecil was on his knees. His bowler was next to him, and he had his hands on his head.'

'Dear God,' said Gertie.

'Wilf had hold of the stick thing with a knob at the end, and it looked as if Wilf had fetched him one off, given him a gonging.'

'Oh dear,' said Maisie.

'Blimey!' Max said.

'Anyway, I scarpered,' Eli said. 'Disappeared sharpish and went on strike. Mother said I did quite right. Anyway, Wilf picked up his bags and tucked away his knobbly stick and set off out of the side door really fast. I heard the punters banging on Cecil's cash desk asking for their money back because of the bad show, but Cecil was still rolling round near the stage looking dizzy.'

Tom and Maisie went to her room to talk. Maisie shed a tear, seeing in her mind her uncle in a cell. Tom tried to reassure her – 'Uncle Wilf's as smart as a whip. He'll have gone to ground.'

They needed time to absorb what Eli had described, and begin to reassess, come to terms with the fact that Wilf the blackleg was in fact someone who had infiltrated, taken the fight to the enemy.

Gertie insisted that Eli have a cup of tea before leaving; she had always mothered him, responded to the child in him. She was filling the kettle when there was a heavy bang on the door at the bottom of the stairs.

Maisie went down and found herself face-to-face with a policeman who asked to come up to the rooms. As he climbed the stairs, Eli, looking terrified, whispered to Gertie: 'Don't tell them he's gone to Darlington, Mrs Pyle!'

The policeman, a brawny man who was breathing heavily from his cycle ride from the station and then his walk upstairs, had a mild manner.

There had been a spot of bother, he said, an assault, and Wilf had been named by the victim. When Gertie asked whether they were sure, as she couldn't imagine her brother being involved in anything like assault, the policeman said: 'I take it he's gone. Where was he headed?'

'Darlington,' said Gertie.

Eli stifled a feeble whinny and somehow turned it into a cough.

'You all right young man?'

'Fine, constable, thank you,' Eli said sheepishly.

'Yes,' said Gertie, 'I gather he'd been booked for a week doing his ventriloquism act. Yes, it was Darlington.'

When the policeman cycled off to use the new station telephone to pass on inquiries to Darlington (if indeed they had a phone up there; the constable knew that some places in the sticks were way behind the times), the atmosphere in the rooms fell flat.

Max had been silent throughout the events of the morning, and Tom had been subdued. From time to time Gertie glared at each in turn. How could they have misjudged Wilf?

Max finally settled to read his Comet; there was a big article on the front page about the spread of the strike.

Reaching for his tin of tobacco from the mantelpiece, he noticed that there was paper under the porcelain spaniel ornament. When he lifted it, he saw that it was a sheet of notepaper, wrapped around a £5 note.

In Wilf's handwriting was the message: 'To help a little, while we are out.' He had underlined the 'we.'

Max wondered whether Wilf had written it that way to express solidarity, or – more likely – to make him feel contrite.

16

The sight of a fashionable young woman stepping from a tram in the Strand added to Max Pyle's conviction that he must do everything in his power to make it effective.

For the woman with the long stride, the swing of the shoulders and disdainful look, he recognised as The Boneless Woman of Brazil.

She wore a bottle green coat with dark fur trim, and a huge orange hat festooned with a tower of ostrich feathers that trembled as she hurried through hissing pickets and into the sanctuary of the Tivoli booking office.

Max had begun to feel comfortable with striking and he was damned if he was going to stand by and see someone with such paltry talent cash in by betraying proper artistes.

In the moments when his fighting spirit waned, he only had to think of Cecil, of the dud half-crown and of the night he hid Razzle in his office and made Maisie cry, to feel vengeful anger rising inside him.

'Who's the blackleg?' shouted a swarthy man in the crowd of pickets, who jeered as the stage door slammed. 'Make sure we get her moniker!'

Max picked his way through the crowd to the man and said: 'She's called Blanche something or other, hails from Tring. She's billed as The Boneless Woman. Contortionist and Posturer.'

'Boneless? Spineless, I'll give you. Thank you brother. She'll go on the list.'

He pointed across the road and said with satisfaction: 'They've just persuaded another two turning up over there at the Adelphi to go home. One's some singer. Top of the bill. I gather they've got no stagehands for tonight. They'll struggle to get a show on.'

Max felt that his old sense of duty to those who ran the halls had waned. Now he was warming to the fight. He hadn't felt quite fired up enough to go leafleting with Tom, who had thrown himself headlong into things, but he was now enlisted – and it felt good. He had said many times, usually to Tom, 'Artistes are not striking types' but he was proof that this was not true.

He liked this new feeling of being disobedient, set adrift with others in the same boat. He was buoyed up by the noise around him, the placards, and the whispered guerilla tactics. He supposed that it must feel like that in war, when you were bound by reliance on each other. Maybe the newspapers weren't being too fanciful talking about Music Hall Warriors...

It was clear that not everyone felt liberated by the fight. At the edge of the group of pickets, Max picked out the forlorn figure of Brendan Cassidy, a portly man famed for his jollity in the wings at halls throughout London, and for his lyrical tenor voice. Today he looked so solitary and anxious, tensing and relaxing his jaw. Brendan had eight children.

Suddenly Max's confidence evaporated. He felt a tremor of fear over the future.

The strike would not go on forever; invading his thoughts was the question: 'What happens after all this? Will those who came out ever work again? Will halls close? Where would next month's rent come from?

Looking over the road, he saw the young, blonde-haired Highland dancers, twins, who had been on at the Astoria a week before, crossing to join the pickets outside the Adelphi. They were holding hands and giggling, nimbly picking their way through the traffic. He envied their freedom from the fear of being ruined. They had everything in front of them.

Max was distracted as a stagehand he knew from somewhere or other arrived with a pole holding a notice saying: 'Come in here for a good night's sleep,' and took up a position outside the main entrance of the Tivoli. Another sign, lodged on masonry beneath a window, bore the words 'This way in – if you want to waste your money'; one propped up beside the entrance said: 'Here, every night is Amateur Night.'

He thought with pride of Maisie, out there somewhere with pickets, but especially of Tom who had gone off leafleting at other halls.

His pride in Tom was growing each day. At the end of that morning's union meeting – as Max had turned to leave – the boy had summoned up the nerve to make a short, impromptu speech to a knot of pickets at the back of the hall.

Max, waiting at the door, had looked back and seen him hooking together his forefingers and tugging, talking about a chain being only as strong as its weakest link. At that moment Max had accepted that the young son had vanished and been replaced by a man.

Afterwards Tom had then stepped out so eagerly to get to the West End theatres that Max had been forced to ask him to slow down. Unheeding, Tom had bustled ahead towards the Tivoli, outpacing a stilt walker in a jacket made of colourful patches and wearing a notice round his neck saying 'HOLD YOUR HEAD UP HIGH.'

Max was chilled, and he was not feeling useful, so decided to head back to the East End, to see how strong the strike was there. He was especially keen to check on the Paragon in the Mile End Road.

Of all the halls he had played in, the Paragon was dearest to his heart and, to his eyes, the most beautiful.

Max had never been abroad, no further than Tilbury Docks to be truthful, but going into the Paragon made him feel as if he was entering some parched exotic land. He almost expected to feel sand under your feet. There was colour and light everywhere in the Paragon. Salmons and browns and creams, and blue pots filled with ferns, and on a summer's evening the sun would beat down through the domed glass cupola where, if you looked up, you could pick out Arab figures holding drapery.

The Paragon stage was as big as a bowling green. He called up a memory of walking on to that stage for the first time, as a young solo act, and of his confidence in commanding it.

He remembered being flanked by the huge elephant heads that supported the stage-side pillars, a lad of seventeen, with a red, spotted silk scarf round his neck, worn in the mistaken belief that it was what a Gipsy fiddler would wear.

He had not been in the least disconcerted by the knowledge that he was on his own, with just his violin, a stool and a carpenter's saw, and that a packed auditorium and 300 faces in the gallery were looking down on him, hushed and expectant, waiting to be amazed by musicianship.

He wondered whether there were still painted flamingos in flight set against a bright blue on the ceiling of the crush room, and whether the downstairs 'Paragon Dive' was still a bar that was full to bursting each night.

He had not been back for years. Perhaps now he would never see inside again, or get even as far as the marble foyer. Shame. He would have liked to have shown Tom and Maisie what a special place a really topping music hall could be, even though he knew they could not share the wistfulness he felt.

There were a couple of dozen pickets near the Paragon doors as he approached. Max was hailed by Jimmy Templeton, a comic conjurer, waving his hat. He was puzzled for a moment by his appearance, then it dawned on him that in twenty years he had never seen Jimmy in anything but the evening dress he wore on stage. Today he was wrapped in a bulky woollen coat with another of tweed beneath it. His breath turned to steam in the frosty air.

'Only two in so far, Max. A woman with three fancy dogs, and a chap carrying banjo case. Amateurs at a guess. Nothing approaching a bill for tonight.'

A stagehand from the Star in Steatham joined them and they swapped tales for a while. Rumours were related, re-told, rehashed, seasoned with unfounded detail, and sent on their way.

Jimmy said: 'They tell me that Sir Oswald Stoll has been riding about in his new Rolls Royce Silver Ghost just to demoralise the pickets...' (in other versions it was Edward Moss in his Wolseley, or Adney Payne in his Imperial with his wife at the wheel).

Word spread that Adge Braithwaite, The Pocket Goliath, had sprung up and cracked the heads of two pickets together when they barred his way, and that Marie Lloyd was coming out to sing for the pickets in the West End.

There was even some tale going round – one that most took with more than a pinch of salt – that a Zulu, the genuine article, had gone doolally, jumped off the stage and poleaxed Cecil Threadgold at the Astoria with some sort of club.

As Jimmy gossiped malevolently about Adney Payne, the Paragon owner, Max looked over his shoulder and saw someone familiar approaching. He could tell by the fiddle case and the sway of his pendulum walk that it was Issy Bass – or rather what seemed to Max to be a decrepit manifestation of him.

Max averted his eyes but Issy sashayed up to him, and, peering into his face through thick-lensed glasses, said: 'My life! If it isn't... dear... old...Maxie Pyle!' He swopped his fiddle case to the opposite hand and grasped Max's, shaking it time and again, euphoric, as if Max had come back from the dead.

Jimmy and the stagehand moved away, noting this man's instrument case, and sensing that it signalled an awkward conversation was about to take place.

'So, Maxie, old chum, are you still caressing the cat-gut?' Issy said. 'Or have you made your pile and sailed off to Little Venice?' Issy's laughter, to Max's hearing, had connotations of a death rattle. His sunken cheeks had the appearance of raw pastry, his wild moustache had been stained yellow by nicotine.

'Still fiddling, Issy, but with the family now. Multi-instrumental act. That is, when we're working.'

'So you're not on tonight, Maxie?'

'No, Issy.'

'Just come to see how this strike business is framing?'

'Well, no...'

'Don't tell me you're a picket, that you've turned into a Red! You, Max? That was never old Maxie's style!'

'And yourself Issy?' Max said, piqued, and trying to hurry things to some sort of conclusion. 'Surely you're not going on tonight are you? You know, while we're out.'

For a moment Issy looked if he was searching for words that would not endanger an old friendship. It was too late in the day for falling out; best to keep things boxed, untarnishd, to enjoy revisiting them time and time again.

'Well, it's like this Maxie. I'll give it to you straight. I'm skint. On the balls of my arse. My fingers have turned to claws. A lifetime of work and I haven't a pot to piss in.'

'Sorry about that, Issy.' Max girded himself to grasp the nettle. 'But if you went in, you know how it would look? It's out of my hands, all of it, but the union's talking of getting back at blacklegs after it's over. They're making lists, Issy.'

'So – persecution is it? Hounding. Now why should that bother me at my stage Maxie? I got through it once as a young-fella-me-lad. But back then the oppressors were professionals, killers, not just rag-arsed scene-shifters and old comics turned into union tyrants.'

Issy stared contemptuously into Max's face. Max looked to his left and then to his right, working out a route round the impasse, hoping that there would be a way of saving what had been, leaving intact the kinship of two old fiddlers who had lived parallel lives in the halls. They faced each other in dumb embarrassment.

'I'll tell you what Maxie. I refuse to fall out with you. I will not let it happen, even if I have to go without baccy money. We'll still be pals even if I fall into bed tonight without a wet or a wad. Now. If you ask me to turn away, I'll go, and we'll still be friends. Just say.'

Max thought: What would Tom do?

He knew. Tom would say: 'Sorry, Issy, but you must not go in. We're at war, and we're fighting for a principle and for the future of the halls.' Maisie would be behind him saying: 'I agree' but would have a tear in her eye.

At last, Max put his head towards Issy's and said as quietly as he could: 'Look, I'm going to move away now, Issy, and when I do, I want you to go in there. Go on, earn a bob or two.'

Max turned away and rejoined Jimmy and two other pickets at a side door to the Paragon.

Jimmy raised his eyebrows quizzically. Max wondered whether guilt showed on his face. He spoke up before the question could be asked: 'No luck. Try as I might I couldn't get the stubborn old buffer to understand what we're doing. In the end he told me to go to hell. Short of knocking him down, there was nothing I could do to stop him.'

Jimmy and three other pickets were diverted, breaking off to approach a middle-aged woman carrying a music case, to challenge her as she headed for the main door of the Tivoli. Max took his chance to move on.

For a moment he regretted sending Issy in because he knew that Tom would have been disappointed in him. Then he remembered Haim Cohen's gift of fish and his kindness in suspending the rent and felt vindicated. Surely there was still a time for compassion?

Tonight Issy would have a smoke, a bit of bread and a swill of tea in exchange for his scratchy fiddling. So what?

Max was happy that, in what was after all just a little bit of an argy-bargy in the big scheme of things, that he had done what he knew was right, even if he had betrayed the cause.

My journal

January 24

I have reclaimed the sofa, clear now of Uncle Wilf's bedclothes. I miss him and fear for him.

Great excitement today, and not only because the strike is working. I was with the pickets at Euston Palace when Marie Lloyd arrived and gave us a song! She really lifted everyone's spirits, and raised a laugh when a couple of elephants were being led into the theatre. She shouted 'Blacklegs!' at them.

They say she's not only sacrificing her fees but she's donating money to keep the strike going, and most of the other stars are coughing up.

It was good-humoured on the streets for the most part today but twice there were flare-ups, once when two military musicians turned up to undermine us. They were given an earful and retreated at the double.

The confrontations have told me that I am, after all, more of a suffragist by nature than a suffragette. I could never say, like Emmeline Pankhurst, 'I am a hooligan.' I'm not. I simply could NOT say to a policemen: 'Arrest me.' I confess – I am a coward.

Eli told me that Les Bicyclettes had moved on to the very smart Palace in Cambridge Circus. I believe this hall will weather the strike because they have started to go in for cinema shows in quite a big way, mixing it with top-hole acts.

Quite by chance I arrived near the Palace as the metal tracks and the bicycles were being carried into the side doors, and I caught sight first of Yvette and Delphine and then Guillaume, who was supervising.

Even though the dreaded spot on my chin has returned with fiery vengeance, I felt it only polite to go up say 'Hello.' Somehow we made ourselves understood, and had such a happy talk. Our giggles rang round the empty auditorium.

Guillaume was SO understanding about the strike, and told me he admired our stand but that they must honour their contract or they would go back penniless to France. He shook my hand as I was about to leave and then a moment later shook it again for no apparent reason. He has a very intense way of looking at you.

I decided it was not 'blacklegging' to go into the stage wings and chat as they worked, and when all the equipment was in order, Yvette showed me her bicycle, knowing how I yearn to have one.

She did some slow riding for me at the edge of the stage and balanced for ages, somehow, on the spot!

Then came the supreme moment. Yvette took the cycle on to the central aisle of the auditorium and held it while I sat on the saddle.

'Allez!' she shouted, and urged me forward, helping to keep me upright. Guillaume sat on the edge of the stage laughing but in a goodhearted way.

When I reached the back of the theatre, up the slope, he jumped down and said: 'Regard! Maisie maintenant returnez!' Then he held the saddle and the handlebars and scorched me down to the stage.

I am just descending from heaven! My kingdom for a bicycle!

Guillaume and Yvette seem very close and I cannot work out where Delphine fits in. Perhaps they are sisters and he is their brother. I did not ask in case it seemed rather forward.

PS: Why do men believe that every young woman is a delicate creature whose gossamer ears cannot be befouled by the parlance they use every day?

Today, outside the Euston Palace, Percy Silvester, the man who does mindreading, was talking loudly about Adney Payne, and his womanising.

He told his companion that he had heard two of Payne's dancers talking. One had confessed: 'I'm going to have a baby,' to which the other inquired ' 'ad any pain?' only to be told 'No, it's my boyfriend's.'

For a moment there was silence, then Percy said: 'Get the joke? Adney Payne...'ad any pain!' and they laughed like buffoons.

Percy, suddenly realising I had been within earshot, intoned solemnly: 'I'm so very sorry, miss. Do forgive us.'

17

For the next ten days, Max Pyle lived two lives. By day he was the staunch fighter, helping to besiege theatres, huddling with the rest in the cold – defiant, unrepentant, hopeful. Each evening, he sat in his chair beside the fire with a pipe of pigtail, staring ahead, clasping a mug of Bovril – fearful, and resigned to penury when the strike ended.

Maisie and Tom would come home talking twenty-to-the-dozen about the strike, and the growing support that was making some sort of a victory a possibility. Sometimes they sounded drunk, they were so exhilarated.

They would be all right, Max knew. Whatever the outcome, the young ones would flourish. But what about Gertie and him?

Gertie appeared not only uninvolved; she seemed uninterested when the day was reviewed. It was not that she didn't care. Max was sure that she cared too much. She was consumed by fear for the family, and by whatever affliction had befallen her.

Max had tried to reach out to her, so they could share the worry. She had repelled him. Once, she had turned on him, looking desolate, and said: 'And are you sure that at the end of all this business that we'll not be signing in at the workhouse?'

'Of course I can't but then...'

'And can you tell me right now that Wilf isn't in jail somewhere?' Her tone was challenging.

'We can't be absolutely sure of anything...'

'Until you have answers just let me be, Max,' she said.

Only the daytime camaraderie on the picket line stopped Max from joining her in the slide into despair.

Each day, threw up a reunion. Within a couple of days he had bumped into Harry Taft, the Musical Tramp, and George 'Beau Brummel' Lashwood (looking, as usual, as if he were about to dine at the Ritz), neither of whom he had seen for years.

He'd even come across old Gus Lewis, now grey and bent. To Max's surprise, he said that he was still doing his act with his Musical Pug ('Actually, Maxie, he's my fourth, and he's been the very devil to train').

Every conversation Max had consolidated the idea that he was part of a community but Gertie, out of the fray, failed to share his excitement over these daily encounters.

As soon as he was home, his elation turned to melancholy, so it was an effort even to muster a smile when Maisie burst in chattering endlessly about incidents that were making the strike a wonderful adventure for her and Tom.

'And guess what, father... I saw Eli, who has a friend who's a stagehand at the Tivoli. This chap told him that the show there was an absolute disaster!'

Tom said: 'They should have had the sense to shut up shop like the rest of them.'

Maisie said excitedly: 'Camille Clifford got a tempting invitation from the management to appear but when she talked with the pickets she jumped into her car and drove off.'

All three looked up expectantly as Gertie began to speak but it was only to chastise the dogs for getting under her feet, and to say 'It's ready,' as she dished up rissoles and gravy.

Maisie was almost breathless as she related how the Salvation Army had now refused to allow their musicians to fill in for strikers, and that the Tivoli orchestra now consisted of just four violins, a piano and a badly played clarinet.

Maisie said: 'Eli told us that when a woman called Miss Walker sang a song called "Does Your Heart Ache Tonight?" the audience shouted: "Yes! And we want our money back!" Then there was a comedian who didn't get a single laugh. They kept yelling at him: "Buck up!"'

With more than twenty theatres closed, Marie Lloyd and Arthur Roberts trying to negotiate with the owners, and fresh damage being inflicted night after night, Max should have been optimistic, and he was – until he came home to Gertie's silence.

One night, Maisie brought news of Harry Relph, who had abandoned his contract to go on as Little Tich, telling the management he was unable to appear because he was busy learning a cornet solo.

'Imagine that, mother!' she said. 'Isn't it inspiring? A big star! Nearly as good as Marie's excuse for not working. The Comet says she told them that she was far too busy sewing flounces on a dress to break off to perform!'

'That shows she's not forgotten her roots,' Gertie said.

'Same with Harry,' said Max. 'He knew poverty for years before he dreamed up Little Tich with the long boots,' Max said.

Tom said: 'I'll hand it to Marie. She's really giving it a go. That said, I keep thinking that she could hardly have left us marooned. Must be thinking that unless the minnows get fed, the big fish will eventually starve as well.'

Maisie told Tom that he was being cynical. She had been touched by Marie's pledge in the newspapers to refuse to go back on stage unless the conditions of every artiste and musician and stagehand was improved – that, and by being alongside the people she was championing.

'I won't have you doubting her sincerity Tom!' Maisie protested.

Tom sounded unconvinced but said: 'To be fair, she's spending a lot to help us. But what about that Battling Nelson, a boxer of all people, not even a music hall artiste, standing up for us? He could have gone on at the Holborn Empire and picked up a fortune for doing next to nothing. They say he'd been offered five thousand to put on a bit of a show.'

'And?' Max said.

'He told them they could keep their money. He said he'd rather turn it down than be known as a scab.'

After washing up, Gertie went to bed early complaining of a headache. Maisie did her nightly writing on the sofa, and then went to her room. Tom had gone off earlier to compose a letter to Keir Hardie, ostensibly thanking him for speaking out for the strikers, but really in the hope that he would receive a reply (any sort of a reply would do) signed by his hero.

Tom also planned to write another letter, to the editor of the Comet, demanding that now that the theatre owners were taking a beating, they do what Somerset Maugham was suggesting and go to arbitration. After all, there had already been more than a dozen fruitless meetings to discuss a settlement.

Finally alone with his pipe, the dogs, and the fire, Max sat back and nursed his sense of foreboding. He couldn't deny that he had found his daily contact with fellow strikers heartwarming but the price was high, and the language of strife was bitter.

Scab. Blackleg. Traitor. These were words he had never heard uttered around the halls. Then there were the skirmishes, and Wilf's episode that could easily have put him been behind bars, and probably had.

Only yesterday, two pickets had been hauled before the beaks and fined ten bob each for getting up a chant in the street, and singing some harmless ditty.

Max wouldn't have believed it before the strike, but Tom had it right: The police and the courts are instruments of the state and they are paid not only to administer justice but to make sure the natives don't get too out of hand.

Max poked the fire, toasted his toes and ruminated.

Once, it had been so simple. You did a turn, people clapped, and more came along and paid to see you. The hall was happy to have you on the bill, and see more money come over the front desk. It didn't matter that the manager was an unpleasant lackey for some faceless theatre magnate. You got your fee, and sometimes a pat on the back to go with it.

If only those times could return, Max said to himself. He would give a lot to be younger and back on the road, in better times, with Gertie and the children in tow, going from town to town, sometimes topping the bill, sometimes being one of the 'little twinklers' that they slotted in between the stars.

The best moment of every day back then was after Gertie had fed and watered Tom and Maisie and tried to diffuse their excitement as they explored digs that might be in Dorking, or Portsmouth, or some smoky industrial city.

Each night, Max would tell the children a story, always about the music hall because that was all he knew, before leaving to do his evening shows. The ritual would involve cocoa and, almost always, a mock stern warning that the tale could not begin until they were quiet.

Sometimes there would be requests for a particular yarn to be re-told, perhaps about the artiste who swallowed swords, or about the magician's assistant who, late at night, was accosted on a tram by a woman who said: 'Ere laidy! You're in one bally piece! How come? Oive just seen your 'usband sawing your bleedin' 'ed orf!'

Maisie loved to hear Pa do an impression of the woman, and loved to hear about the elephant nudging the fat lady off the stage at Coventry.

They never tired of hearing about the Hungarian who would get someone in the balcony to throw down a swede which he could catch on a fork held between his teeth, but who was concussed one night when someone threw the swede too early. They would laugh hysterically over this.

'Don't get them giddy, Max! It's me left with them,' Gertie would say.

Years later, Tom and Maisie demanded stronger meat, and so he would describe, with great gravity, the night at The Oxford when Ling Look, The Great Salamander, Lord of Fire, Sword and Cannon, told a boy in the gallery that he must sit down, and how the lad was so enthralled by the lighting of the cannon fuse he stood up for a second time – and had his head blown off.

Max would tell the children: 'So you see, curiosity doesn't only kill cats! And never trust a man with a cannon!'

He remembered how Tom, a scrap of a boy, had offered a moral point. When he was told that a judge had later decided that Ling Look was not to blame, he said: 'But he was, Pa. He was a grown-up and it was his cannon, and he fired it.'

Max had always regarded this as the first indication that Tom possessed rare integrity and a keen sense of justice. At eight, he was wiser than a judge.

Now he was seeing Tom's qualities in action each day, and Maisie was at his shoulder, an eager apprentice.

The look on Isobel McBride's face when she opened the front door of her little terraced house brought home to Wilf the extent of his plight.

She gasped on seeing him. He was white-faced, swaying, and on the point of collapse after a night on the train. She took him by the elbow and led him to a chair beside a grate in which a small mound of coal struggled to stay alight.

'It's Wilf. Wilf!' Isobel said as if she was unable to quite accept that he was there, this apparition, a mere suggestion of the hale specimen she remembered seeing perhaps ten years before. It might have been at some sort of party Morag had arranged. She was sure it had not been Morag's funeral; she had been ill and couldn't make that.

It was the same old Wilf, she decided, but how had he turned into this refugee, arriving in the night with his big bags, trudging in as if his feet were burning?

For a moment they looked at each other – Wilf's expression one of resigned amusement, Isobel's a mixture of puzzlement and pity – before she said: 'You're saying nothing until I get some hot tea and a wee bite intae ye!' And then: 'Will ye have potted heid?'

Wilf felt himself revived by the sweet tea and the thick bread topped with brawn. When, between mouthfuls and coughing, he tried to speak, Isobel said gently 'Whisht a minute. Breathe man.'

Isobel had few visitors and little drama in her life. Wilf would have a lot to tell, and there was time for her to enjoy the detail.

Wilf began by explaining that he had come from London, setting off 12 hours before. He had been working there at a music hall but decided to return home to be available when the solicitor completed work on Morag's affairs.

With each turn of the tale, Isobel sucked in air, encouraging, showing empathy.

He had lost the key, the only one, to the house in Braid Street. Yet he'd had it, he said, when he had boarded the train.

He'd been away so much that there was no one in the area

he knew well enough to ask for help. He could not break in, he said, because the solicitor had told him firmly that while searches for Morag's relatives were continuing, he should not regard the marital house as his.

So he was homeless. 'I could only think of you for help. Yours was the only address I could bring to mind, and even then I was walking up and down out there because I was at the wrong end of your street.'

And so, once again, Wilf found himself asking a favour, stressing that he would be no trouble, that it would be for just a couple of days, that he could sleep in the chair, and that he'd like to acknowledge Isobel's kindness when Morag's affairs were settled.

'Och away you puir man,' Isobel said finally. 'Morag would have wanted me to share my roof. What are friends for?'

For the time being, her craving for some piquancy to enlive the dull diet of her life was sated. Now she would simply enjoy having company.

Wilf imagined how wider her eyes would have been, and how many more little breathy noises she would have made, if she had heard the full the story, if he had explained that, during one week, he had finally found the perfect act, been disowned by his family, and – while dressed as a Zulu – had flattened a theatre manager with a club. He could hardly believe it himself.

My journal

January 25

Took a tram to a lunchtime gathering of suffrage supporters at the home of a spirited 'Honourable' lady of perhaps seventy years.

I came away recharged and holding a leaflet about a massive London protest that is planned for next week. I will be there.

Someone remarked that men don't wish to empower us but want to protect us, and they feel redundant when we show that we are quite capable of walking without the support of a gentleman's arm.

It is true. A lady parachutist is killed and I see we now have a government ban on women parachuting, and more wind-baggery about the physical damage lacrosse and hockey do to the fragile feminine form.

Tom said that I am in good company. Keir Hardie is also angered by this kind of thing – women being regarded as 'half angel, half idiot.'

On my way back from the meeting, to rejoin the pickets for the afternoon, I diverted to the Barclay Brothers cycle emporium to drool over the beautiful machines, and was alarmed to come across a display card at the top of which it said:

A WOMAN MUST NOT RIDE, and (in smaller writing) '...on the ordinary bicycle saddle!'

The text daintily hinted that there are differences between men and women (such sensational news!) and insisted that a young lady bicyclist must always be sure that she is sitting upon her situpon bones.

Elsewhere there were descriptive cards about special saddles for the fair sex, pneumatic saddles, 'healthful' saddles recommended by doctors intent on sparing women riders brain-scrambling and threats to fertility.

PS Mother retreats further and further into herself. She waits for the letter she knows Uncle Wilf will send. So far, nothing.

Perhaps after a search of Darlington, the police bloodhounds sniffed a scent that took them to Glasgow and (God forbid) that Uncle Wilf is locked up.

At least the charge would not be murder. Yesterday Tom spotted Cecil with his brother (men Mr Darwin would describe as simian) roaming Spitalfields, red-faced with drink.

A frightening thought: Cecil will not be content to leave matters with the police.

18

All was silent in the rooms except for the occasional snore, snort and ping of a bedspring, and incomprehensible utterances from unguarded mouths.

Gertie was gathering harebells on Crail golf course in her dreams and Max was senseless in a deep, warm well of oblivion. Razzle and Dazzle were asleep, side by side on their blanket in the blackness at the top of the stairs.

But Maisie was restless, her sleep shallow. So when the shock of the crash came, she knew immediately that it was the main window, where Mr Cohen displayed his fish on a tilted board.

The initial implosion, and then the tinkling of the glass fragments, was followed by footsteps that came from somewhere near the privy. Maisie dare not move. She lay, listening, frozen with fear.

Gertie sat up in bed. She was puzzled. Had she dreamed it, or had she heard some sort of a bump? She shook Max by the shoulder and demanded to know whether he had heard a noise. He surfaced and said irritably: 'No, I bally well didn't! I was asleep.' He turned on his side and once more fell into stupefaction.

Gertie was not satisfied. She felt her way to Maisie's room. As she opened the door, Maisie let out a cry and curled into a ball.

'Did you hear a bang?' Gertie whispered.

'Mother!' Maisie said. 'What a relief! Someone's down there's just broken Mr Cohen's big window.'

Gertie sat on the bed and speculated, deciding that this was a malicious act, and that, even though nothing could be done until dawn when Mr Cohen came in to start frying, Max should be woken.

Gertie lit the lights in the main room and made a pot of tea and they sat together, Max gruff and monosyllabic.

'The thing is,' Gertie said, 'we don't know who or why. Is it because of the strike? If they did it to get at us, what do we say to

Mr Cohen? How do we pay for a new window? And will they do it again?' She had picked up a tea towel and began to crumple it, her habit when she was agitated.

Max was now fully awake and trying to make sense of the incident. Gertie needed calming.

'It might be to do with the Cohens,' he said. 'Jews have trouble with other Jews. You get Jew-haters. We might never know.'

At first light they heard below them the shop door being unbolted. Gertie put on a housecoat and, with Max at her side, went downstairs and out to the shop front.

They found Mr Cohen shaking his head, and looking closely at the pile of glass shards covering the slabs where his fish was displayed.

'No stone, no brick in there. Looks as if someone hammered it in, Max, or hit it with a stick.' He looked composed, curious rather than angry.

'Glass can be replaced,' he said calmly, 'but if there's a grudge out there somewhere, it will have to be tracked and wiped clean.'

Gertie could not restrain herself. Mr Cohen was so decent, he would find it difficult to suggest that the strike, or Wilf, might be the reason his shop had been targeted.

She said: 'If we thought for a moment that this was done because of us, we would be so sorry. We'd do our best to make the window right.'

Mr Cohen offered a half-smile and there was generosity in the big, dark eyes.

'You mustn't blame yourselves, especially as we do not know who did this. For the time being, I will have the window repaired, and I will ask two of my young and strong nephews to lie in wait here for two nights so that you feel secure.'

Max and Gertie dressed and then helped Mr Cohen to shovel the broken glass out of the window.

As they worked Mr Cohen said: 'Think of it this way. We, the Cohens, might have done something to incur bad blood. Jews can hate fellow Jews you know; we are not angels. We have factions, family conflict. Or, of course, someone might be opposed to your strike, or even have a vendetta against the uncle with wig and the coconuts!'

He was greatly amused, picturing Wilf, and hooted with laughter. He said that if it were discovered that the Pyles were indeed the target, and not the Cohens, he would demand that Max play a tune or two for his family by way of compensation.

'I have not had the pleasure of hearing the famous fiddle,' he said. 'We must unite against bullies wherever we find them. Use your fiddle as a weapon!'

They had just finished clearing the glass when Maisie joined them. She was in her housecoat and she was crying.

'I can't find Razzle. He's gone!' she sobbed. 'They've taken him.'

My journal

January 26

We lost Razzle today, or he has been kidnapped. We searched the entire neighbourhood but there was no sign of him. I cannot stop crying. I stand at the window, waiting, hoping to see him coming home.

Mother is terribly upset, father is angry and Dazzle is mystified, waiting expectantly at the top of the stairs.

I could not believe that the noise of the window being broken can have frightened him so much that he ran away. He is used to the noisy halls after all. When mother found the note on the stairs we had our worst fears concerned.

How can just five words have the power to instill such terrible fear into us all? 'ZULU WE WILL FIND YOU'

Whoever it was wished to hurt me has succeeded. It can only be Cecil, or Artie.

I do not believe that any of the strikers would feel so outraged about Uncle Wilf blacklegging that they would terrorise us in this way.

Razzle is easily identified by his ribbon Could it be that they took him rather than Dazzle to cause maximum pain?

Tonight I will sleep with Dazzle in my arms, assured that Mr Cohen's nephews, two enormous young men, are sitting in the darkness of the shop, keeping guard.

I will pray that my dear Razzle simply had a terrible fright and is back in time for his breakfast rissole.

19

The rolling waves of protest that had pounded London music halls for almost two weeks were gradually breaking down the defences thrown up by the owners.

Meeting after meeting, some involving the biggest stars of the day and the most powerful owners, ended in stalemate but everyone concerned knew that things had begun to shift in favour of the strikers, for many validating the action.

Tom was now hoarse each day, rallying the pickets, and helping union officials to monitor progress. Maisie walked from theatre to theatre and had holes in the soles of both boots. Each day battles were won. Audiences grew tired of shabby shows featuring amateurs even when the entrance price had been lowered.

The majority of the public could see the injustice of the demands being made by the owners. Many workers who sacrificed lunch, or worked a little overtime to pay for a music hall visit, and knew the true value of two bob, felt sympathy for the cause.

They were also influenced by the fact that many stars were on the side of the strikers.

They had read how Marie Lloyd had mocked Belle Elmore as she went into the Euston Palace to perform. She urged the strikers to let her in as she would empty the place with her voice. Marie had then begun to sing in the street, drawing the audience out of the theatre.

On the tenth day of the strike there had been moment that, for Tom, symbolised the vulnerability of the managers. It was when Adney Payne's wife, in a gesture of support for her beleaguered husband, volunteered to go on stage as a stand-in act. As the newspapers reported, her rendering of The Holy City was judged an unholy row, and was drowned out by booing.

'Desperation,' Tom told Maisie, over supper. 'The cracks are widening.'

As Gertie solemnly ladled dumplings into bowls, at the end of a long day's picketing, Max said that he'd heard that two orchestras in Manchester theatres had staged a walk-out – 'One conductor just had a harpist to wave his stick at!' And in the Comet a performer in the north had spoken up for the London strikers. He said he was doing 16 performances a week, and having to contend with heckling and lighted fireworks being thrown at him on stage, all for a pittance.

Gertie sat down but showed little interest in her food. However, her interest quickened at Tom's mention of Glasgow.

He said: 'They've had a meeting up there, more than 100 people in the business, and they're going to give us five per cent of their fees.'

Gertie thought of Wilf and wondered whether he had been at the meeting when the decision to help had been taken. She knew that if he had been, he would have voted to donate the money.

Tom said: 'Oh, and we had a message from America today. America! From some entertainment organisation, saying "Our hearts are with you."'

'That's so touching,' Maisie said.

Tom devoured his meal in minutes, and Gertie re-filled his bowl from hers. He had not eaten all day.

'It really is biting now, Ma. We have so many people on our side. Anyone trying to get around several halls to work is on a hiding to nothing; now the tram and bus unions are refusing to carry them.'

'Good, son. Good,' Gertie said. 'It may mean that it's over soon.' Her face reverted to customary glumness; Max knew that the mention of Scotland had stirred up her worry over Wilf.

'We're putting on our own shows at the Scala, mother. The Alliance. We've leased it for a while. Marie Lloyd's going to be on in a couple of days. Want to come? We could go by Tillings.'

The invitation fell flat. He expected nothing more; Ma was becoming unreachable. He felt ashamed that he had been so absorbed with the fight that he had refused to allow her plight intrude. They (Pa and Maisie and him) would have to do something to save her. But for now, the strike had to come first.

Tom finished his second bowl of dinner. He plonked his elbows on the table and put his head in his hands.

'You know what, Pa. If we win, when we win, I'll be very interested to see how many blacklegs refuse on principle to accept any pay rises. Surely they can't really be seen to be benefiting from any gain won by what they regard as foul means...'

Maisie enjoyed hearing Tom and her father being conversational. There had been an armistice, brought on by the demands of the strike, and she believed that they would never return to hostilities.

'You watch, son, they'll grab it and still sleep sound in their beds,' Max said. 'Principle is a foreign word to some. Any decent person would give the extra to Boots For The Bairns, or the Sally Army.'

Max was about to say that those who had worked through the dispute should remember that they would be on bills with those who had lost money during the strike – he nearly said 'they'd be working alongside us' and remembered, with a pang of regret, that Musical Mayhem was no more.

That night, when Maisie had finished her writing and Tom had trooped off to bed exhausted, Gertie wiped the last of the dishes, sighed heavily and said that she would have an early night. She was nonplussed when, as she settled in bed, Max joined her and encircled her with an arm.

She gently prised it off. 'Don't cramp me, Max, I'm suffocating,' she said, gasping . Max felt Gertie edge away.

'I know you never want to talk, Gert,' he said, into her hair. 'But we need to think about what we're going to do when it's over, when the last bit of money goes. We need to get you sorted, get you a doctor or somebody who knows about nerves...well, whatever it is that's dragging you down...

'Doctor? I'll be all right. I just need to be left alone for a while,' she said impatiently. 'I'll pull round.'

'But what about me, Gert?'

'I can only be as I am, Max.'

'I know. But I'm, well, lonely, I suppose. I'm scared for us all. I hoped you'd give me a hand working it all out. You would have done, once.'

'I would still if I could. I can't help how I feel, Max.'

'But we'll need a plan, Gert, and soon. Mr Cohen's not a charity. And anyway, you know me and charity.'

'Not now Max. Please. I'm not in a talking mood. And anyway, what's the use of talking? We're sunk. And it's because of me.'

'No, Gert!'

'Can't perform properly, can't go anywhere without being scared witless. Can't even show my own children a bit of affection.'

'Or me.'

'Or you.'

'When it's over, will you talk with me, and Tom and Maisie? Will you help me to sort out what can be done?'

'I'll try. Right now I'm just trying not to think about Wilf. Where he might be and how he is. Goodnight Max.'

She moved further away and puffed up the pillow under her chin. 'Can you get your arm away?' He obeyed. 'It's not you, Max. It's just that I get panicky. It feel trapped.'

My journal

February 3

The only excuse I have for breaking my resolution to make a journal entry each day is that we have been consumed by the strike, absolutely consumed.

We have been returning to the rooms battle-weary each night, and sometimes on the point of sleep while eating our dinner. The strike has become our way of life.

A week has gone by in a whirl of activity – walking to the theatres, mounting pickets, leafleting, spreading information.

I understand perfectly now when Tom talks about brotherhood and sisterhood. Out there at the theatre doors we are a beleaguered tribe, grimly united as we huff and puff and try to blow the house down.

Tom, especially, is tireless, and is getting a name for himself as an organiser. Father is all for the cause and turns up to picket each day, purging anger he has been carrying around for years.

Mr Cohen has been most supportive throughout although, poor man, he tells us that his sister-in-law has just died. She was the wife of the man who smokes salmon for Fortnum's.

He told us this evening that he is shutting the shop tomorrow because of the bereavement. His dark eyes were even more soulful that usual. Mother touched his forearm as he told us his news.

We did not ask but for some reason Mr Cohen told us about the funeral. It would be over very quickly; there would be psalms and a eulogy and, afterwards, mourning phased in a particular way.

Mother said: 'May we offer some flowers from the family?'

I am glad she said this, although Mr Cohen knew as well as us that we have no money for flowers. He declined with thanks for the thought, explaining that flowers had no place at Jewish funerals.

Tonight I have been thinking of Aunt Morag's passing and of Uncle Wilf's insistence on making her funeral a flourish, a happy remembrance of what she had been – free-spirited, vibrant, colourful and, in her illness, uncomplaining.

With typical panache, uncle had decided that she would be returned to Kirkintilloch, whatever the cost, and via a notice in the local newspaper decreed that on no account would black be acceptable at the service but that laughter would be insisted upon. He arranged for a jolly concert to be held in the evening ('so bring your best voices,' he demanded!)

On the morning of the service he asked Tom and I to accompany him on a walk that Aunt Morag had taken many times as a child.

She had been fascinated by the fact that the Luggie Water, a local stream, fed the River Kelvin and in turn the Clyde, and finally blended into the ocean.

Uncle Wilf said that sometimes, as a little girl, she used to launch a leaf or a twig to send it merrily on its way to America.

Before the concert, I was touched when we spotted Uncle Wilf walking with a posy towards the Luggie.

Behind me at the service was an ancient lady with a stoop. As it ended she told her friend that she had brought her ribbons, and was 'awa to tell the bees.'

Later we London 'townies' learned of an ancient country custom involving the tying of ribbons to hives and the instruction to the bees to fly off and spread the news of a death.

I have kept a picture in my mind of this old lady, bent like a bow, leaning towards the hive and whispering: 'Spread the news. Morag has passed.'

20

Maisie was on her way to a meeting where plans for the great London winter march in support of women's suffrage were being discussed when, passing the Vaudeville on the Strand, she saw above the door a crudely-made message in two-foot-high letters.

It said: PEACE! ALL THE STARS RETURN TONIGHT.

She could barely wait to discover what settlement had been

reached.

Had the union caved in – or had the music hall owners made an offer? She was tempted to hurry home for news but decided that hearing plans for the great demonstration was too important to miss.

So one battle was over. But she had read that a greater one was about to reach a high point. After the march from Hyde Park to Exeter Hall in a couple of days, there would be another rally of major figures in the suffrage movement, in Caxton Hall, and there was growing fear that this would be a flashpoint. Civil disobedience was expected.

When Maisie made her way out of the stinging rain and into the hall, a small group at the door began singing. The words – to the tune John Brown – brought a lump to her throat.

> *Rise up, women – for the fight is hard and long;*
> *Rise in thousands, singing loud a battle song.*
> *Right is might, and in its strength we shall be strong,*
> *And the cause goes marching on.*

Maisie said to herself: Who would not be moved by this little circle of women? By the fervour in their voices and their bright-eyed conviction?

But much as she was stirred by the singers – and thrilled by the sight of Mrs Pankhurst on stage – she was apprehensive.

Her worry was over means and ends. She had witnessed conflict first hand and had learned that simple ideals and aims often led to violence, and she felt repelled and cowed by it.

She thought of Uncle Wilf, the most good-natured of men, lashing out and of Cecil hitting the floor. She recalled the startled face of an American who did a lariat act being manhandled the other day by two stagehands at a theatre door. She could hear again him pleading: 'But fellas, please – I'm only trying to work!'

There was menace in the faces of pickets – once pleasant fellow entertainers – when they shouted at blacklegs going into theatres, threatening that there would be a day of reckoning. It would be so easy to walk into trouble on the stepping stones between argument and protest, and onwards to bloodshed or even jail.

As she looked for a vacant chair in the hall, Maisie reminded herself that she was a suffragist and not a suffragette and that there was no shame in that.

She took off her waterlogged felt hat, put it under her chair, and sat fretting with her hands to her face, knowing her cheeks would be bright red from the cold.

A large, expensively dressed woman sitting next to her for some reason presumed that Maisie was in the vanguard of action. Her voice was cultured and her manner imperious. Her hat was dry; obviously she had come by motor car.

'Dear girl,' she said 'have you been asked yet to help with, you know, the plan?' She touched her lips with a gloved finger as if she feared being overheard. 'The rally. After the King's Speech? Are you in one of the groups?'

'No, I haven't been asked.'

'But you must get involved. I have two northern ladies staying with me. Brave girls, working girls, down here with the firm intention of jolly well going to jail.'

Maisie replied that she was simply a supporter of the fight for suffrage, not really an activist. She had merely come to hear about the arrangements for the big march starting in Hyde Park. She had heard nothing of duties for the second protest rally, which, she began to suspect, would be more like a planned affray.

'Then you really must ask, my dear! If there's nothing offered to us in the King's Speech we will act, mark my words. You must not miss the chance to make history.'

The woman looked up at the stage where Mrs Pankhurst now stood at the lectern, preparing to speak, then, leaning towards Maisie and giving off a whiff of expensive scent, she dropped her voice and pointed a gloved finger.

'There's your model. A nice, educated, civilised lady who is quite prepared to spit in the face of a policeman – or bite like a tiger.'

While Maisie listened to the speeches she grew excited about the next day's march. There would be thousands taking part. There were calls for banners and badges to give the best possible showing, for cars and bicycles to join in, for the spirit of the day to reflect a classless sisterhood bound by a noble aim.

An organiser announced above the din of people about to leave the hall that the marchers should expect insults from the crowds lining the route. Everyone should try to wear galoshes; the bad weather looked well and truly set.

Tom, meanwhile, was in the Mile End Road having the first pint of beer bought for him by his father to mark the end of the strike. The long mahogany bar of the White Hart was lined with drinkers, who shuffled constantly, gathering frothing pints from a brass sheet in front of the ornate pumps.

Max and Tom were comfortable together. The awkwardness between them had gone. The shared experience of the strike had somehow knocked off the sharp edges of their interchanges; now they could sit and be themselves.

They settled in a quiet corner and speculated about what might come out of the Board of Trade Arbitration.

Max expressed concern about how long it might be before any award was made, and whether there would be a stampede of acts anxious to get back working, and earning, again. Tom said that what really mattered was that they had put up such a fight that, whatever the outcome in terms of money and conditions, the managements had learned that the union had teeth.

'I admire what you did, son,' Max said bashfully before downing a long draught of beer to mask the discomfiture he felt in voicing something that was difficult for him.

'It was easy for me, Pa. I knew which side I was on from the start. You didn't. You have to take credit for putting your penn'orth in, once the scrap started.'

Max was inwardly pleased but tried to divert the conversation. He sought a topic that was less personal, more practical.

'So the question is: What now?'

Max took out his pipe and dug around in his pocket for his penknife and a length of pigtail.

When Tom didn't not reply, Max said: 'I'll be John Bull with you, Tom. The money's running out, and would have by now if Haim had not given us a rent-free month. He'll be looking for rent in a week or so, and quite right too.'

Tom thought for a moment, took a sip from his glass, and said: 'Look Pa, mother's far from well. All things considered, it might be best going solo again. I'll be off, and Maisie could help out with rent, get a job.'

By the time Max and Tom arrived home, Maisie was back from her meeting, sitting holding Dazzle, on the sofa. She was bright and expectant as Max and Tom walked in and before they had taken their coats off, said: 'So?'

Tom said that the whole dispute was going to be looked at by an arbitration board. They would report back and the managements would be bound by their findings. He was confident that there would be gains all round for performers and music hall staff.

Max walked towards Gertie who was enveloped in steam as she poured water from a pan of potatoes, and pulled her to him.

'That's it, Gert. It really is over.'

He was surprised by her smile, relieved to think she might be happier now that she did not have to hear each day about conflict involving so many people she knew and cared for.

The smile did not last.

'But what will happen now? To us,' she asked pointedly.

'Well, we all have to talk. Decide.'

'When we do, and it needs to be quick, we ought to have a good think about what Wilf's suggesting,' she said, pointing to the mantelpiece. 'There was a letter today.'

On top of the letter were the words: Wing No 4, Barlinnie Prison, Glasgow (convict in solitary).

As he read this, Max spun round in shock towards Gertie, who was doling out mince and potatoes, and looking decidedly relaxed.

'Read on,' she called. 'Ignore the first bit. You know what he's like...' The letter said:

'Dear Gertie,

They are treating me quite well here, very well in fact. They say I look good in the uniform. The arrows suit me.

A nice warder has just woken me sweetly and given me a mug of tea while I decide what I would like for breakfast. I was going to ask for the kippers but they make my cell smelly for hours after, and so I've gone for lorne sausage, potato scones and a coddled egg.

If the weather holds they're going to take us by motor to Lunderston Bay beach for a wee sniff of sea air. The nice warders have promised to buy us an ice cream and then a few drinks, and we'll round it off with a fish supper and a sing song.'

Wilf then confessed that, far from being locked up, he had found a new freedom back in Glasgow – 'but I'm lying low for a while, like a Zulu in the grass.'

Having spent a couple of nights with Mrs Ewart ('Gertie – remember Morag's old friend?' the letter said), he had visited Mr Ritchie who was dealing with Morag's affairs. The lawyer had sent letters to the Braid Street but Wilf had not been back there since he went down to London and so was unaware of developments.

'Mr Ritchie tells me that, as we suspected, Morag has no living relatives and so the house, and the money that my dear wee lassie had squirrelled away for a rainy day, is passing to me, along with the house. The rainy day has come. This will change things for us all.'

Wilf said that he had a suggestion for the family to consider and, at risk of 'killing off Max with a bout of apoplexy,' he wanted the family to consider it.

'When the strike ends, why not make a fresh start up here? There's sure to be bitterness in the London halls whichever way it goes. You could get away, and live rent-free. There's work round every corner here. It would get you back on your feet.'

He listed some of the Glasgow theatres, described in glowing terms the new Coliseum. He boasted about the Hippodrome in Sauchiehall Street where people could now book their seats by telephone. At the newly-built Alhambra, aquatic tank acts were all the rage. Glasgow was showing the way.

He went into raptures over the Panopticon and the amazing Mr Pickard. His latest stunt to get in the newspapers, he wrote, was to arrange for a giantess, normally a 'living exhibit,' to slide down a water chute for the benefit of press photographers – 'Genius! He's never out of the news.'

There was a footnote for Tom, who, he believed, might be influential in tempting the family to Glasgow – 'The new Mitchell Library is VAST. You could lose yourself in the maze of shelves. And there's enough political unrest up here to last you a lifetime!'

As Max read the letter, he was overcome by a feeling of dread and Gertie had to tell him twice to get to the table before his dinner went cold. He could not shake out of his mind the words 'This will change things for all of us.'

He looked towards the table and noted that Gertie was listening – actually listening – to Tom and Maisie as they speculated about what the arbitration would decide. She was curious, attentive, nodding, almost back to the Gertie of old.

My journal

February 4

I go to bed feeling proud of Pa and Tom and everyone who conquered their fear and stood up to the rich and the powerful.

Whatever the tribunal rules, father and Tom have indeed behaved like warriors – and perhaps I can also be proud of myself.

After all the threats and attempts at intimidation, our little ragbag army forced the owners to the negotiating table time and time again, and then to impartial judgment.

Tom says that he'd heard that when one owner confessed himself beaten he pleaded with the union not to boast to the press about his humbling. How are the mighty fallen.

There's a song that sums up our victory: Two lovely black eyes – and, oh what a surprise!

PS The Pyles are at the crossroads, and Uncle Wilf is beckoning, pleading for us to 'tak the high road' to join him. I confess that I am intrigued by the idea, and hopeful that it would bring about a miraculous recovery in mother, but I can foresee Pa having other ideas.

21

Next day, the feeling of relief in the Pyle household that the strike was over lasted only as long as it took Gertie to dish out broth that had been bubbling on the trivet of the range all afternoon.

Tom had been thinking all day and was already considering options for his future as he sat down at the table.

He had greatly enjoyed pitting himself against the owners of the halls. Now that fight was over it was time to move on and stand up for others who were being treated badly, and to show them how to stand up for themselves. There was a big dispute in the offing in the Belfast docks, a major set-to. He might look for a niche there.

As she sipped her soup, Maisie was more absorbed by the immediate crisis the family faced than with her own ambitions. She sat breaking bread into bits and debating whether she would choose to move to Glasgow if father and mother decided to go.

Max and Gertie were silent throughout the meal but as Gertie washed the dishes, Max could hear a breathy little musical noise she used to make as she did household tasks, hardly a tune but the sound of someone content in doing something mundane.

He knew that, in her head, Gertie was already half way to Scotland. He sucked on his pipe, seeking solace as a teething baby might find comfort gnawing on a hard, sweet biscuit.

Tom and Maisie left the table and went into Maisie's room. Max knew they would be speculating about the future. He was sure he overheard Maisie say: 'Yes, but what happens to Pa if refuses to go?' Tom's answer was an inaudible drone but Maisie's question reminded Max that he had to make a decision, and it had to be made quickly. In fact, he had made it earlier, as soon as he read Wilf's letter.

It was that – whatever privations he might have to bear, whatever the pain of parting, the loneliness and desolation – he would not be going to Glasgow. He would not be reliant on Wilf or on his new-found prosperity.

He congratulated himself on his decisiveness but then doubts crept in; the implications, and the reality, of living alone, of losing everything that he and Gertie shared, nibbled away at his resolve.

Wilf's assurance in his letter that Morag's money would change life 'for all of us' still filled him with dread. His talent had always kept his belly full; he was too long in the tooth to start being a sponger.

If he was going to be in debt, it would never, ever, be to Wilf. He especially hated the idea of being steered into work by a guiding hand, especially if that hand was Wilf's.

Max had barely spoken to Gertie about the letter. He had hoped that if he left the matter in the air, a solution might present itself. But as he took to his chair and began to rub up a wad of tobacco, once more he rehearsed the stark truth of the situation: Going to Glasgow, and suffering Wilf, or losing Gertie.

As for Gertie, she chose not to spoil her new optimism by looking too deeply into implications. But as had happened so many times before, what was unspoken between them tormented them when they got into bed and lay cloaked in darkness, out of earshot of Tom and Maisie.

'Well,' Gertie said, 'what do you make of Wilf's idea?'

Max didn't reply immediately. The enormity of the issue

overwhelmed him for a moment. This was a conversation that could end his marriage.

'Don't you think we should give it a go? There's not much left for us here. The rent's due and we haven't got it.'

'I know that.'

'Just think, up there we'd not need to worry about money, staying with Wilf. And there's work. Wilf's making contacts.'

'All right. We're on our uppers. But just because he clicks his fingers we don't have to up sticks and accept his charity.'

'Is that what you're going to say to Mr Cohen when he comes up for his money a week next Friday?'

'No. I'll say that even though my brother-in-law has tainted our name by clubbing a manager half to death, and my wife is ready to ruin our marriage, good old Max is still good old Max, and he's ready to get up off his backside and pay his debts.'

He could hear that Gertie had begun to cry but was trying to do it soundlessly.

'That's not fair, Max,' she sniffled.

'Look. What I think, Gert, is that once you get up there it will be over. We'll be finished.'

'So you'll deny me a bit of happiness?'

'That's blackmail, Gert. Anyway, there's something that you've not thought of.'

'The children? They're off. Making their own lives.'

'No, not the children. How on earth are you going to get to Scotland without going on a train? The thing you're scared of? Or are you going to hire a bally horse-bus?'

'There must be a way for me to get there.'

'So you're going?'

Gertie didn't answer but Max heard a sob, stifled by the pillow. Max got up.

Outside there was a cutting wind. Icicles as hard as glass hung over the privy door and the latch needed force to release it from its anchorage of hoar frost.

Hurrying back inside, Max lit the gas mantle and sat beside the fire. He needed to think but within minutes he could see that there was nothing to debate. It was still resolutely black-and-white: To go, or to stay.

He thought of all the years of companionship he had enjoyed with Gertie, and the way they had come through hard times together, and educated the children, equipped them for life.

He appreciated that there was genuine kindness behind Wilf's offer (as well as self-interest) and accepted that, to Gertie, his own attitude must seem churlish and ungrateful.

He turned off the light and as he felt his way towards the bedroom he confirmed his final, final, and momentous, decision: He would not go to Glasgow.

Max eased himself under the eiderdown, his teeth chattering, and the couple moved towards each other for mutual warmth – and, simultaneously, farther away from each other than they had ever been.

My journal

February 7

I am writing this in my bed having caught a rotten chill on the big march (my excuse for more missed entries).

No regrets. I will remember it until the day I die (which if my sniffling does not subside might be quite soon).

Pneumonia would have been a small price to pay for the joy of being with 3,000 like-minded people laughing at the rain and the mud.

The rich marched side by side with domestics. Titled ladies and textile workers, shoulder to shoulder, bore the weight of the waterlogged banners.

There were posies everywhere, and a cavalcade of cars and carriages joined the mud-spattered walkers.

Tom was envious when I told him that I was within yards of Keir Hardie for a few minutes when I moved to the front of the procession.

In fact for a time I was close enough to name those in the vanguard – Millicent Fawcett, Lady Strachey and Lady Balfour – all of them bedraggled.

There were catcalls from some who came to mock us. Young men eyed us and shouted in a good-natured way: 'Are your sweethearts with you?' and 'Oh, you lovely girls!'

I walked for a time with a girl called Millie, who is with a household in the West End. Recently she discovered that two other servants, men, were receiving several pennies more each day for doing the same work as her, and she had become outraged.

She said she wondered what was so special about the way a young man, rather than a girl, emptied the master's bedpan that commanded this extra pay.

It seems to have struck Dazzle, finally, that we are not working! This morning as I retreated to bed with my linctus I saw him sniffing around in the mouth of the tuba.

He simply stood and stared long and hard into the instrument, tilting his head in puzzlement, perhaps believing in his doggy way that it had died, which in a way it has. He resembled that little dog Nipper, in that painting called His Master's Voice.

PS I do not know whether we will be taking up Wilf's offer of digs in Glasgow but I have seen the effect his letter is having: Pa's been digging his heels in, and mother was heard to hum a tune when she filled the hot water bottles tonight. I do believe it was something Scottish.

22

AE Pickard was smaller than Wilf had expected. He had presumed that such a notorious self-publicist would have had an imposing frame to match the personality. Not only that, his clothes – smartly sharp but unremarkable, the dress of a bank manager – lacked the razzmatazz Wilf expected, having seen the newspaper reports about the master self-publicist.

Judging by his appearance, he might have been an accountant.

'Come in lad,' AE said, opening the door to his office, leading from the entrance to the Panopticon. He left the door wide open and, putting up a forefinger, looked out and said: 'Here. Just watch...'

Wilf found to his surprise that he was a little nervous. He flicked back his hair and buttoned his jacket before taking the seat AE had steered him to.

He watched. There was nothing to see for a moment, but then a man and his wife walked into the entrance area, stopped, and looked down at the floor near the pay desk. They then stared at each other, raised their eyebrows, shrugged and walked on, disconcerted, edgy, looking behind them.

AE observed them, fascinated, then chuckled and turned to lower himself into the big chair behind the desk littered with paper.

'People are such funny buggers! You put down a sign on a perfectly flat floor. It says "Mind the step" but it's clear there's not a step in sight. Yet instead of believing their own eyes, they believe the sign, and keep looking for the step!'

He turned to Wilf, who felt uncomfortable under AE's searching gaze. He knew that he was about to be assessed.

'You're in the business, Wilfred, so you'll have guessed that this place is packed full with little illusions, life's oddities, and with what some would call lies and trickery. Brimming with it – and folks come back time and time again wanting to believe it all! I think you'd agree that it would be silly of me to refuse their money...'

He took out his pocket watch and then put it back without looking at it.

'Mind you, to pull them in and hold them, so they stay loyal, you've got to join in a bit yourself, while you're indulging them. Play the fool, show you don't take yourself too seriously, show you don't mind being a bit of an aunt sally.'

He leaned across his desk and held up a piece of paper and read aloud: "Visit the Britannia Panopticon, the pharmacy to cure all ills. Testimonials from crowned heads, soft heads, bald heads and stairheads." That's what it'll say in my next advert.'

As AE talked, Wilf glanced around the room. The walls were covered with newspaper cuttings and photographs, mounted, framed and glazed.

In one newspaper picture, AE was shown standing with a horse, like some Wild West hero; in another he was stooping, holding the hand of a dwarf, in another looking up into the face of a towering, dough-faced giant in billowing trousers.

'I get the customers to insult me. Invite it. One's just addressed a note to me calling me The Skinless Sausage. Where's the harm in that? And here's one that says "To the Aberdonian Skinflint." Only half right – I haven't been to Aberdeen. It's just daft fun to keep them interested.'

Once again he drew his watch from his waistcoat pocket, looked at it this time, flipped the lid shut and then, leaning forward with an earnestness that alarmed Wilf, said: 'Now. What's it that you say you do, lad?'

Wilf remembered that accent; it was from when he was doing the vent act in Leeds, or was it Huddersfield?

'Some sort of Zulu business...?' The eyes were eagerly expectant. 'We once had a Dahomey warrior here for a while. Went down really well.'

Wilf explained as graphically as he could how he would introduce his act ('it's a little one-man play really') as an English army veteran, swathed in a big Union Jack, hiding his blacked-up body. He would create a tense atmosphere, and then – to drumming, and with the stage darkened – would disappear and re-emerge, black-faced, in a loincloth and wig, as a Zulu chief.

He found himself dropping in phrases from his script and, seeing that AE was absorbed, put a few dramatic flourishes into his delivery as he described the knobkerrie and how he would use it in a symbolic way to smash the coconut, and would then fall dead on the sound of a crack on the drum.

AE looked thoughtful. His head was rocking slightly, as if sieving what he'd heard, so he ended up with the essence of the act.

'This is a shocker,' he said finally. 'A frightener. Especially with the darkness and the drumming and the way you tell the story. From what I'm to understand, there's this decent soldier, guilty as hell after killing a brave native lad. But the laddie's only brave because he has no alternative. He's a victim not a hero. To prove the point you have this mighty Zulu chief caving in the head of another young coward and then being shot by our lot. In a nutshell, war's just bloody stupid tit-for-tat.'

'Yes.'

'To be frank, Wilfred, it's disturbing. I can see this upsetting anybody who sees it. It would keep people awake at night.' Wilf's spirits sank.

After a moment AE stood up and said: 'So, yes. Let's give it a go. Murray upstairs will sort out the staging and the drums and such. Talk to him. Iron out any wrinkles. Give it a week. Three quid. Two shows a day.'

He led Wilf by the arm to the office door.

'And... now... what do you call yourself?'

'Wilf.'

'No, for the act.'

'I used to be The Crazed Zulu but I'd like to change it. How does The Zulu Executioner sound to you?'

'Nice ring to it. We'll bill you as a hero of Rorke's Drift. We'll say you witnessed it all.'

'But I wasn't actually at Rorke's Drift, Mr Pickard. I was at Isandlwana.'

'No matter. Same war. We'll say: "Not for those with dicky hearts. No refunds if you conk out." There's nothing like a dire warning to pull them in. Curiosity. They'll roll up in droves.'

Wilf felt a glowing pride spread through him. He had impressed an ultimate arbiter of public entertainment. He wanted to tell Morag, to say that her belief in him had been well founded.

'And I'll tell you what, lad. If this works I might find a corner for you later, in the statics. I can see it – a bit of a stage near the Sleeping Princess, with you leaping out three times a day to frighten the bejabers out of them. We'd send somebody up to shoot you at the times we decide.'

AE frowned, then nodded. 'You know, I think it'll have to be a gun, not a drum. More realistic. Behind the curtain. Yes, a gunshot into a sandbag. I've got a gun. Once had to shoot a bear on the roof. Escaped from the zoo. Couldn't have an exhibit eating the bloody customers! Yes, a gun would get the buggers jumping. Oh, and we'll get in a job lot of coconuts from the Fruitmarket.'

AE nudged Wilf a little nearer to the office door. He had to push on, he said, to telephone the Herald about a dog with two heads, and then look at a mechanical cigar-smoking monkey being offered for sale by a fairground man in Bearsden.

Before he ushered Wilf out, he said: 'Oh, and Wilf. I take it you're draping the coconut shy in African stuff, material, to make it more like a real Zulu youngster? And why don't you get a saw and cut through the coconut shells, just enough to make sure that when you hit them they crack open nicely. With luck, you'll get some spillage. You know, a bit like brains.'

My journal

February 8

What a thrilling start to the day! When I joined Ma and Pa for breakfast there was an envelope propped against the clock on the mantelpiece. Ma pointed to it as I came in, and said: 'For you.'

The writing was spidery and unusually curvy and was addressed to 'Mlle Maisie.' I was sure it would be from Yvette.

I felt Ma's eyes on my back as I began to open the letter and so I went out and stood on the doorstep. To my surprise it was from Guillaume.

Bicyclettes have several dates in London and he had encountered Eli who passed on our address.

My, the wording of the letter is so very formal! But the terms are truly charming as well, as if taken from a book of etiquette. He asked after me and my family and said how much he admired our backing of the strike.

He says that Les Bicyclettes will soon have confirmed bookings for three more London halls before travelling to Carlisle, Edinburgh, Dundee and GLASGOW! He would count it an honour (an honour!) if we could meet at any of the venues.

As if that wasn't exciting enough, he said that Yvette and Delphine, his SISTERS, were greatly looking forward to seeing me again.

He gave a forwarding address of The Oxford where Les Bicyclettes are appearing next week, and so expects a reply from me. I will write tonight giving him all my news, including my new intended location once we settle that matter tomorrow.

23

A solemn breakfast preceded the family chat that would decide the future of the Pyles. It seemed strange to every member of the family, this sitting down round a table, almost like at a creditors' meeting to dismantle a business.

No one knew how issues would be broached, nor how to start the process.

Maisie hovered at her bedroom door, fingering a length of hair and looking distracted; Gertie was washing the porridge bowls. Tom was at the table reading. Max had skimmed through the Comet and was restless, anxious to get on, to discover where the future lay.

He also needed to discuss with Gertie the state of funds. He had just raised this, even before he was fully awake, as they lay on their backs in bed like two strangers being forced to share a room. Gertie had turned a deaf ear.

'Leave the bally dishes, Gertie, please!' he snapped. 'Let's get started.'

Gertie levelled an angry look in Max's direction, but put down the bowls, and dried her hands. She perched on the edge of a seat at the table, clutching a tea towel, as if she might have to get back to her housework at any moment.

'This seems like one of your union meetings instead of a family talking together,' she said coldly.

Max ignored her, and, sitting to face Tom and Maisie, said: 'All right. First, Mayhem is dead and gone. You two have plans for your lives, and quite right too. No good if your heart's not in performing.'

He said that Uncle Wilf's invitation to join him in Glasgow was meant kindly and, things being as they were, it had to be seriously considered. By the sound of it, Max said, he had room at his house for three, four at a pinch.

Tom interjected: 'Count me out Pa. I'll be moving anyway, probably to Belfast.'

Gertie's face fell.

'That came out of the blue. Are you sure, Tom? Are you ready?' she asked, twisting the tea cloth.

'Never been surer of anything, Ma. There's the first conference of the Labour Party coming up, and there's union work to be had, openings. I've got a friend who says that he can get me into a paid position. Big things are going to happen.'

Max put aside his disappointment that Tom was going, at a time he had come to understand him so much better.

'So, that leaves Ma and me, and you Maisie.'

'I'd be willing to move up there,' said Maisie, cheerfully. 'I can't think of anything I do in London that I couldn't do in Glasgow. For me it would be the same fight on a different battleground. It would be exciting, different. An adventure.'

'And that brings things to Ma and me,' Max said. 'Right. We

can't live on fresh air, and so Uncle Wilf's offer might seem like the perfect solution. He wants to help sort out mother's health, and he'd be trying to get me on to a few bills. A fresh start...'

Max looked thoughtful, as if he was being struck forcibly by the logic behind Wilf's plan that his resistance was weakening.

'He's right about one thing; there'll be a lot of bitterness, old scores being settled in the London halls. It'll never be the same.'

Maisie and Tom looked expectant. Had Pa already made his decision?

'You're keen to give it a go up there, aren't you mother?' he said, turning to Gertie.

'Well, all other things being equal.' There was no confidence in her voice.

'I understand that,' Max said, turning to Tom and Maisie. 'But as your mother will have guessed, I can't go to Glasgow...'

He stopped mid-sentence, seeing Maisie's face flush, and immediately feeling a pressure to give reasons that the children might accept as acceptable grounds for separation, something that he knew would come as a cruel blow to them.

'The thing is, I'd find it hard to be in debt to Uncle Wilf. I'd be a fish out of water up there. It's very...well, foreign. Anyway, it would be a crush at the house, all of us on top of one another again.'

Maisie's eyes began to fill with tears. Tom showed no emotion, as if he had predicted this outcome.

'So I plan to soldier on here. Do some solo bits. Keep a London base, in case Glasgow doesn't work out.'

Maisie said: 'Father. Are you really saying that mother would be up there, and you would be in London?'

'No decision has been made,' Gertie said hurriedly. She turned to Max and, sounding hurt, protested: 'I didn't know that you wouldn't go up at any price. You never actually said that, Max.'

'I'm saying it now. I can't go. But I know you'd go in a shot.'

'Yes. I would. There's no option. We won't be earning a living here. Wilf's not well, and I'd want to keep an eye on him.'

She looked down at the tea towel in her lap, wondering whether she should have mentioned Wilf's need at a time when her husband was being abandoned.

'And anyway, Scotland's my home. My real home.'

Max bridled.

'Home? You mean you've been homesick for twenty-odd years? Never settled here? Been living a lie all that time?' He threw back his head disdainfully.

Gertie didn't answer. This discussion, for both of them, felt uncomfortably like washing marital laundry in public. To be rowing like this in front of Tom and Maisie showed just how separate they had become, and how willing they had become to contemplate separation.

Gertie could see that Maisie was wounded by their disagreement.

'Well, I'll tell you all now: I wouldn't move without father,' Maisie said firmly, and buried her face in her hands. She reached down and picked up Dazzle and sat motionless nursing him.

Gertie said: 'I haven't even said I'm definitely going, Maisie. And if I did, I'd want your father to come, of course I would. Moving is the best solution for the situation we're in, that's all.'

The discussion petered out into uneasy silence lasting minutes. At last, Tom retreated to his bedroom. Gertie stood up and busied herself at the food cupboard. Maisie sat on the sofa, petting Dazzle to comfort herself; Max was aware of her eyes following him in mute support.

Not knowing how to proceed, Max thumbed some tobacco into it his pipe, put on his coat and without saying goodbye strode out, past the privy and on to the Mile End Road, near-deserted in a gloaming of fine drizzle.

He tried to keep his mind blank, in the hope that a path ahead would show itself. Instead, the pain of impending loneliness encroached and filled his mind.

There had been another time in his life when he had felt this bitter pang, this sense of his own vulnerability.

It was when he was eleven and his father's unvarying daily routine (breakfast; retreat to his study for violin practice, while the skivvy was in; lunch; nap; tutoring of students; dinner) fell into chaos.

Father, a spindly man whose bony elbows formed sharp triangles when he played the violin, had slowly become even more angular, and Max noticed a large gap where his neck no longer filled his collars.

He had always been quiet but hardly spoke at all; the violin practices petered out, family life was suspended.

Young as he was, Max understood that all his mother's attention had to be turned to the matter of helping father to die but he had hoped that, after the funeral, she would know how to ease the ache in him. He soon accepted she had no feeling to spare, no way of seeing into his emptiness.

Father's friends ensured that Max continued to play music, encouraging him to do a solo or two and take a bow when they performed in local halls, but when his mother began to go to tea and to bridge with a silvery widower with transparent charm and no visible means of support, Max knew that it was time to make a life for himself.

He also knew that he had to begin to think of the motherly love he had once known as a phase, like the passing of a single glorious summer.

By the age of sixteen, while his mother, now re-married, helplessly watched the family money leak away, Max was playing solo at concerts and socials. A year later one of his father's friends put in a word for him after a Masonic meeting and he found himself at the Paragon, between the big, stage-side lions, looking out at a sea of caps and floral hats.

Instead of caprices and sonatas he was teasing comic sounds out of the violin, and the saw, punctuating the playful routine with short bursts of dazzling virtuoso playing to make the audience sit up and pay respect.

His father's bequest turned out not to be monetary (his mother's suitor had seen to that) but the training he had instilled. It was a legacy that ensured that Max never had cause to doubt his mastery of his instrument, or the need to fear any audience.

Sometimes he was haunted by the thought that his father would have disapproved of the way he used his talent, and where he chose to play. But the old saying that the violin sings, and the fiddle dances, pointed to a distinction he did not observe. It was all music, and, for Max, music had no lines of division.

Father had gone so long ago. Mother had followed him a year after, almost hurrying away from the mistake she had made with his replacement.

It was only when Max met Gertie that he experienced again the sustenance that came from someone caring for him. She was the treasured companion on the road he had chosen for himself, and he rediscovered what it was to be sustained by the attentiveness another person offered.

As Max braced himself for what was ahead, without Gertie beside him, there seemed to be little reason to soldier on. He would not see where the future led but he was sure (almost absolutely sure) about one thing: It would not be in Scotland.

My journal

February 9

Suddenly our family seems broken beyond repair. Father has hardened his heart. Being beholden to Uncle Wilf is just too must to ask of him. Mother will go to Glasgow, I know it, and, in her current state of mind, abandon poor old Pa if necessary.

I will stay at father's side, even if I have to become a typist to help with the rent.

PS What an irony that we should win so many battles in the strike and then find this crisis wiping us out.

24

Eli Sherman's impact on the world had been inconsequential. In response, he expected little from life, especially for himself. His quiet humility went largely unnoticed in the brash and noisy world of the music hall.

Eli was a scene shifter who tended to be part of the scenery, to blend in like a worn backcloth. He was there to serve but he went further; he offered himself as an untenanted space for others to inhabit with their opinions, their jokes and their orders.

The gammy leg completed the persona he presented – of someone who always followed, rather than led, and who presumed that others always knew better.

Yet Eli was not entirely devoid of self-esteem. He prided himself on always finding work; he was an efficient facilitator enabling others to perform on stage. He excelled especially at following orders (even Cecil had admitted that), and he was a loyal son to his mother in her needy dotage; a little saint, she would have said.

Lately, he had even been able to claim a little extra kudos from a gesture of defiance. Somehow – and to this day he didn't know how – he had found the courage to flee from the Astoria when Cecil, blundering around like a bewildered beast, had ordered him to fetch his brother to exact vengeance on Wilf.

Looking back, Eli still marvelled – and trembled – at the thought of his recklessness in hobbling into the night, leaving his livelihood behind.

Over the years, Eli had come to regard Gertie and Max as confidantes. They were watchful over him, like distant but protective relatives, and that was why he decided that the Pyles would be the first to know that, with the strike over, he had landed a job at the Fortune.

Eli would never know it, but by calling on them, he inadvertently accomplished something that he would have regarded as the pinnacle of his modest attainments, even greater than running away from the Astoria. He saved their marriage.

Eli stayed an hour, ramblingly regaling Gertie and Max with news of the halls and describing the uneasy peace marking the passing of time until the arbitration board announced their ruling. He reported that Cecil was still hungry to avenge Wilf's attack.

'They say he tells everybody that bobbies are useless, that even with their telephones and their fancy new fingerprinting they couldn't even collar Wilf in a little place like Darlington. He's talked of sending Artie up there, so you'd better tell Wilf to watch out!'

Gertie hoped that the conversation would move away from Wilf but then Eli asked blithely: 'Is there word of him? Your brother?'

'No. We lost track of him... after Darlington,' Gertie said haltingly.

Maisie and Tom were out, Tom at the Musicians' Union office helping staff deal with a flood of enrolment requests, and Maisie at a suffragist fund-raising event.

When Eli asked after them, Max took the opportunity to pass on news that he knew would devastate Eli: that things had changed, that Maisie and Tom had ambitions away from the music hall, and that Musical Mayhem was no more.

Eli was nonplussed. 'Finished? You're finished? That's terrible news. Everyone loved your show.' His voice quaked with emotion. 'Everyone.'

His dismay then showed itself in petulance. He shook his greying, childish head in disbelief. 'It's not fair. Maisie was wonderful. Her and the dog. You all were.'

Max said: 'It might have happened even without the strike, Eli, but to be honest, Wilf clubbing Cecil to the floor didn't do a lot for the Pyle reputation.'

Gertie cut in sharply. 'You can't blame Wilf, Max! Be honest, the act's gone because I'm useless, and because the children have other fish to fry. That and all the nastiness we'll be getting in the halls.'

She turned to Eli, who had raised his eyebrows in alarm at Gertie's tartness, and said, more softly: 'Tom wants to go off and do union work, Eli. Maisie has dreams of, well, just helping people. She's got a bee in her bonnet. Wants to be some sort of do-gooder.'

'Maisie will be good at that. She's a good person,' Eli said, a little dreamily. It had been obvious to Gertie and Max for a couple of years that Eli was besotted with Maisie.

Max and Gertie looked at each other and then Max said: 'Eli. Look. The fact is, we might have to move. Move away. Just for a bit. Gertie needs to stay up in Scotland, family crisis, and I might end up finding a cheap room and doing my old fiddle act somewhere until things sort themselves out.'

Eli looked first into Max's face and then into Gertie's, searching for a truth he knew was there but which he didn't want to hear.

'Please don't tell me that the family's breaking up. Not you and Gertie, Max!'

Eli tilted his head and made a face. 'But you need each other.'

Max touched Eli's shoulder and said: 'It's not settled Eli, old son. Far from it. But these are tricky times for us.'

Eli was not to be comforted. 'But there'll be no family left. You'll be like me, Max. On your tod, or as good as, because Ma is no real company for me, bless her. It's a waste.'

Gertie gathered the teacups and Eli stood up and put his cap on. He looked grave. He shook hands solemnly with Max and gave a little wave towards Gertie at the sink.

'And will Maisie be going up there with you, Gertie?' Eli called, as casually as he could manage.

'Too soon to know, Eli. But we'll get in touch and tell you when things are worked out,' Gertie said.

'Promise?'

'Promise.'

Eli had wanted it to be a happy morning, telling the Pyles his good news and, maybe, finding Maisie at home. He limped home briskly, to check that his mother was all right, with a heavy heart.

Gertie and Max pottered about the main room, and although they did not talk, they both felt an easing of the tension that had been building for days.

'Telling Eli brought it home to me,' Max said. 'You know, how serious it is, Gert.'

Gertie looked at him and nodded. A moment later she suggested that perhaps they should have tea early, just them, and talk before Tom and Maisie came home. Max responded benignly, noting the mildness in her voice – 'Why not, Gert?'

When Max showed Eli out, he had found another letter from Wilf on the doormat. It was addressed this time to 'Gertie and Max Pyle' leading Max to speculate that Wilf, having presented Gertie with an offer that she would want to take, was now drawing him in, as part of the master plan.

In the letter, Wilf leapfrogged any stumbling blocks. He spoke of "when you come," and it was clear he had even worked out the living arrangements ('Would Maisie mind taking the truckle bed, all being well?').

Max resented this presumption. It was a tactic to remove any doubt about whether the family should move to Glasgow, and hurry matters on to the how and the when.

Wilf had settled the question of how by enclosing a £20 note that Gertie drew from the envelope, held delicately by the corner, and stared at in wonderment. She couldn't remember when she had last seen a £20 note.

The letter said: 'The enclosed sum should cover the cost of the flit... I expect you will need a trunk for all your gubbins as well the tickets.'

Gertie folded the large, white banknote, tucked it under the spaniel ornament on the mantelpiece, thinking: 'Four of us would have had to sweat for six weeks to get one of those from Cecil.'

Her thoughts turned to Morag. She was overcome, quite

suddenly, and to her surprise, first with sadness that the poor woman had not gained any enjoyment from having been so prudent, and then with gratitude for the security her legacy might bring for her and Max if he relented and saw sense.

Max betrayed no emotion as he read the letter. He put it back in the envelope and said: 'So it's just about cut and dried. You're half way there.' There was no resentment in his voice; it was a statement.

Gertie chose her words carefully. The prospect of Glasgow was irresistible but could she really live without Max? Would they ever uncover the accustomed, well-trodden path of their marriage, or had it disappeared completely among the barbs and prickles of recent times? And if Max joined her in Scotland, would Max be forever at Wilf's throat?

Tom arrived home ravenously hungry but deliriously happy about the surge in applications to join the union in the wake of the strike. Then Maisie trooped in, apple-cheeked from the cold wind. She seemed forlorn. As she came through the door, she looked anxiously first at Gertie and then at her father, to try to gauge whether the deadlock between them had been broken.

Unusually, Gertie seemed energised as she ladled out soup and then began briskly slicing a loaf of bread. Max could see the change in her and it left him dispirited. He wondered whether, like a prisoner, she was mentally ticking off the last days of a sentence.

Over the meal, Tom talked from time to time but somehow circumvented the issue of the day (the future of his parents' marriage). Maisie remained detached and silent throughout. She picked up Dazzle and went to her room leaving her soup. Max and Gertie were left alone. In the absence of conversation, and having read the Comet thoroughly, Max decided to go for a walk.

Gertie challenged him: 'A walk? At this time? In the dark?'

Max did not answer but as he started to go downstairs she called after him: 'It's no good running away from it, Max. We have to talk. We have to give notice to Mr Cohen, it's only fair. We have to let Wilf know.'

Max set off towards the Mile End Road, walking quickly to keep warm but with no destination in mind. He was trying to exhaust his mind and his legs, to lose himself but he knew the area too well for that. There were landmarks at every turn – White Horse Lane, the Anchor Brewery, Beaumont Square, the hospital.

When Max had been walking for two hours and knew he was at least a mile from the rooms, he regretted having walked so far. His legs were heavy, his head felt no clearer, and he was still as undecided about the future as when he had set off.

He stepped it out on the most direct route to the rooms and, trudging upstairs to the darkened main room, recovered for a few minutes in front of the fire.

When he eased into bed, the warmth from Gertie was comforting. He had always enjoyed that moment of the day, the juncture when troubles fell away and tiredness overtook him.

Max was aware that Gertie was still awake; he could tell by the cadence of her breathing. He wondered why tonight she was not feigning sleep. Her silent alertness prevented him settling.

He turned away from Gertie's back, pummelled the bolster, and lay listening to the silence willing sleep to come.

Suddenly, Gertie spoke. It was a wide-awake voice.

'I've been thinking, Max. Eli is right. It would be a damned waste. A criminal waste.'

Max chose not to reply. He knew that Gertie would say more but the interval that followed was unnervingly long.

'Stupid! Years and years down the drain, with us ending up hundreds of miles apart at a time of life when we will need each other more than ever.'

Max turned on his back to show that, although he was not talking, he was listening. He was relieved to hear Gertie's doubts but especially the valuing of their marriage.

'Tonight, for the first time, I saw it all clearly. It was frightening. It was when I looked at poor Maisie. That lassie's face! And then I thought of little Eli soldiering on. Coping alone.'

Still Max kept his silence but Gertie forced him to respond, with a question.

'Can you see any way ahead?' she said, turning towards him. The hardness in her voice had gone.

Max had still not consciously thought out a strategy, or really chosen an option about the future but as he began to talk, he outlined a proposal with a firmness that suggested a great deal of forethought and some determination.

He told Gertie she had become a stranger but that this was not her fault; she needed help over her nerves. He explained how his pride was hurt by the very idea that Wilf would be providing for both of them, how for him moving from London would be a terrible wrench. The place was in his blood.

When there was a lull, Gertie said: 'You make me feel ashamed.'

'Bosh! There's no need for you to feel like that. But for a long time you've not been the Gertie I used to know.'

They lay in the darkness for some time, Max fighting his need to sleep but afraid to miss this chance of some sort of resolution. He knew that Gertie might not be as conciliatory in the morning.

'Actually, I'm a bit ashamed of the way I feel about Wilf,' Max said, to balance Gertie's guilt. She did not pick up this thread but said: 'Do you hate me for wanting to be away, to go back up there?'

'I don't hate you. But I want to be here. Actually, to be honest, I think that I'm a bit pettish about you wanting to go to be with Wilf, and not putting me first.'

'It's not like that Max. It's just that I've always protected him. From the time we were wee. He seems full of himself but he's a very sad man if you get under all that tomfoolery.'

She sat up and said: 'I've come to one conclusion. What will govern us in the end is money. We've got to eat, Max, we've got to live. Sad to say, money makes the plans, not us.'

Max took this to be an assertion that the prospect of poverty made the move to Scotland inevitable.

'I'd get by, don't you worry,' he said. 'You know it, Gert. I'd find work, always have,' he added, more testily than he intended.

Gertie wanted to say that yes, he was right, he would get by, but that lately it had been a hand-to-mouth existence, the halls were changing, and anyway, she was pining for Scotland, and that feeling would not go away. Instead she said: 'What would suit you best?'

Max was taken aback by the immediacy of his reply and his assertive tone.

'I'd want you healthy, as you were, so first I'd get help for you. Then, so long as you agreed to do what was good for you, I'd go up there with you. I'd give it a try for six months. Strictly six months, but only on condition that you get yourself right.'

Gertie lay down again. She turned away from Max and drew up her knees.

'You're right. I've been avoiding it. I'll do something about it, mark my words. We'll give it a try. Maisie will be so relieved.'

'Maisie? But what about you?'

'I'm relieved. So very relieved.'

Max shifted to find the warm expanse of Gertie's back. He laid his arm across her shoulder and waited, sure that she would move it but she left it where it was, pulled it tighter round her as sleep overtook them.

My journal

February 10

Pa, poor man, seems to be just an onlooker as Ma merrily wheedles her way towards Scotland. He went striding off into the night to think.

They say Eli had visited. I didn't ask, but I did wonder whether they told him that they might go their separate ways. He would be devastated to learn it.

Father was back late.

We will see what the morning brings but I fear it might not be good news for me and for Ma and Pa's marriage.

25

Max and Gertie had known Horace Webb – International Mesmerist, Hypnotist and Mind Reader – for almost 20 years. They had been on the same bill many times.

Their friendship had endured mainly because Horace regarded Max as the best fiddler he'd seen on the halls, and Max held Horace in the highest esteem as a master entertainer – the mutual admiration of fellow professionals.

Horace exercised his mysterious art with such skill that invariably audiences were left baffled, and admiring. Max had witnessed this many times.

What Horace didn't do, something Max found especially admirable, was to place stooges in the audience. He had no need to; he found it easy enough to strip volunteers of their volition and to turn them to his ends.

Hecklers were a speciality. Max had lost count of the times he had seen Horace lure a rowdy gasbag, usually the worse for drink, up on to the stage and within a minute have him on their hands and knees meowing and licking up milk from a bowl.

The genuinely curious and good-hearted were spared humiliation when they volunteered. Horace would set up a line of bashful seamstresses singing like canaries, or get them dancing around with an imaginary mouse in their skirts but that was innocent fun.

Horace was still sometimes surprised by his powers. In fact, he was not sure where his limits lay but he steered clear of performing cures. He believed this was best left to lesser performers and tricksters, along with those Germanic professors who, in their vanity, seemed to believe that they had the key to the unfathomable workings of the mind.

However, he sometimes agreed to help in cases where a habit had become a problem, or some irrational fear was blighting someone's life. This occasional service was limited to friends and acquaintances, people like Max, who that morning had called on him to ask advice.

And that was how Horace came to be sitting on the Pyles' sofa eating warm, homemade shortbread and having a second cup of tea poured out by Gertie Pyle.

Horace reminded Gertie of a laird, with his ruddy cheeks, mass of crinkly hair swept back as if he was permanently walking into a stiff wind, and his coarse tweed suit the colour of dead bracken.

He was a kindly, avuncular man with an air of other-worldliness. Gertie found reassurance in his plumpness and in his kind, watery blue eyes.

After small-talk round the table about the weather and the way the days were lengthening, Horace picked crumbs from his hairy trousers and said: 'But now – to business...'

Max began: 'Well, it's like this, Horace....'

Horace interrupted. 'No, Max. Not a word! I always like to come at things with an empty head. Tackle it like a scientist would, objectively, not as an old chum. It all has to come from Gertie. For all I know you might be the problem, Max!'

Horace laughed wheezily and turned a worrying red for a moment. 'Just joshing,' he said, patting Max's arm.

Max went off out in search of a copy of the Comet, and Horace asked Gertie to sit on the sofa. He drew up a chair to face her and said: 'So, Gertie, I gather you've been a bit out of sorts. Nervy. And I hear you have a journey to make soon, and you're not a good traveller...?'

Gertie felt herself flushing. How much had Max said? The situation was disturbingly intimate, Horace's eyes far too invasive.

'I'm petrified in anything but a horse-bus, Horace. Silly, I know, but I'm petrified.'

Horace slowly and patiently began to delve, each question peeling off the protective layers Gertie kept in place around her fragile feelings.

'I won't go on trams, or the Tube. I hate cars. Trains scare me because of all the crashes. And I wouldn't go within a mile of that Aldwych lift.' She blushed at what she thought Horace must regard as foolishness but Horace remained earnest.

'That's a considerable handicap,' he said, and then, fixing Gertie with an inquisitive stare, asked: 'Tell me, what's the worst, the very worst, thing that could happen in your life?'

Gertie's reply was hurried: 'That we're in a crash. That we die. Or we're in a fire, and Max dies or the children die and it's my fault...' She laughed to show that she knew how irrational she was being.

At last, Horace said: 'You know, Gertie, cleverer people than me now believe that the things that happen to us, events that shock us or disturb us in some frightening way, can leave a scar – not a real scar of course but a bit of damage that won't heal. That wounded bit can start playing up and give us grief, sometimes at the most unlikely times.'

'And do you think that I've got a scar.'

'Perhaps,' he said. 'But our task today is just to get you fit to face a journey. Glasgow awaits!'

Horace took from his waistcoat pocket a silver chain with a globe of jet on the end. He asked Gertie to breath slowly and deeply and to follow the arc of the black ball as it swung. She obeyed, and after a few moments he whispered: 'You've seen me work Gertie. You know you can trust me.'

'I know I can.'

'Well then, tell me about whatever it was that made you afraid to travel. An accident, perhaps?'

Gertie replied that she had not been in an accident but that they were happening all over. There was danger everywhere.

She said that this sort of fear had come suddenly. She had first felt the terror two years before, on the train home from visiting her brother in Scotland.

She was alone and had been tempted to leap from the door of the moving train. She had cowered in the carriage for nine hours.

Horace asked if anything had happened in Scotland to upset

her and in an unemotional drone she described being with Wilf the previous day and coming across the boarding house fire in Watson Street, and seeing the bodies being taken away.

When Horace asked what thoughts on the train home had made her so anxious, she said: 'I suppose that seeing the fire did something to me, set something off. When the train left Glasgow, I was upset and sitting there thinking of the fire and then my mind moved on, to picture another train, one I went on when I was wee.'

'Tell me, Gertie.'

'It was when we left Crail. We'd gone off in a terrible hurry. Wilf was left behind, poor wee boy. Mother was in a panic, fair yanking me by the arm to the cart that was taking us to the station.'

Horace asked why that childhood trip should have stuck in her mind. 'Yes, it was quite a rush. But most children love a trip on a train,' he said. 'Wasn't this an adventure?'

'No. Mother was frightened. She was white. I think we were being chased. I wanted the train to go faster and faster because mother said he would kill us if he ever caught us.'

'Who would kill you, Gertie?'

'I shouldn't say.'

'Say it, Gertie. Who?'

'Faither.'

Horace had found the scar. He decided he had no need to probe further.

He would use his powers to instil in Gertie the idea that in future she would feel differently about train carriages, that she would think of them as cosy cabins on wheels, safe places in which there were seats that rocked you to sleep.

He had come across this sort of case before. The mind had somehow commingled the tragic boarding house fire and the train journey that followed.

He told Gertie that he had the power to put her dreadful

memories into a sturdy safe at the back of her mind – 'I will lock it, and I'll keep the key.'

He counted Gertie back to consciousness. She shook her head as if to clear it and said: 'Did I say anything silly, Horace?'

'No, Gertie, what you said made sense. I think you'll find that now you will have no fear on that journey north.'

Max returned, the Comet under his arm, as Horace was putting on his greatcoat. They walked together to the foot of the stairs and stood at the privy door.

Max said: 'Good of you to come, Horace. Appreciated. Could I offer you something for your trouble?'

'Certainly not, Max. Friends don't make money out of friends.'

That's the sort of brotherly spirit that I'm going to miss, Max thought ruefully.

'Thanks. But Horace, I don't suppose you can tell me…well, how it went? Whether she's going to be better.'

'No, Max. I wouldn't dream of telling you. Suffice it to say that she should be a better traveller now. I say should be. Sometimes you uncover some mental injury and you put a hypnotic ointment on it, so to speak, but it simply refuses to heal.'

He said, despite that, hypnotism was far healthier than the lithium bromide doctors had started prescribing, and it cost nothing. He was sure Gertie would relax on the train and might even enjoy the journey.

'But with the mind, you never know, Max. So why not take some strong drink just in case there's still a little agitation there? Tonic wine's an idea. Something like that. Calming. It's such a long journey and it would take the edge off things in the unlikely event of her growing fretful.'

There were few refuges in Glasgow in the darkest months of the year when the weather would not test the thickness of your coat. Few nights when the abstemious would resist the temptation to tip a dram into their hot milk, when even the hardiest of the hardy poor would not shiver and dream of hot broth and a woollen blanket.

One such place was an airy palace made of glass, another a sweltering room where the wealthy reclined in calm and silence and under a bejewelled ceiling.

Both refuges lay in Glasgow's West End, an area of the city Wilf had not known well until his advancement to prosperity and stability. Recently he had gone exploring, experiencing the places he had always known were there but which had seemed to him to be the domain of the rich.

The bitter winter was taking its toll on Wilf's ailing chest. A fit of coughing had ruined his second appearance with his Zulu act at the Panopticon. Despite superhuman efforts to control his breathing, his monologue – contrived to build an atmosphere of drama – had descended into farce. Someone in the audience had shouted 'Quick! Owbridge's Lung Tonic and a spoon!' and laughter erupted throughout the hall.

AE had been displeased, and told Wilf that he shouldn't appear again until he could do a convincing act – 'Get yourself into some heat, man. Tell you what, get to the Arlington Baths and lie around in the Turkish Suite for a couple of days and we'll get you back on.'

Wilf thought of the Arlington as an elite hub, where the owners of the mansions nearby took their leisure and sweated out the excesses of the dinner table and the drinks cabinet.

But it was not out of bounds for him; he encountered no barrier when he arrived with his newly acquired striped bathing suit of light wool to join the club. Duly approved, and subscription paid, he diffidently joined the swimmers, and virile men exercising on the hoops hanging above the water.

He found that when he swam, he coughed. Climbing from the pool, with the swimming costume clinging to his long, angular frame, he was struck by his own frailty. He noticed he was thinner than a month ago. Everyone around him appeared to be in rude health.

He found his way to the Turkish Suite – and felt at once that he had entered heaven. The walls of the room and the floor were tiled and he was immediately embraced by almost overwhelming heat. He could see, in the half-light, motionless draped figures in deckchairs, ranged around a central, tinkling fountain. What a wonderful place to lie and think, embroider little worlds in his head...

Wilf lowered himself into a reclined seat and breathed almost effortlessly. The urge to cough had gone. He lay back and silently offered thanks to AE for steering him here, to what he felt must be the anteroom to paradise.

He resolved that this was where his cure was to be found, here and perhaps at the Botanical Gardens, another place he had yet to visit. Elspeth, the Woman With Half A Body, suggested that he really should take a good book and spend a few hours there, in the Kibble Palace glasshouse. It was like being in a huge bubble, she said; some of the plants grew so well in the heat they were as tall as houses.

He resolved to spend time there relaxing, getting better, and would make make a habit of taking trips to the Arlington in the morning, gaining strength for performances.

Lying prone, Wilf looked up at the beehive ceiling of the Turkish Suite, enjoying the exoticism of the place, feeling again the excitement he experienced when first he basked in the heat of Zululand.

He fixed his eyes on the pure, bright lozenges of coloured glass set in what could easily have been the night sky above him and felt all vexation and sensation fall away, like a tide going out inside him.

My journal

February 11

Green with envy this morning. In White Horse Lane two girls of my age (probably sisters) hurtled past me on what looked to be BRAND NEW bicycles. They had on identical hats with trailing ribbons, and plum-coloured serge skirts with raised hems that flapped round high enough to suggest that they might have KNEES!

Of course, I thought of Guillaume and Yvette and the other Bicyclettes.

This morning I left the house as quickly as possible and used my time profitably by going to the Endowed Library to find out more about the Second City of The Empire. My real reason was to escape the tension between mother and father as they continue to brood.

I discovered that Glasgow is very much like London in that it has a West and East, housing the rich and the poor.

What I found remarkable, coming across a very revealing report, is that people from the poorest families are about four inches, yes, four INCHES, shorter than their betters in the West End. So it turns out I am as big as many Glaswegian men!

When we go, IF we go, I will be finding out how I can help to lift up the 'little people,' for whom (understandably) I have special sympathy!

Coming home, to my amazement I found that some magical breeze had wafted away the twitchiness that, lately, has been making it difficult to have even the plainest of conversations.

Ma and Pa, if not companionable, were civil and soft-spoken with each other. The say hope springs eternal.

PS If I do find myself in bonnie Scotland I will look forward to visiting the Skating Palace in Sauchiehall Street. I told mother, and she said with a smile (a SMILE, mind you!) that Sauchiehall was not pronounced 'Sorchi' but 'Socki'.

A suffragist friend in London goes rinking in Lambeth and says it is the most enormous fun, although a terrible generator of perspiration.

I could not find any mention in the library of a cycling school in Glasgow, yet there must be hundreds of young Scottish women, like me, aching to learn to cycle. Perhaps one day I'll start one. Surely they don't have steep hills everywhere?

26

Two days after Max's Pyle's marriage had been revived by a combining of negotiation, pledges, recrimination, apologies, and then by Gertie's returning affection, he was frantically clinging to her elbows, restraining her flight from her demons. Dazzle barked and Maisie looked on, horrified, with tears in her eyes.

The train journey to Scotland had gone well for the entire first leg – but then came a fateful stop at Crewe. There, Max's belief that good fortune is inevitably followed by misfortune (or worse) was validated once again.

Gertie had boarded the train at Euston with no trepidation, to the astonishment and relief of Max and Maisie. She had plonked herself down in the carriage and gasped: 'There! Let's be off.' She looked pleased with herself.

As the train gathered speed, Gertie looked out of the window. Max and Maisie had her under observation. She seemed so tranquil, nursing a picnic parcel of pretzels, bagels and cold fish, a parting gift from Mr Cohen.

The city was left far behind. The train rushed on through open country with distant copses and church spires punctuating the grey skyline, and bare fields studded with standing water.

The journey seemed to Maisie to be marking the end not merely of a chapter but an entire book, and the beginning of another, to be set in an alien land, 400 miles from the familiarity of London. Every aspect of their life was changing in the duration of a train single journey.

But the augurs were good. Everything to do with the move had been trouble-free. Max had gone to a dealer in Denmark Street and sold the tuba and a bag of smaller instruments, and had given money to Tom to travel to his union job in Belfast, and for his first week's rent there. Gertie had been tearful as they left, pleading with Tom to find a job in Scotland as soon as the industrial trouble in Northern Ireland dies down.

Mr Cohen had offered a large, battered trunk (one that had carried his late mother's possessions across Europe) for a token sum, and with a teasing smile explained that the new Aliens Act would mean that Max could now sleep easy in his bed – 'No need for you Pyles to escape to Scotland! They have now voted to stop foreigners like us invading you!'

This had made Max feel ashamed. He never thought he'd say it but he believed the country could do with more Haim Cohens.

When Max and Haim had shaken hands, they stared intently at one another, with eyes that showed feeling, two middle-aged men who knew what it was to have to pull up roots.

The saving on the cost of a trunk, which would hold most of the possessions the Pyles could not bring themselves to part with, allowed Max to give Maisie thirty shillings rather than the pound he had promised for her work with the turn at the Astoria.

She had decided she would treat herself. She took herself off and ventured into the beauty hall at Liberty's and, trying to appear assured, bought a small bottle of Atkin's lavender, some pearl powder and some pale lip rouge.

No one would have challenged her indulgence but she chose not to show what she had bought. During the journey, the make-up nestled alongside her books – including her journal – in a cloth bag, along with her hairbrush and favourite crimson velveteen hat, which she feared might be crushed to ruin in the trunk.

In a smaller bag, at the request of her father, she carried a bottle of Wincarnis Tonic Wine and his copy of the Comet, his last (he had been disappointed to learn that its circulation did not extend to Scotland).

When the train reached the outskirts of Crewe, Max dug around in his pocket for change for cups of tea during the break at the station.

'Tea would be nice,' Gertie said, 'I'm parched,' and asked him to look out for some of the new Dairy Milk chocolate.

The thundering of the engine and the rattle of the rails

diminished and was replaced by hissing and the opening and slamming of doors, and the shout of a railway man announcing that this was the train for Glasgow departing in fifteen minutes.

Max got out and stretched his legs, and then hurried to a refreshment servery, returning with teas and chocolate. Maisie had Dazzle on a lead and was walking him briskly along the platform.

Maisie gathered up Dazzle and re-boarded the train joining Gertie in the carriage. Max followed, having returned the empty cups. There was an echoing whistle and shouting and the train jolted forward, slowly gaining speed, rolling through clouds of smoke.

An hour or so hour later, Max, without thinking, turned the leisurely journey into a nightmare, casting a careless handful of words.

'I've always respected Horace, you know Gert,' he said, 'but I have to say I count it a near-miracle what he's done with you. He should take a bow. Imagine, getting you on a bally train with not a spot of bother.'

Gertie seemed to be thinking long and hard over what Max had said. Then her face contorted in terror. She stood up and rushed towards the corridor, pleading to be let off the train. Max had her by the elbows, pulling her back on to the seat then taking her face in his hands.

'Gert! Steady girl. You're safe. We're here.'

He tilted her back and held her still and Maisie looked into her face and made reassuring noises.

'Maisie – the Wincarnis,' Max said.

Gertie was trembling and crying quietly. 'It all came back,' she sobbed.

'It was me. I broke the spell,' Max said.

'What's this? Wincarnis? What for?' Gertie said in a quaking voice.

'Horace said it would help if you had a turn. Soothe you until we get to Glasgow.'

Gertie let out a childlike wail and squeezed Max's hand. 'I can't make it to Glasgow. All that way! I have to get off. We'll crash. Look how fast we're going...'

Max had taken the top off the bottle of Wincarnis and pleaded with Gertie to have a sip. She shut her lips tight like a child resisting a dose of castor oil.

'One sip,' he said. 'And don't look out of the window.'

'I hate wine. You know that Max. No!'

'This stuff isn't really wine, Gert. It's got herbs and things in for your nerves. Just a sip. One!'

Max tilted the bottle and Gertie gulped down a mouthful and coughed.

'Well done, Ma. It really will help,' said Maisie.

'Another drink. Just a small one, for me,' Max said, and Gertie took a little more but then began to struggle, as if she was throwing off chains.

'I want you to have a drop or two more, just a little, more. Think about something nice. Think about Wilf meeting us in Glasgow.'

Gertie relaxed a little at this, and took two or three gulps of Wincarnis. She sat back and seemed more composed. Max sat alongside her with his arm round her shoulders and holding the bottle in front of her.

'More. Just a little more,' he said and she began to comply.

When Max reached for her hand he noticed that she was no longer trembling. She stared ahead, to the other side of the carriage, determined to avoid looking out of the window. A few minutes later, when he put the bottle near her, she reached forward to drink without being prompted.

By the time the train rattled its way towards the tall smoking chimneys of Lancashire, Gertie had removed her hat, and taken two or three more slurps of the tonic wine. She was now holding the half-empty bottle and resting her head on the carriage side.

Max began reading the Comet, giving off an air of calm but

feeling anxious and vigilant. Maisie was talking non-stop with her mother to divert her. She took the wrapper from the chocolate. Gertie accepted a square, asked for another, and washed it down with a slurp of Wincarnis.

Maisie noticed that her mother's eyelids had become heavy, and that she fumbled the chocolate as she took it. She was rocking with the movement of the train and once, when she tried to take another drink, she found it difficult to get mouth and bottle to meet. At that point, Max, looking on, waved his outstretched hands to Maisie and said: 'No more, Gertie.'

Maisie claimed the bottle and, very slowly, her mother lay down, full length along one carriage seat.

'That's it Ma. You have a little nap,' Maisie said. Gertie emitted a deep guttural sound and then fell silent.

Maisie opened the paper parcel Mr Cohen had given them. She bit into a bagel and gagged when she found that it was filled with smoked salmon. She wondered why on earth people who were rich enough to have any food in the world chose to pay Fortnum's for this flabby stuff with its oily smell. Then she remembered that Scotland was famous for salmon; she hoped it wouldn't be a staple food in Glasgow or she would surely starve.

She ate a piece of cold fried fish instead, and then broke off a square of Gertie's chocolate to take away the taste. She looked back fondly to mother's neck of mutton stew bubbling on the hob back at the rooms and felt homesick, and then she thought of rissoles and in turn thought fondly of Razzle.

Gertie tried to sit up as the train arrived at Carlisle and passengers came and went, slamming doors, but then sank back, comatose.

When, late at night, the train hissed and groaned its way into the Glasgow Central Station, Gertie was still deeply asleep and Max and Maisie were travel-weary and bleary-eyed.

Max and Maisie tried to raise Gertie, to no avail. When Maisie looked out, she saw Wilf at the window making a comical face and mouthing words they could not hear. Maisie waved for him to come. He stepped into the carriage and was aghast to find Gertie struggling even to sit up, and her head rolling.

'She's ill!' he said.

'No, just a bit tipsy,' said Max.

'But she doesn't drink.'

'Medicine. For the journey. It's been a nightmare. Let's get her off,' Max said wearily. This was all a mistake. He thought of the rooms back in London – his chair, the fire, his pipe – and bitterly regretted ever having reached the agreement with Gertie about the move.

Once Gertie had been manhandled from the carriage, the sharp air revived her and she saw that it was Wilf who had his hand round her waist, steadying her. She let out a cry of delight and began to talk and laugh.

They stood at the station front while Wilf supervised the collection of the trunk from the goods van and then tipped the porter who brought it. They waited for a horse bus and Wilf again took out a coin or two to persuade the driver to accept the big trunk, upended, on the journey.

At the house, Max gave Wilf a hand with the trunk and Maisie helped her mother to the door. Max could see above the roofs of the single-storey houses what looked like the prow of an enormous ship and towering cranes and tall chimneys picked out by the moonlight.

Six months, he'd said. He wouldn't break his promise to Gertie but he couldn't see him settling.

My journal

February 16

Thirteen hours have passed since we left Euston, and here I am on what they call a truckle bed, a pull-out affair, surely intended for a child. I am small yet my ankles spill over the end. Privacy will not be an easy matter. I can only settle to sleep when everyone else is tucked up.

Strangely, I do not feel exhausted now, hence the journal entry. I have a new lease of life from the excitement of landing in Braid Street.

The little house is cosy enough but Morag's invisible presence, and evidence of her at every turn, gives it an air of a mausoleum.

On the mantelpiece in a crystal bowl are some crisp, dried flowers (perhaps a gift when she was nearing the end) which Wilf either chooses to keep, or fails to notice.

There are sepia photographs on the walls, Morag's books, including the collected works of Sir Walter Scott, are ranged along a shelf. There are china souvenirs and over the mantelpiece a sampler showing mountains and, written in the sky, 'Listen to the wind upon the hill till the waters abate.'

Perhaps it means 'Be patient.' If so it is so fitting. Aunty Morag was patience personified, over her illness and the vagaries of her husband's career.

Uncle Wilf kindly had made a bold attempt at concocting some ham hock soup for our midnight supper but it was too thin and much too salty but luckily he had bought for us some wonderful savouries called Forfar Bridies and warmed them. I left not a crumb!

Uncle Wilf has lost weight and his face in the gas light is quite ghostly. Ma chastised him, saying he must have been neglecting himself. I expect she will take over kitchen duties tomorrow.

Father seemed worn to a frazzle by the journey and Ma's antics on the train. He looked almost meek sipping his soup, as Wilf's reluctant guest.

Mother, now refreshed and with her terrors behind her, was annoyingly bright and talkative. I noticed that her Scots dialect is returning by the minute ('I dinna ken why I was so feart, Wilf.').

Uncle Wilf had thoughtfully bought a wicker basket and lined it with an old piece of velvet but Dazzle took one look and decided that he would rather share what little space there is on my bed. He will be a comfort, although he will never replace Razzle in my heart.

Tonight I began to think of Tom, who by now will be on his way to Belfast and to an unfamiliar bed and strange surroundings, but I told myself to stop at once.

I'm still embarrassed by my clinging farewell to him, and the tears I left on his new jacket. I must have made the parting much harder for him than it needed to be.

I must write to dear Eli. I did not have chance to explain our move and say goodbye.

I'll try to sleep now but expect to be given a rude awakening quite soon. Uncle Wilf says that the house is situated close to a shipbuilders and engineering works.

You won't just hear one or two big hammers going at dawn, he tells me, you'll hear screeching and clanging, a full industrial orchestra. He plugs his ears each night with cotton wool and he advises me to.

27

Maisie couldn't wait to explore Glasgow and Wilf was keen to show her the wonders of The Britannia and Grand Panopticon, in his view a grand title that in no way exaggerated the excitement to be found within every recess of Pickard's emporium of pleasure.

He knew that she would be amazed, as he had been. If they were lucky, they might bump into the man himself, Mr Albert Ernest Pickard.

Before they had finished their porridge he was urging her and Max and Gertie to come with him for a quick visit to Trongate that morning. He was like an excited schoolboy.

Ideally, he would have liked to show all three of them around but he sensed that Max would not want to confront the unique combination of entertainment there; a place where music hall kept company with a freak show, waxworks, zoo and amusement arcade. Wilf knew that Max would have especially disapproved of the new attraction at the Panopticon – 'Real Singing Pictures via the Chronomegaphone.'

Max liked his music hall traditional, unadorned, straight

John Bull. Without telling Wilf, he planned to explore the city's theatres, walking on his own and working out the tram routes.

Gertie was keen to go with Wilf, and was on the verge of agreeing, then remembered that the trip would involve tram rides, and – knowing Wilf – random diversions, involving stop-offs wherever took his fancy. She backed out – 'Better not. My ankles are up this morning.'

Max professed himself too tired after yesterday's journey. He asked where he might buy a newspaper and, as Wilf and Maisie prepared to leave, returned to the house having walked Dazzle and settled with the Herald.

Wilf and Maisie smiled as they left; they could hear Max complaining to Gertie that he wasn't going to get along with the Herald as it was full of Scottish news ('It's as if London doesn't exist!').

Wilf asked 'Got your walking boots on? Thought I'd give you a glimpse or two of the place before we step into the strange world Mr Pickard inhabits...'

'Please!' Maisie said.

It was clear to Maisie that Wilf had planned a route that enabled him to boast about the city. It involved two tram journeys and walking that entailed many twists and turns.

They set off in weak sunshine without speaking as they could not compete with the cacophony of metallic banging. Soon this was replaced by the background hum and rattle of the trams, the roar of cars and clatter of horses' hoofs.

Maisie was oblivious to the hubbub, absorbed with the grandeur of the buildings, and the landmarks Wilf pointed out.

'First there was Athens, then Rome, and then Glasgow!' he said as they passed the church of St Andrews in The Square, with its neo-classical columns.

Wilf talked of the phenomenal wealth accumulated by merchants in the city, and of the reverse side of the coin; the hordes of abjectly poor – 'I picture the Merchant City as a shiny new ship ploughing the seven seas, going full steam ahead, with the thousands of paupers and weakly weans drowning in its wake.'

Maisie, riled by such extremes of inequality, silently bridled. There was much to be done here.

Wilf had slowed down but his commentary flowed; he had not lost his knack of story telling, or of using irony to illuminate the contrariness of life.

He stopped Maisie in her tracks, holding her shoulders, and said: 'What about this, Maisie? A boy from Fife, a weaver's son, goes to America. He becomes the richest man in the world, and – far from forgetting his roots – bestows on his homeland the priceless boon of literacy. What a gift. There, look! Bridgeton Library! Spanking new and just one of hundreds of libraries Andrew Carnegie coughed up for.'

Maisie longed to look inside but Wilf was keen to move on and for her to learn more. Rather breathlessly he wended his way, with Maisie in tow, towards Glasgow Cross and its old Tolbooth Steeple.

On the way he remarked that the city was in constant flux. The old City Poor House had just closed. He raised his hand above his head and pointed – 'Over that way, somewhere. Townhead.'

He began to laugh and said: 'You know how we had to queue for a wash at your rooms in London? Well, we should have thought ourselves lucky. I hear tell that the Poor House had just two baths, and three hundred men had to share them once a week. Your father would have been very impatient! They say it took twelve hours to give them all a quick dip. And then people wondered why we got the bubonic plague back...'

'Plague! Here?' Maisie exclaimed.

'Not so long ago. It would have been when you were eight or nine. Sickness flourishes among the poor. People on top of each other. Same with TB.

They're starting to fine people a fortune for spitting on the buses.'

He stopped and considered whether to say what had come into his head but he said it anyway.

'Makes you nervous. I sometimes wonder about myself...'

'Don't say that!'

'Och no, Maisie!' he said, sorry that he had alarmed her. 'Mine's just an awfie, awfie chest – just as that doctor decided before he took my money!' He chuckled and tapped his breastbone.

Mother was right. Laughter was Uncle Wilf's response to fear. He laughed when he lost his toes, he laughed when he was heckled, he laughed when he was sacked.

Of course, he had not laughed when Morag died but he turned her funeral into a laughter-filled party.

Maisie suggested that they have a cup of tea; she didn't need one but she was concerned that in his excitement, Wilf might; he was exhausting himself.

The café was empty. They chose a window seat and sat and talked, about the strike, about Max, about the revival of Wilf's career, and the worrying state of Gertie's nerves.

'I'm determined to bring her back. It's no life being stuck in the house, frightened to take a ride to do a bit of shopping. She's not the woman she was.'

He said that he had inquired at the new Stobhill Hospital and, yes, there were medical pioneers there who were fathoming the mysteries of the mind. He was ready to pay any price to see his sister healthy and happy again. Morag would have wanted the money spent in that way.

Maisie sipped her tea and they chatted easily, like equals, not like typical young niece and mature uncle. Looking across at Wilf with his pallid face, the hank of hair flopping over his eyebrows, and holding his cap on his bony knees, she felt tenderness for him.

She was touched by his dogged determination to help her mother back to health even though, plainly, he himself was ailing.

'The problem with the mind is that you can't get to it with a bandage,' he said. 'If your mother was a soldier, she'd be down in the book as wounded in action. I suppose so would I, if I think about it, even if I hadn't carelessly mislaid my toes.'

Maisie wondered whether Wilf was referring to the way his army service had affected him.

'I'm puzzled, Uncle Wilf,' she said. 'I know that horrible things must have happened when you were fighting but I can't understand why you have an act that must remind you of those times, every day...'

Wilf thought for one minute. He slowly lowered his teacup and said:'Well, you know they say that familiarity breeds contempt? Well, the Zulu stuff helps me to keep a sane...'

'Sane?' Maisie said, raising her eyebrows, to tease him.

They laughed. 'Well, my kind of sane!'

'You know how it is Maisie. Some things can be packed up and put in the attic and they'll lie there forgotten. Others can break out in the night and make their way to your bed to haunt your sleep, or leap into your mind at any time to terrify you, on a motor-bus or when you're buying a loaf.'

Maisie looked hard into Wilf's face and he turned away. She wondered whether she had been too inquisitive.

'My Zulu business keeps me in touch with what was a dire time, keeps me close to what happened. I can deal with it each day, rather than hiding it away only to have it come out and take me by the throat while I'm shaving or tying up my bootlaces.'

'I understand,' Maisie said.

Wilf led the way to Trongate, having to pause occasionally for a moment to catch his breath. Finally, he extended an arm extravagantly and watched for Maisie's reaction as the Panopticon, with its arched recesses and pale limestone frontage, lit up by slanting sunlight, came into view.

'Here, in all its glory – the Pots and Pans!' he announced.

At the front door was a chimpanzee, standing upright, in a man's clothing. As Wilf and Maisie approached another chimp appeared, followed by a tall, bearded man who was carrying a leather satchel full of sheets of paper she presumed were flyers.

'Murray!' Wilf called to him.

'Morning! We're away to drum up some custom,' Murray shouted, leading the chimpanzees down Trongate.

He took the hand of the smaller chimp and, pretending to be annoyed with the larger one, said: 'Betsy, now where on earth did Solomon leave his bowler hat? No wee treat for him. Now come on you two – keep up!'

Wilf ushered Maisie into the entrance, saying 'They're some of AE's favourites. He claims they've been educated. Bills them as The Missing Links. Solomon's usually better dressed than me.'

The hall itself was deserted. It was far too early for the Panopticon to be open to the public. The smells of the previous night (sweat, smoke, fish, scent, beer) hung in the air.

Maisie detected another smell, something indefinable, but unpleasant. Wilf saw her sniffing and said: 'Animals. There's forty cages full of them down in the basement. Sometimes the whiff is appalling, even up here.'

Wilf explained that the zoo was just one more way that AE kept the Panopticon pulling in audiences in a city where there was intense competition for customers.

'He's often out and about in other halls, weighing up the acts and generally making a nuisance of himself. He's been escorted out before now for disrupting a rival show. There was a barney one night at the King's. He was sitting near the front blowing bubbles while the turns were on. He's a law unto himself!'

Maisie looked round at the empty balcony and the bare benches and imagined it packed with people, and Uncle Wilf in his black wig, with his scrawny physique, trying to tame them with his Zulu monologue.

He had not been a military hero in Zululand but she thought of him now as valiant, indomitable, picturing him on the Panopticon stage, struggling not to cough.

Wilf led the way to the attic space above the balcony. Maisie became child-like as she explored the amusements assembled there – rifle shooting, a coconut shy, fortune-telling machines, observed by dead eyes of wax figures of notables, including the last man in Scotland to be hanged.

'I'll show you where Mr Pickard's putting me, now I've come off the bill,' Wilf said, moving to another, smaller room, and pointing to black curtains round a small stage against a wall.

'I'll be dying here, on cue, three times a day, Maisie. And it will be a proper gun going off, the real McCoy.'

In the centre of the room was a tomb-like bed covered by a tent of semi-opaque net. Above it, fixed to the rail from which material hung like a white tent, was a sign saying:

THE SLEEPING PRINCESS
This young lady rests eternally. She is in a state between life and death, a condition that defies modern science. Warning: Please show respect. Attempting to wake or attract her attention **MAY PROVE FATAL.**

Maisie approached the bed gingerly, almost afraid to peep through the mesh falling down the sides of the bed. When she did, she saw that there was no one there.

'She's not due in until noon,' Wilf said matter-of-factly. 'But she'll be settled in bed well before the doors open. Which reminds me – I must get a move on. I'm a Zulu at two o'clock.'

Wilf had stepped out of the front doors of the Panopticon when he saw AE bustling towards them. He was carrying a newspaper and seemed deep in thought. Wilf bid him good morning and AE recoiled then responded apologetically – 'So sorry – I was somewhere else.' He looked at Maisie and turned to Wilf for her to be introduced.

'My niece,' Wilf said. 'A musician, from London. Maisie.'

'I have a women's orchestra for the hall at the moment. Let me know if you need to earn a crust, young lady.'

Maisie said thank you. She felt shy in the presence of this legendary character whose impression on Wilf had been so marked. She could see that he had charisma and that Wilf was enraptured by the dapper man with the high white collar and the perfectly shaped moustache with its waxed wings drawn into points.

'Actually, it's her father who might be looking for work, Mr Pickard,' Wilf said. 'Wonderful fiddler. Trained. Comedy and virtuoso playing combined. Max Pyle. Been on all the big halls in London.'

'Well, the sign says it all!' Mr Pickard pointed to the billboard at the side of the main entrance: GOOD ACTS WANTED.

He peered intently at Maisie through the oval lenses of his glasses and said: 'You've probably heard how badly the public treat me, young lady. They delight in calling me names. Yesterday I was The Knock-kneed Kipper and this morning I had a letter addressed to The Prince of Paddy's Market. But also in the morning post came a poem that soothed my troubled breast....'

Wilf laughed obligingly with AE, who pulled from his pocket a letter.

'Just look what this kind Glaswegian maiden penned...albeit in the hope of winning a five bob prize from me!'

Maisie took the letter. Wilf looked over her shoulder and they read as AE looked on, puffed up, pleased with himself...

I have been to a Grecian Lyceum
And have wandered thro' Rome's Colosseum
But I ne'er yet have seen
Where'er I have been,
Aught to rival the Pickard's Museum

Wilf folded the paper and was on the verge of saying something complementary but AE's attention had shifted, and he turned to go into the Panopticon.

'I must be away. My golden eagle got out of the zoo last week and she's been spotted. I'm just off in the motor car, accompanied by a few dead mice, to bring her home.'

He called over his shoulder: 'You know, you'd have thought that with all of bonnie Scotland beneath her, the blessed bird would have chosen to drop in to somewhere more salubrious than Alloa...

My journal

February 17

The most exciting day! A letter arrived from Tom. He is happily installed in digs near Sailortown, next to Belfast docks, along with another official who is an assistant to James Larkin, the union leader from Liverpool. Tom says that the mission is to unionise the poor, unskilled workers like labourers and carters who work up to 75 hours a week in bad conditions with no holidays.

I was so proud to hear that he has a role (albeit a small one) in this plan. I noticed that father nodded after reading the letter as if giving silent approval.

Tom worried me by saying that we were not to worry if the dispute boiled over into something nasty – the adversary is a powerful man who owns ships and factories and there are religious conflicts between groups of workers.

Spent much of the day in the company of Uncle Wilf who took me roaming round Glasgow – and acted as if he owned it!

Visited the Panopticon, an intriguing place, part Noah's Ark, part fairground and waxworks, and part zoo – with a music hall at its centre.

We bumped into the sorcerer who formulated this mixture of amusements, AE. He is energetic and has sparkly eyes and his mind flits endlessly hither and thither.

I noticed something intriguing...that Uncle Wilf was at the point of doffing his cap when AE appeared! He had hold of the brim but then corrected himself.

Now Uncle Wilf has never been a cap doffer and so that reflex showed how much admiration he has for the great AE. It also shows that he sees in AE something of himself.

Both are rule-breakers, outsiders, initiators, men who do not give a fig for the approval of others. Both have bats in their respective belfries.

Mother is quite at home in Braid Street, humming away as she reorders Uncle Wilf's kitchen and hints that perhaps it is time for him to remove some of the reminders of Morag.

I suspect Pa is homesick but at least mother is now less sharp with him. She seems dedicated to ensuring that he adjusts (and does not abscond to London).

When I returned from the Panopticon there was violin music coming from the room Pa shares with mother. Perhaps he's preparing to look for solo work. I didn't tell him that Wilf had broached that subject with AE today; it really would have been waving the proverbial red rag to the bull.

Pa is fiercely proud of always having made his own way. He is looking in at a music hall tonight but has not mentioned it to Wilf, and I suspect he was in the city centre this morning weighing up opportunities.

When he gave the Herald a second look this evening he came across a strange advertisement that he pointed out to Wilf. 'I think this must be your man.' (I noted that he said YOUR man, to distance himself.)

I snipped the announcement out. It is yet another teaser by AE, the inventive Kaiser of Candleriggs!

YOUNG lady of 23 years wishes to meet a young gentleman. The lady in question weighs 40 stones 7lbs, has a waist of 83 inches and a bust of 97 inches – apply to Mr Pickard, Trongate.

28

The exiled Max Pyle found himself in dire need of certainties. He felt he was dragging his anchor, drifting with no sign of land. London was behind him, along with the old crowd. Tom had gone. Maisie was loyally supportive but her eyes were on far horizons,

Gertie had mellowed but her pleasure in being on home ground was almost a source of annoyance to him.

It was at times like this, when the hard facts of his existence hit him in the face, that Max opened up the old, velvet-lined fiddle case, the one his father used. He would tune up, without enthusiasm. He would rosin the bow his father used, the pencil-thin bow of Brazilian pernambuco, unsurpassed for flexibility and resistance to warping, and costing half as much as the violin he inherited.

And then he would play. Anything. A mazurka, a waltz, a snatch of some concerto, a popular song of the day decorated with ornamental flourishes to introduce a challenge and to keep the fingers flexing.

Playing did not change circumstances, and he did not expect it to. But when, after half an hour or so, he placed the violin back into the black, scuffed case and stowed the bow safely behind its clamps, he had been reminded that, come what may, the sublime could always be found.

What was fine and pure in life, qualities to be found in music, was always there, waiting to be rediscovered. For Max there was constant solace in the bliss that came from beautiful sound and rhythm bound together by emotion. He had no religion but there was a sanctuary he could go to.

Here, in alien surroundings, with the old life he had known lost without trace, he needed the balm of music more than he ever had.

Max and Gertie had planned a short walk to a cake shop that was a quarter of a mile from Wilf's House. It had been at Max's insistence. Gertie showed no inclination to see how Glasgow was changing, and no curiosity about the places she had known.

They had turned out of Braid Street when Gertie stopped and let out a cry, spinning round, her hands to her mouth, hurrying back towards the house.

Max held her shoulders and guided her to the fireside where

she sat, white-faced and desolate. Max stood beside her, his arm round her shoulders, unsure about what to say.

'I thought it would be better here. I thought I would be over it,' Gertie said.

'We'll find a way of getting you right, you'll see' Max replied, not believing it. He had trusted Horace, a great performer, a marvellous man when it came to matters of the mind, to sort it out.

He'd failed with Gertie and that was a big disappointment, and it made Max wonder whether her collywobbles might be beyond reach, or at least calling for expert treatment.

Wilf had gone out shopping for mutton and vegetables so that Gertie could make a meal. They heard him whistling as he opened the front door. He passed a copy of the Herald to Max, and noticed as he did so that Gertie's eyes were red and that she looked unwell.

Gertie spotted his inquiring glance and said: 'I've just had another turn.'

'On a tram?' Wilf asked.

'No, just walking this time. Wilf – it's getting worse.'

Wilf made a pot of tea and said over his shoulder: 'I don't want to interfere. It's up to you and Max. But I want to see you right, Gert.'

'We all do,' Max said. 'Of course we do.'

'As I see it, there's an option. But it's a matter for you, both of you.'

He poured out the tea and talked as Max scanned the Herald, almost ostentatiously (Wilf took this a signal of non-cooperation, one of Max's little gestures of defiance).

'We have a brand new hospital on our doorstep, Stobhill, and one bit of it is full of doctors who are experts in...'

'No hospitals for me, Wilf!' Gertie said with urgency. 'No. It's just nerves. I have to get a grip somehow, that's all.'

'So there's the hospital, or there's a man you'll have heard of,

Dr Bodie. He's on at the Pots and Pans. I've met him. I'd be happy to pay any expenses whichever one you chose, Gertie. You know very well that Morag would have been more than happy to do that herself.'

'Dr Bodie?' Max said. His smile was derisive. 'Bodie? The bloke in black who looks like Count Dracula? The Electrical Wizard chap who wears a cloak?'

Wilf said: 'He's gifted. A magician who does all sorts of things, hypnotism, healing. But really he's a scientist with a gift for showmanship.'

Gertie said: 'Isn't he the one women throw themselves at. He's been in the newspapers. He seems to have some power over them, and they lose their way.'

Max dredged up a little muck to throw at Dr Bodie.

'Oh yes, a big womaniser. They say he gave his wife a baby and then fathered one with her sister so she didn't feel left out. Been in hot water because he puts MD after his name but isn't really a doctor. There was a big thing in the Comet about him.'

'Misunderstood genius, more like,' Wilf countered. 'I take some convincing but I saw him get a cripple on to the stage, work on him and then saw the laddie jump off, actually jump off and then trot out of the orchestra pit like a spring chicken.'

'He'd have been planted.'

'No, Bodie got the audience to choose who to go up. He didn't choose the invalid.'

'But there's something fishy if a man's always involved in some dispute or other. Wasn't he in court not long ago? Quackery?'

Wilf admitted that Walford Bodie was controversial but he reminded Max that the judge had come down on Bodie's side, telling the jury that doctors tend to be jealous people and that it was high time people stopped calling Dr Bodie a quack.

'You know well enough, Max, if you're ahead of the field, lesser mortals want to stop you.'

'And you saying you think he could cure Gertie?'

'Yes.'

'Well, she's not going near him.'

Gertie said: 'Here you are again, Max, telling me what's good for me. I'll decide. It's my head that needs looking at, not yours.'

'All I'm saying Gert is that if Horace couldn't sort out the problem, nobody can. We thought he'd bottomed it but, next thing, you're squealing like a stuck pig and trying to bolt out of the bally train.'

'That's damned cruel, Max!' Gertie protested. 'I was crying, not squealing.' She dabbed her eyes and looked out of the window.

Max said: 'It's just that I'm at my wit's end, Gert. It's because I care.' Max hated to appear helpless in front of Wilf.

After an uneasy silence, Wilf said: 'Look, I don't know this Horace but I don't think that he ranks with Bodie. The man's a legend. He commands fat fees. Got a big house in Macduff. And I hear he does bits of private stuff.'

'So how much is he going to charge to sort Gertie out?'

'I'd have to see but all I know is that Morag would have wanted it and that she's left enough to make it happen, and more besides.'

There was a sniffle from Gertie. 'And do I have a say in my cure?' she asked a voice laden with hurt.

'Of course Gert. By all means. Sorry, we're running ahead...'

'I'm grateful Wilf but, first, I will not step inside a hospital, and second, I won't have you frittering money on me.'

'But the money's there, and the man has a track record,' said Wilf, becoming exasperated.

'The other thing is, I couldn't let anybody near me with electricity.'

This curbed Wilf's plan. Electricity was Bodie's forte. Only the night before he had leaned back in his famous electric chair, attached to wires, and La Belle Elektra, his assistant, had thrown a switch. The doctor's face had contorted, his back had arched and a dozen light bulbs in his hands lit up. Then he had stood up, large as life, swirled his cloak round his shoulders, and basked in the acclaim from a packed house.

'That's all right, Gert,' Wilf said. 'He doesn't always use electricity. He's got all sorts of other skills. He's mainly a faith healer.'

Max said that he was surprised that Wilf, who was a man of the world, couldn't see through Bodie's showmanship. Wilf replied that it could be that if people had faith, absolute trust, in someone to help them, and believed totally that they had special powers, then that belief became the very cure they needed. All the same, he did think all the claims for Bodie's 'bloodless surgery' were dubious.

Gertie said that she trusted Wilf's view, prompting Max to scowl and look down at his feet. She didn't need surgery, bloodless or otherwise. But she wanted the fear removed so she was no longer a prisoner and a burden. Surely there was nothing to lose by seeing Dr Bodie, except Wilf's money (which he seemed anxious to part with)?

She had seen a photograph of the doctor once in The Performer when he had been given some civic honour and she remembered his eyes. Black. Searching. Devilish, actually, above that moustache drawn out to upward-turning points. Max's comparison with Dracula was not far off but perhaps he meant Svengali, a man with the power to manipulate women.

Remembering those eyes she wasn't at all surprised to hear that women, weak women, melted in his brooding presence.

Since arriving in Glasgow, Gertie had not once mentioned missing London and the old life, so Max did not feel free to voice the emptiness he felt in his new surroundings, nor his curiosity about the life in London he was not longer part of. And so when a letter with a London post-mark arrived he felt an inner quickening – before noticing with dismay that it was addressed to Maisie.

She was out, having set off to find a shop run by suffragists, in Bath Street, and did not return until lunchtime by which time Max, having discarded the Herald, largely unread, was desperately curious to find out who the letter was from and what it said.

Gertie had looked at the envelope and said: 'It's a child's writing. Who an earth do we know with a young child?'

Max handed the letter to Maisie as soon as she had taken off her coat.

'It's from Eli!' she said, chuckling with pleasure, having read a few lines of the meandering script. 'Dear man, he's written straight back to me!'

The letter said that although he was glad that the Pyles were settled, he hoped it would not be too long before they returned to London. Things were not the same. He asked Maisie to promise that if ever she visited London that she would get in touch and said that anyone she was going to give time to with her good works was very lucky.

He asked Maisie to tell her father that Issy Bass, the fiddler, had died. He was found in his room when his landlady smelled something even more unpleasant than usual at the top of the stairs.

Maisie broke off reading to tell Max this. His regret at the news was coupled with relief that when he had been picketing he had not turned the old boy away. The strike seemed such a little matter when compared to the death of a friend of such long standing.

Reading on, she came across the word IMPORTANT, written in capitals and underlined. Beneath it, Eli had written –'Tell Wilf its in The Performer paper that he is a Zulu in Glasgow so he better watch out.'

Before signing off he wrote: 'Inside will tell you what happened to Adney Payne.'

A folded newspaper cutting fell at her feet from the envelope. The heading was The Death And Inquest Of Mr George Adney Payne. While Max and Gertie looked at Eli's letter, she read the newspaper report.

It told how Mr Payne, who had done much in his career with his 'dominating temperament and shrewdness' to turn rough music halls into more palatial places of pleasure, had been trapped beneath the overturned car driven by his wife, Ethel. He had been taken to the Mount Ephrion Hotel, Tunbridge Wells, to recover.

After a few days the doctor judged he was well enough to lie on a couch and have a little poached sole for breakfast.

'It was lovely to see him back to his dear old self,' his widow told the newspaper. But then, she said, he was snatched from her as she held his hand. ('Yet now I still seem to hear his little whistle calling me...' she told the correspondent.).

When questioned at the inquest, the report said, she claimed she had driven thousands of miles and was familiar with the road where the accident had occurred, but a cyclist had come out of a side road.

She said she was travelling at only nine miles an hour because she did not want to churn up dust as she approached churchgoers in the road.

She denied that she was going so fast that she would have hit the group, and that she had turned into a bank to avoid them. She had been sounding her hooter, she asserted.

Maisie read the report in silence until she reached the last paragraph when she snorted contemptuously and alarmed her parents by shouting 'Utter rubbish!'

She had just read the conclusion reached by a local policeman who attended the scene, and who put the cause of the accident down not to the wealthy, well-known and well-connected Ethel Adney Payne's irresponsible driving but to the local cyclist 'losing his nerve'.

My journal

February 18

I am growing used to my small and rather hard truckle bed. It is like trying to sleep on a shelf.

Woke to a glorious bright morning and stepped out into the city centre with Uncle Wilf who was heading to the West End and the baths.

I asked about bathing clothes and he tells me that frequenters of the Turkish Suite are naked but are issued with a wrapping sheet to soak up perspiration in the desert heat as they lie on their reclining chairs like Egyptian mummies.

Today I met a new friend who educated me about the network of suffrage groups here, so I am now in a position to put my shoulder to the wheel once more. There is a growing spirit here.

Nan is the daughter of the woman who cleans out the Panopticon hall (poor lady!) and Wilf has got to know her and mentioned my interests.

She is training to be a teacher but her raging passion is the suffrage cause.

We met by arrangement for a cup of tea, she having told Wilf, via her mother, to say I would recognise her by her red hair and her green melton cloth cloak, if the tea-room happened to be crowded.

As it turned out, we were in stitches before we even said hello because the café was deserted apart from us, and two waitresses!

'Maisie, I presume,' she said, and the ice was broken.

We had finished two pots of tea before there was any mention of suffrage. The Scots call it blethering – and how we blethered!

We walked in the sunshine and blethered some more. I had heard that there was a suffrage campaign centre in Bath Street (it turned out to be the HQ of the militant agitators) but Nan led me instead to Sauchiehall Street where the Women's Freedom League have a tea shop.

There, over slices of cake, we showed our respective suffrage colours. They happened to match! We are both determined, and both angry enough to act but preferring stealth and argument to outrageous acts.

She said she would introduce me to Teresa Billington, one of the League stalwarts and a powerful advocate of passive disobedience.

One character I must meet is Flora Drummond, a formidable woman who was recently locked up in Holloway for popping into 10 Downing Street uninvited. Nan seems really taken with her.

What was immediately appealing about this lady was that she is tiny like me. In fact, Nan says that she had heard that Flora's fiery sense of injustice was ignited by a silly rule about height.

Evidently, she qualified as a postmistress but was told that at five feet and one inch she was an inch below what the rules allowed and could not take up her post. I am not surprised she is hopping mad!

When we parted, Nan mentioned a saying – 'A gude cause maks a strong arm.' It will make a heartening rallying cry in the suffrage fight and I think the Music Hall Warriors proved the truth of it.

There are plans for the first women's suffrage procession in Scotland in the autumn. It promises to be a huge event. Nan will keep me informed, and, as a 'local' says she will try to locate a cycling school in Glasgow.

Coincidentally, on the noticeboard at the WFL teashop was a short obituary of Susan B Anthony, the American champion for emancipation. It seems she once said: 'Cycling has done more for the emancipation of women than anything else in the world.'

29

Max Pyle had polished the new act to his satisfaction. It worked – his instinct told him that – but of course you could never know for certain until you put it before an audience and felt the first wave of laughter coming up at you like a warm breeze.

Some of the old comedy act was in there somewhere but it was all fresher. He knew where the trigger for laughter was; once you knew that, you just had to pull.

Sitting in the bedroom in Braid Street he devised an opening not unlike the one dreamed up for Maisie, with the tuba, a tension builder leading to release and the first laugh.

He would come on with a stool and his fiddle and, looking serious, play a well-known tune, probably There's No Place Like Home, beautifully but with the occasional off-key note. Some would think he was simply a poor musician, others would be intrigued to find out whether he was teasing.

He would go off and come back with a saw, put the fiddle on the stool and make movements as if he was going to saw it in half. Then he would look thoughtful, move the fiddle, sit down and – tucking the saw between his legs – would tease out of it a tender, mellifluous rendering of Ye Banks and Braes o' Bonnie Doon.

Then would come the silly stuff, holding a deadpan face while playing the fiddle behind his neck, and through his legs, making it cry like a baby and wail like a cat on heat.

He would add facial expressions as he made the violin create like a gate on rusty hinges, then use the back of his instrument to bat ping pong balls into the audience. He'd end playing a medley of jigs and reels at full pelt – the Scots and Irish, he knew full well, loved a toe-tapper, so he was sure to go off to applause.

'That sounded so good, Max,' Gertie said as he returned to the kitchen having gone through the act in the bedroom. 'You've never lost it, you know. You really should go on at the Panopticon.' And then she spoiled the compliment: 'Wilf could have a word.'

Max strode out of the house without replying, banging the door behind him. Gertie, who was peeling potatoes, stopped and watched him go.

He strode out, spurred on by burning anger. Loving people were destroying him, killing him with ill-judged kindness and concern. They seemed to want to strip him his self-respect.

When he had covered a few hundred yards he decided to take a tram to Renfield Street. He had liked the look of the Pavilion Theatre there when he passed it the day before, and thought he might ask to speak to the manager.

He pulled at the big brass handles of the front door then stopped and stepped back and let the door close, realising that he hadn't yet decided what to call himself on theatre bills when – if – he was offered work.

Hector McKay was friendly but brisk. He knew of many of the people Max had worked with and had a vague memory of having read good things somewhere about Musical Mayhem.

He was about to sort out the bill for the following week and, he said, there might be an opening. Would Max mind bringing his fiddle and giving him a taste of the turn (just a formality to see where he might go on the bill)?

'So what are you calling yourself nowadays?' Hector asked, showing Max the door.

'Oh, I use my own name because so many people in the game know me,' he said nonchalantly, as if he had never given up his solo act.

'They usually bill me as Max Pyle – A Funny Sort of Fiddler.'

'I like that, Max,' said Hector. 'Tells them exactly what you're about.'

When Max returned to Braid Street, Gertie took two bridies from the oven as he took off his coat, and said: 'Here. Get these down you. I'll make you a hot drink.' She was being contrite, patching things up.

'You know, Max,' she said, filling the kettle at the scullery sink, 'you should stop being so touchy. Wilf only tries to help.'

This reminded Max that the gulf between what he felt, and what Gertie and Wilf perceived as help, was as wide as ever. Talking was a waste of time. He said 'Forget it, Gert.'

He lay out the Herald on the table and ate the bridies while scanning the news, then took his mug of tea to the room he shared with Gertie and had one more run-through of the new act, practicing the facial expressions in the mirror fixed to the front of the wardrobe.

As he was putting the fiddle away, he heard Wilf return having called at the Panopticon that morning, after his relaxation in the Turkish Suite at the Arlington.

He heard Wilf cough and then call out: 'I've talked with him, Gert. He was with two of his harem setting up his electric chair and the other gear for tonight.'

'Harem?' Gertie said, wondering whether she had misheard.

'One was probably his wife Jeannie but I think the other was Isabella, a real beauty, the one he electrocutes, the woman he calls La Belle Electra. But there's so many sisters working for him you can't tell who's who.'

'And?' Gertie said.

'He'll do it. He agreed to give it an hour, here, before the show. No electricity, no gadgets. We'd better take this chance, Gert. He's on in Aberdeen from tomorrow.'

'I feel so bad about this! Is he charging you the earth?' Gertie said.

Max listened particularly intently, keen to hear how much Wilf was willing to cough up for what Max believed was fraud dressed up as therapy.

'Well, Bodie doesn't come cheap wherever he works, and I've agreed to pay for a motor both ways so he's back in time for his first show tonight. I just told him a little bit about your problem and he says he's sure he can help.'

Gertie sighed. She was excited. She had total confidence in Dr Bodie. She had heard about the crutches left outside theatres when the halt and the lame had gone home rejoicing.

'He says that he wants no one, absolutely no one, in the house except you. From what he says, any distraction could wreck the whole thing.'

Wilf looked thoughtful. 'You know what, Gert, he looks different close up and without his black gear. Very normal. I think the tash is dyed, and the eyebrows. But his eyes are like drills. They bore into you.'

Max joined them and said: 'Did I hear that Dracula's dropping in on us? I trust you know what you're dabbling with Gertie?'

'It's my problem, and my head. And it's Wilf's money.'

'I can imagine what old Horace would say...'

'But Horace didn't make me better, Max. This man has cured dozens of people of all sorts of ailments. I'd heard a lot about him. I believe in him. Horace was too much of a family friend. There was no mystery.'

Wilf looked sheepish. Picking up the smell of the hot bridies, he took one from the oven and sat at the table eating it.

'You must have money to burn, Wilf,' Max said sourly. 'There's a very big question mark over Bodie and his miracles. I want Gertie well but it makes me feel bad that you're having to pay through the nose to help my wife all because I...'

'Well, she's my sister, Max, as well as your wife, so she's welcome to it. Money should be used, not hoarded. Yes, Morag was over-careful but she saved up with the idea that someone, some day would get pleasure and security out of her foresight.'

Max retorted: 'Talking about security, I think you should put some by for a bit of protection from some big Glasgow pug if Cecil's brother's paying a visit. It's only a matter of time before you're rumbled by Artie, or the Old Bill.'

Wilf looked philosophical. 'Life has thrown me worse surprises and I'm still here.'

Max's expression softened. He was thinking carefully about his words, trying to find a way to show that he appreciated his brother-in-law's good intentions but without giving ground.

'Look, Wilf. I have to say something. I'm grateful for having a roof over my head but I'm not happy about living rent free. Kind of you, I know, but Gertie will tell you that it eats away at me, not being able to hand a bit of something over. Living here feels like sponging.'

Hearing this, Wilf felt for Max, knowing that he really was troubled over something that really shouldn't bother him; Morag had left the house to him and, as a family, they were simply sharing that loving bequest. And hadn't Max and Gertie always given him a bed?

He moved to shake Max's hand as a gesture of goodwill but Max turned away, perhaps coincidentally, but possibly out of awkwardness.

'Can I speak frankly Max? Can I tell you what I think? You should be using your talent. I'd have given an arm to have what you have.'

'Might have made it difficult to hold the fiddle,' Max responded, with not a trace of humour in his voice.

'You're going to be bored, Max, and you're in danger of wasting yourself, feeling useless. And that's why I've taken a liberty. I know you'll give me an earful but I don't care. And what I'm going to say has nothing to do with rent but...'

He hurried the rest of the sentence: '...the thing is I've had a word with AE and he's happy for you to do your solo stuff for a couple of nights next week.'

Gertie held her breath and Wilf straightened his back, ready to soak up the eruption they knew would surely come but Max responded cordially, looking Wilf in the eyes.

'That's typical of your kindness Wilf. But would you please thank Mr Pickard for the offer and tell him that I'm unavailable as I've been booked by the Pavilion.'

For moment the only sound was the tick of Morag's old pendulum wall clock.

'But do tell him that I might be free for another date at some time.'
'But you never said, Max!' Gertie protested.
'You never asked,' Max replied.

Suddenly, Max felt empowered, more alive. He could only hope now that once Hector had seen a bit of the act, he liked it and booked him.

My journal

February 20

Today mother had some private treatment from Dr Bodie, the famous music hall mystic with powers that nobody seems to be able to explain away. It was like a royal visit. We all had to get out of the house while Dr Bodie, who is very controversial, was there, so I decided to go to a bicycle shop in Argyle Street and then stroll to see Wilf's late afternoon Zulu act upstairs at the Panopticon.

Two dozen people gathered round the little stage as the curtains opened. They were spellbound by Uncle Wilf and by his words as much as by his rather frightening presence.

There were shouts of alarm as 'the Zulu chief' clubbed the coconut 'head,' and screams as the gun went off and Wilf fell down dead. The gunshot was deafening; it echoed throughout the entire building.

After Uncle Wilf had changed, we passed time by having tea, and the conversation turned to cycling.

Out of the blue, uncle said: 'Let me buy you a bicycle, Maisie.'

I said that I couldn't possibly consider it but I felt my heart (and my imagination!) racing. But if uncle even so much as helped me to fund the purchase of a cycle, father's feelings would be terribly hurt.

Pa is no longer the provider and is beholden to Uncle Wilf. This reliance also bothers me, so I have started looking around for a job so that I can save for a cycle.

I sent Uncle Wilf in to one of his coughing fits by making him laugh while reading out from a leaflet I'd picked up at McNair's, the cycle shop. It was an advertisement from The Featherweight Cycle Co. To add interest, the company had listed all the things women bicyclists should not do.

So... once I own a bicycle, evidently I mustn't be a fright, or faint on the road, or wear a man's cap. I mustn't criticise the legs of fellow riders and mustn't wear kid gloves, as silk is the thing now.

When coasting, as a lady I should on no account throw my legs over the handlebars, something Uncle Wilf was particularly amused to learn – 'Not relevant, Maisie – yours wouldn't reach,' he said, setting us off laughing once again.

More serious for me was the injunction not to cultivate a 'bicycle face.' In most weathers I have precisely that – the face but unfortunately not the bicycle to go with it!

PS Things are turning ugly in Belfast. Tom's latest letter described how many thousands of workers are now involved in the struggle that threatens to descend into violence. In just one incident, 1,000 women simply downed tools.

It makes our musical hall strike appear a piffling little thing but I suppose that the scale is not important; it's the principle is the thing.

30

When the famous Dr Bodie called at Braid Street, he was greeted at the door by an agitated Gertie Pyle, wearing her favourite pea-green velveteen dress over a white cotton blouse.

The blouse had a tall and fine embroidered collar, and she had chosen to wear it knowing that by the time Dr Bodie arrived her customary nervous rash would have appeared.

She had her hair piled high and secured with two mock-tortoiseshell combs and a trace of some colouring on her cheeks. She had taken a guilty dab or two of Maisie's lavender perfume.

Dr Bodie was dressed for his Panopticon performance, entirely in black, and as he got out of the car he folded his cloak over his arm.

He was unsmiling, erect and, with his carefully tended black hair and inky moustache, was every bit as saturnine and charismatic as Gertie had expected.

She called from the doorstep to ask the motor driver to return to the house in an hour, and to make absolutely sure he wasn't late ('It is important – this gentleman is performing at the Panopticon this evening.')

She had tucked Dazzle away in a bedroom, remembering Dr Bodie's instruction that there was to be no interruption during his consultation.

When, an hour later, Dr Bodie had left, Wilf was returning from doing his afternoon shows, and Max was heading along Braid Street from the Pavilion, with a spring in his step, having been signed to appear for five nights.

When Max walked in he stopped in his tracks, forgetting to shut the door behind him.

Gertie had the look of someone who had recently taken a strong opiate. She was slumped in Morag's old upholstered chair with the cabriole legs. There were two teacups on the table and biscuit crumbs on a plate.

There was no sign of strong drink yet Gertie's eyes were unfocussed. Her shoulders had dropped; her head lolled back. The tension had gone out of her jowls.

Max had almost forgotten how Gertie used to look when she smiled – not the perfunctory, everyday smile that had become rare enough, but a smile with some joy behind it, the sort of smile that once he would see perhaps ten times a day.

As he put his fiddle case on the table, he saw that the old smile was back. It was as if he was looking at a photograph of Gertie taken in happier times.

'Well?' Max said. 'How was it? You look a bit squiffy. Was it hypnotism?'

Gertie just smiled and sleepily began trying to form a sentence when Max said: 'No electrical stuff was there, Gert?'

Wilf came in at that moment. He drew back his head in surprise. He had expected to find Gertie pottering round the sink, or cooking at the fire. Yet here she was looking as if she had lost the use of her limbs.

Gertie got up and very slowly went towards the sink, took a tea towel and, holding a corner, put it under the running tap then dabbed her face and forehead.

'No. There was no electricity, although as I'm feeling now, I wouldn't have objected. I think this must be how you feel when you've had laudanum. It's a glow.'

Max and Wilf looked at each other and Gertie aimed a broad, sleepy smile at them both.

'Did he give you a tablet or something to make you relax?' Max inquired. 'Or any advice – you know Gert, for if you get...well, edgy again?'

'I think those days are over. I really do, Max. No. We just had a quick cup of tea once I'd come back.'

'Come back?' Max said.

'You know, out of whatever state he put me in.'

'Sounds even better than my Turkish Suite!' Wilf said, going to Gertie's side and patting her arm. 'I'm so happy it worked. You'll be able to get out, tour the city again, and see how it's grown. It'll be a revelation.'

Gertie explained, drowsily, that Dr Bodie had stressed the importance of leaving the house straight away, while the effect of the treatment was fresh and strong. She would take him at his word, she said. When she could get her legs going again, she would pop along to the Buttercup Dairy for some eggs and some lorne sausage – and she would go alone.

She would confound her fears. Dr Bodie had given her the strength. He had even recommended that she revisit Watson Street, scene of the fire that upset her so much. She could still hear his words, intoned in that dark, languorous voice: 'You're quite over all that now, Gertie dear.'

He had left her with a very good idea of what the Devil must be like, what power he would have, if he existed.

Maisie Pyle knew within a minute of being installed behind the counter in Simpsons department store that she would not slip easily into working life.

She simply did not fit; she was, she thought, rather like a fat hand being forced into the slender, brown, leather glove she was about to place into a small wooden drawer marked TAUPE, just one of perhaps 100 drawers in the Ladies' Glove Department above the chaotic traffic of Argyle Street.

Miss McKinnon – skeletal, ramrod straight and twitchy – prided herself on her introductory talk. This morning she treated Maisie to a lecture on the lore of the glove and its pivotal role in the Robert Simpson department store.

Maisie had stood obediently alongside a blushing co-recruit who, barely audibly, had said that her name was Isla, but who had not dared to say anything since.

Miss McKinnon concluded by mentioning some of the things she wouldn't stand for (as in 'I will not stand for stock being placed in the wrong drawers...') before leading the girls to their posts in the department.

Maisie was keen to earn a little money, and knew that she ought to feel grateful that this, her first job, was in a warm and carpeted environment rather than in noise, smoke and filth. But long before Miss McKinnon had given permission for a ten-minute break for the statutory call of nature she had decided that she would not be there at the end of the week to pick up her first pay packet of ten shillings and tuppence for her forty-seven hours of wasted life.

Much as she wanted to work, as most people had to, she could never tolerate for long the darting eyes of Miss McKinnon who loitered vigilantly as Maisie dipped into boxes lined with tissue paper, separating the chamois and the suede gloves from the silk and the lisle, and the multi-buttoned elbow-length theatre gloves from the flimsy nets.

There were no customers so far, and so no distraction from the sorting and the placing of stock in the regimented cabinets. Maisie worked mechanically while Isla, mute and flushed at

Miss McKinnon's side, did her best to show that she found the department pricing system engrossing.

'These, with twenty buttons,' said Miss McKinnon, 'cost 1s 7d. Make sure you do not confuse them with the twelve-button silk ones at 1s 4d. Any loss through error has to be made up. You must get to know your stock.'

She called over to Maisie: 'Did you hear that Miss Pyle? Any error must be made up from wages. We can't stand for incorrect pricing.'

Maisie pretended to be familiarising herself with all the cabinets and drawers but in fact she was mulling over a question in her head.

She was surrounded by hundreds of pairs of beautifully made gloves, in a city where any lady wishing to be regarded as such wore gloves at all times, except when eating or tending to the most personal matters. But – apart from winter use outdoors, what were the gloves for?

It seemed a radical question but she had never heard it asked before. By the time she had looked in most of the cabinets and forgotten what was in them, she had some answers.

Gloves were used ostensibly to keep a lady's hands pale, smooth, and silky (odd, Maisie decided, as there was no danger of them being anything other than that, as rougher, hired hands did the work). But surely they were really used to show, at a glance, a lady's class – no, more than that: They were to guard against physical contact with the lower classes.

They were a barrier against deadly germs left by those who had only a passing acquaintanceship with soap, or who had already succumbed to the pustules and fleabites that indicated their class.

She had followed the controversy raging in father's Herald about the problem of working people wearing soiled clothing being near those in fine attire in tramway cars. She had seen for herself warnings on the Glasgow trams about spitting, and the heavy fines that would follow.

Maisie wondered whether the poor and the consumptive were now becoming a little too much in evidence in this prospering city, where people were mixing as they moved about, and she began to think of gloves as the soft, encasing of hands that had an iron grip on power.

There really was so much to do out there to change things, and it couldn't be done in the prison called Simpson's Ladies' Glove Department.

Maisie walked up to Miss McKinnon and announced with what confidence she could muster: 'I am afraid that I've discovered that I'm unsuited to the work here and I would like to give notice of leaving.'

Miss McKinnon's head retracted and her penetrating raptor's eyes narrowed.

'I wish you had given your suitability some thought, Miss Pyle, before wasting my time and that of the company. You had better visit the office at once.'

Four hundred miles away, in another warm and carpeted place of work, two typists employed by the Board of Trade were collating the documents that would make up the report into the music hall dispute, and its many recommendations.

Misses Tompkins and Leake enjoyed the total trust of their employers and they understood perfectly the burden of confidentiality on their shoulders.

Miss Tomkins was busy putting together the preamble at the front of the adjudication, and Miss Leake, who was the senior of the two, was typing from a hand-written document the section that listed the key findings that would provide a blueprint for peaceful relations in the music hall industry.

Both young ladies felt privileged to be working on something that called for the word STRICTLY CONFIDENTIAL to be typed on the cover page.

There were few frissons of excitement in the life of Board of Trade typists (in fact Miss Leake could not remember one from the past) but today, as her fingers flitted over the keys of the Remington, she was in a state of eagerness and expectation.

Coincidentally, Miss Leake's father was a music hall enthusiast, a twice-a-week man when he was well, and had been for years. He often boasted that he had seen Dan Leno at his funniest – and laughed so much his ribs ached – but regretted that it was long after Dan had done his clog dancing. ('What a maestro! His feet were so fast that, over sixteen bars, he could tap out more beats than a drummer!').

Mr Leake, who came to London from Manchester, loved a bit of clogging. He also had a soft spot for Lottie Collins, and more than once he had swayed with the rest of the audience when she sang Ta-ra-ra-boom-der-ay at the Tivoli.

Better still, late one night as he passed the Coliseum, Yukio Tani, The Great Japanese Wrestler, World Master of Ju-jitsu, stepped out and bowed to him in the street, something he would remember on his death bed.

He sometimes said that the music hall was like the salt on his breakfast egg; life would be a bland affair without it. He felt a sense of loyalty to those who made him laugh and got him singing, and so, when the artistes went on strike, he did the same, and bally well boycotted the halls.

That night, Miss Leake would be having tea at the table, opposite her father, who had been very ill. Just a month before, the doctor had whispered to Mrs Leake outside the kitchen door that her husband was facing what he described as 'a crisis that involved serious risk.'

Mr Leake was stubborn. He promised his family that he would not give in, and he hadn't, outstaying the tenacity of the pain and the bouts of fever, and confounding the doctor. He was a fighter and he admired other fighters.

Over the last days, weak as he seemed, he had become more alert, and yesterday had asked if there was any news of the Askwith report.

'How long does the man need?' he asked. He tapped the side of his nose to show that he was being too inquisitive and said to his daughter 'I don't suppose you're allowed to say in your position which way the wind's blowing...'

Knowing what her father had been through, how could she possibly contain herself and not give him a slight hint – just a vague tip that the Board had come down on the side of the artistes?

As she sat down at the table, she knew she would end up giving him the wink. No details, mind. Just a pointer that soon the union members would have reason to be pleased with themselves. No more than that.

She would remind him to keep 'things' strictly under his belt although there would be barely anything to hide, and anyway Mr Leake was not likely to be mixing socially for a while, much as he pined to be sitting with a pint of beer inside him, hearing the music striking up at the start of a night in some music hall or other.

Miss Leake knew she would feel guilty when she dropped the hint but she was confident that no one from the Board would ever hear of her little breach of confidentiality, and it would give her dear old father such a tonic.

It was a trifling gift but she knew that he would feel privileged, and also take enormous pride in the fact that his daughter had been selected by the Board to be privy to matters of such importance.

It was worth the guilty feeling, and the flutter of fear that was putting her off her tinned pears, to mark her father's fight against overwhelming odds and being there, as he always had been, smiling at her from across the tea table.

'Father,' she started, 'you must keep this under your hat but...'

My journal

March 12

I return to my much-neglected journal, a casualty of my busy life in Glasgow, to report important news: Today I started work. Unfortunately today I also rejoined the legions of unemployed (and that before tea-time!).

No regrets. I am not a shop person. I am not an office person, a ledger person, or a factory person but neither am I work shy, or ashamed. I am just ambitious to do some good.

There's alarming news in Pa's newspaper about the union battle in Belfast that sounds like civil war. The whole thing has been inflamed by the introduction of blacklegs who are living on a ship for their own safety.

Of course it made me anxious about Tom.

Incredibly, within a minute of putting down the Herald, a letter from him arrived! It was as if it had come to me via some telepathic route propelled by my thought of him.

He's in fine fettle, inspired by the spirit of the people around him, and witnessing acts of courage (eg the refusal by a policeman to guard a blackleg engine driver).

He asks after Wilf and seems to need assurance that Ma and Pa are settling here, and remain together. When I write back tonight I say that father is a different man, having landed a few nights at the Pavilion.

Being 'Mr Independent,' he had objected to Uncle Wilf letting it be known to Mr Pickard that he was looking for work.

How fortuitous then that Mr Pickard was in the Pavilion on the second night, out on one of his spying sorties. While watching Pa's act, the penny dropped as to who he was, and he instructed Uncle Wilf to ask father to come for a chat.

I am becoming more involved with suffragist activities and have now been invited to join a committee putting together plans for the great rally planned for Edinburgh in the autumn.

On hearing this, Ma happened to say that perhaps I might like to become a telegraphist some day (a hint that I should be gainfully employed?). I professed interest but see myself working directly for the betterment of people.

To that end, having passed the Home For Deserted Mothers in Renfrew Street a few times, I acted on the spur of the moment and left my name and address, with a message asking how I might be useful. It is a start.

By second post I received a note from Eli who says that the arbitration report on our strike is due out any day. He will be watching the Comet.

This time he signed his letter 'Your ever loyal friend Eli' in his childish hand and I was touched, just as I am sometimes when I think of Uncle Wilf, and of the vulnerability hidden behind the jaunty way he has.

Actually, my dear and dotty uncle is looking a little pinker lately and coughing less now the weather is milder. He puts the improvement down to what he calls 'Turkish Delight' – his mornings of meditation at the baths he belongs to.

He continues to petrify people with his Zulu act and seems to have become a favourite of Mr Pickard. I noted this, and Uncle Wilf agreed that they are similar in their madcap approach to life.

He says that one day AE said: 'Wilfred, I note that we both enjoy a certain healthy disregard for the ordinary. I sometimes believe we are separate cheeks of a common bottom.' (But Mr Pickard had said a---).

Uncle Wilf has promised to let me know if he hears that Les Bicyclettes are due to appear at any of the Glasgow halls. Ma has also asked him when Dr Bodie will be back performing in the city, as she is very keen to see his act. She is planning to write to his house at Macduff to thank him for changing her life.

31

The news that the arbitration recommendations was just about to be released inflamed wounds that had barely had time to heal during the weeks since a truce was called in the music hall dispute.

Yet both sides were at the point of satiation with the whole affair. The process had involved depositions from 100 witnesses and 23 sittings involving the two sides.

Everyone, including the public, simply wanted to know what Mr George Askwith, the tall, thoughtful barrister with an alarmingly full black moustache, had concluded. On the eve of the publication of his report, only Mr Askwith, and a handful of colleagues (including Miss Leake, who had acted as secretary) knew what it contained.

So which side was the winner, now that full time had been reached? Many wondered whether, in fact, there had been a winner.

Long after Askwith's whistle had stopped play, hurtful niggles and petty fouls went on, unseen. Some managers had already inflicted peevish revenge, in the subtlest of ways, on those who had been prominent in the strike, when halls had resumed what appeared to be normal working.

During the strike, the lines of demarcation had sliced through friendships and marred working relationships that had been trouble free for years.

The bitterness went both ways. In the hectic toing and froing of life in the halls, revenge could be served cold, in the recommended manner, with little effort and maximum discomfort.

A conjurer who had not only worked through the strike but had goaded pickets as he left a hall, waving two £1 notes in the faces of pickets, suffered humiliation in front of 600 people after someone (and no one would ever know who) interfered with the specially designed table he used on stage.

At the point in his act when, holding up a dove, he announced that he would turn it into a white feather duster, the duster was not where it should have been but in undergrowth behind the theatre. He was left with an empty hand and catcalls in his ears.

As artistes, musicians and stage workers gossiped excitedly about the prospect of a pay rise, some decided that they needed bloodletting before normality was achieved.

A page had to be torn out before a new chapter could be begun. And that is how one afternoon three young and wild musicians and an aerialist, who had all been appearing for a week at the Assembly Hall, Aylesbury, came to be crammed into a Standard car parked at the end of Mimosa Road, Tring.

The aerialist (whose rich father owned the car) was at the wheel, and the musicians and their brass instruments formed a fleshy mound beside him on the open seat meant for a single passenger.

They disembarked, stretched and groaned, and walked part way down the road, the aerialist checking the house numbers. Then the three musicians began to play, with the aerialist conducting by waving his forefingers.

Inside the semi-detached Elm Villa, an elderly gentleman and his wife were drinking weak tea and enjoying Garibaldi biscuits, as they did each afternoon once the hall clock had struck four, when they were surprised to hear what they took to be a brass band playing.

'Is it not Tuesday, Maud?' the man said. 'The Salvationists never play on Tuesdays do they?'

Maud cocked an ear. 'It's some sort of band. Unless I'm very much mistaken, that's Handel. Badly played but Handel. The Dead March...'

'Ought we to look, Maud...? Even I can hear it, with my ears...'

'No, dear, I don't like it. People shouldn't be playing the Dead March. It's...well, sinister.'

The music grew louder and Maud and her husband looked at one another. They each took a second Garibaldi.

'You can hear it, Maud, can't you dear?'

'Yes, dear,' Maud said. 'How very odd! Disquieting, actually. Perhaps a neighbour has died. It seems to have stopped now. We must remember to tell Blanche at the weekend.'

They nibbled and sipped distractedly, unaware that the

aerialist had brought from the car a can of white paint and a brush and was at that moment writing in large capitals along the front the wall of their house: BONELESS BLACKLEG.

Maud might have been wrong but a few minutes later, as she took away the china cups, she was sure she heard distant singing and laughing above the burble of a motor engine, as if some rowdy young men were out on the razzle.

She worried that perhaps her mind had begun to play tricks. It sometimes happened when you were old.

When dear Blanche came home from performing in Birmingham she would mention it to her, and ask whether she thought it advisable to have her ears checked by Dr Carter.

They were so very lucky. Blanche was the sweetest of daughters and, as well as being blessed with remarkable physical talent, thanks to being double-jointed, she always knew what was for the best.

George Askwith's weighty findings addressing grievances simmering in the music hall profession landed with a fizz rather than a bang in Braid Street.

Max, grumbling to himself as he read the Herald at the window, stood up suddenly, threw the newspaper on to the breakfast pots and demanded: 'Wilf, tell me where I can get a proper bally paper? It looks as if we've damn well won – and what we get in that is a dozen lines.' He gave the Herald another contemptuous look.

'Won?' Wilf said, sticking a patch of paper on to a shaving cut half way up his long, bony neck. 'What have you won, Max?'

'Won?' Gertie shouted from the kitchen where she was happily pumping away at wet clothes with a posser, drawing on new found and seemingly inexhaustible energy.

'The strike,' Max called. 'Askwith's come out on our side. We've got a new basic, and overtime money, and probably God knows what else. But we'll not find out from that,' he said, pointing to the Herald.

Gertie hurried through, beaming and wiping her hands on her pinny. Wilf picked up the newpaper.

The tiny report, headed: Music Hall Warriors Triumph, was equal in length and prominence to a two-paragraph item stating that the 'Scotch Boat' from Derry, carrying cattle and Irish passengers seeking casual work, had been slightly delayed yesterday by bad weather.

It said simply that performers, musicians and stage staff in London had won concessions as a result of their industrial action during the winter, and that it was hoped that a new Board of Trade report, which ran to 32 pages, would now bring peace and prosperity to the music hall industry.

Artistes' terms would be improved, musicians in London receiving a minimum 30 shillings a week and drummers 28 shillings, and there would be changes to the notorious 'barring clause' employers had imposed.

'Short and sweet,' Wilf said. 'But we won, Max! We'll find out soon enough what else is to be changed. Good to know that this Askwith chap wasn't in the pocket of the owners.'

Max refused to celebrate. 'I want meat on the bones. What about the scene shifters, and the call boys? Anything about matinees? And what happened about holiday pay? I want to see it all in black and white.'

Gertie playfully shoved Max on the shoulder and said: 'Come on you old grump, at least enjoy the thought that we got some justice!' He was forced to smile at her.

She busied herself making tea and then went to the cupboard and brought out (and ceremoniously opened) a circular tin containing a Dundee cake.

She had intended it as a peace offering of sorts to Max, and a thank-you to Wilf, and a luxurious treat to mark, in some way, her gratitude for being given the chance of a new start by Dr Bodie. Now it was also a celebration cake.

She only wished Tom had been around to share the moment, and that Maisie had been back from her meeting so she could enjoy the happy news.

Seeing the cake allowed Max's mood to mellow (he adored Dundee cake). It also cheered him to imagine Cecil at his cash desk at the Astoria, combing through the Askwith report and being appalled at how much more of the profit would be going into the pockets of the staff and the artistes.

He would really try to cheer up. He decided that in future he would try not to say anything negative. He would guard his tongue. How good to see Gertie looking so very relaxed and happy, reverently slicing up the cake as if she was dividing up an empire. Another thing; he would try very hard not to goad poor Wilf.

No, he mustn't spoil this triumphant moment. That said, he really did need to go through every word of the report. He knew managements too well. What they said in public and to the union meant little in the dingy corners of the halls; benefits bestowed by Mr Askwith might be (would be, Max knew) countered by little dodges and evasions. If the owners could wriggle out of anything, they would.

He missed Tom. He fell to mulling over changes affecting the halls, and the way syndicates had taken over and how new attractions were being brought in to replace human beings. Tom had a way of viewing the whole picture. He especially wanted him around today, to see how his commitment had been rewarded.

'It's settled. But they'll try to punish us,' Max said, maintaining his smile as he reached for his tea, looking across at Gertie chatting away and handing round wedges of Dundee cake.

With some incredulity, as he took a second wedge of cake, he remembered that actually, he was no longer on the London circuit; he would not witness the outcome of Mr Askwith's new regime for the halls.

His regret was tempered by the knowledge that it
was just a matter of time before he won his own spot on the Panopticon bill, and he had earned it without relying on Wilf to put a word in.

Soon he'd be working for the celebrated Mr Pickard, who was as straight as a poker and really knew the business, and not the shifty Cecil.

My journal

March 15

This has been a day when three wishes that I might have made have come true.

First, I came home to a HAPPY mother and father and the wonderful news of our victory and the improvements Mr Askwith wants to see initiated in the halls.

I thought of Tom first, and then of Eli, our comrades in arms, and all the people I had fought alongside, and was SO happy for them!

Father was ravenous for precise details of the settlement and when I opened a letter from Eli and it contained a cutting of a full report taken from the Comet father could barely wait to take it and study every word.

I am sending the report to Tom who, I'm sure, will be so encouraged. We were stronger in the fight than I had thought; the report says that around 300 artistes and more 200 musicians supported the strike with the backing of 90 stage staff. Warrior heroes all!

Another cause for my happiness is that Ma has been out and about, unaccompanied. Evidently she ventured to the dairy shop on her own and (according to Pa who kept a vigil at the window) she returned looking composed.

Yet another reason why I go to my truckle bed smiling tonight is that Guillaume has written once more!

It is a long and elegantly written letter in a charming version of English.

He says that Les Bicyclettes are indeed coming north and that he would love me to meet his sisters once more and to see them when they appear at the Empire. I will not need to be asked twice.

He signed the letter 'William (Gautier – the goat keeper).' He seems to think that 'Guillaume' might be beyond my linguistic limit!

I will sleep well tonight.

32

Spring had finally shown its nose after a numbing Scottish winter. It nuzzled into the airy space of the Kibble Palace glasshouse, warming plants and people and scattering morning light that was dazzlingly bright after the long grey days.

With typical contrariness, Wilf – breathing in the damp peatiness and the primeval smell from exotic vegetation stirring in the heat, and sitting back on a slatted bench – chose to travel in his head to Antarctica.

The impulse, that led to an image in his mind of endless snowy wastes, had first come to him when he was in the Turkish Suite the day before but he had put it on one side when Tom, and the terrible industrial trouble in Belfast, invaded his thoughts.

He had been bothered about Tom. He was not so much worried for his safety but simply wanted to see him, shake his hand, hold him in a manly way for a moment. He felt a strong bond with the lad, one forged over years, and he knew Tom felt it too. Belfast was not far away but it might as well have been some distant country.

He had also felt his fondness for Maisie growing when he had thought it impossible for him to enjoy her company more. He loved her goodness, her honesty and her selflessness. He had pressed her once more to allow him to buy her a bicycle as she was desperate to have one but again she thought this was over-generous and had worried that her father would have felt shamed that he had not been the one to help her.

In fact, Wilf had a bigger plan.

Maisie had once said that in her ideal future she would be combining good works and campaigning with teaching young women how to ride a bicycle. She had no doubt that she would quickly become a good rider and believed she had what it took to run what would be a small business hiring out bikes and acting as an agent for bicycle sales.

Wilf knew of a building, an old cotton-finishing factory in Anderston, that would be the perfect place for an indoor cycling school. What was now the Saltire Hall had been a mill when there were more than 150 cotton mills around Glasgow. It had then become a cotton-dyeing works, and then a roller skating rink, before the craze died.

Now, Wilf had discovered, it was used as a Highland dance school on two evenings each week and the owner, a businessman from the West End, regretted having installed the expensive maple floor. He received little rent and lived in the hope that roller skating would soon enjoy a revival.

Wilf planned to take Maisie to see the hall, and to tell her that he would like to pay rent for the daytime use of it. She would refuse, he knew, and would hide her bitter disappointment but he would not let the plan go.

Soon he would confront Max about the matter. But now, Antarctica, and the possibilities it might offer, once more filled his consciousness.

The Zulu act was going well. That afternoon there would be another huddle of punters waiting to be drawn into his imaginings, then hanging on his words and finally recoiling in shock at the gunshot (so many children had been traumatised by the bang that a sign had gone up saying: 'WARNING: Cover your wean's ears straight after the coconut execution!').

AE was delighted with the attraction and had not even hinted to Wilf that he wanted it to end but he was a man who thrived on change. Wilf thought it prudent to have a card up his sleeve and to play it before AE started to wonder whether the routine was growing stale.

Wilf hadn't worked it out, certainly not in any detail, but he wondered whether there was a second dramatic act to be contrived from another real-life adventure, an event during the Discovery Expedition. After all, the newspapers had been full of it, and people loved to hear of plucky men risking all to put places on the map, while suffering frostbite, gnawing hunger, scurvy, panic, and snow blindness.

There was something especially poignant, something he had half-remembered, an incident he would look up at the Mitchell Library, concerning the shocking death of a young able seaman, one of the Discovery crew.

How gripping it would be if it was implied in the act that the restless ghost of this young boy, killed at the outset, travelled with the explorers, and was responsible for the many aspects that went tragically awry.

You couldn't really go wrong with the supernatural. Wilf had learned that. When people weren't fleeing in fear from it, they were getting thrills from stepping nearer and nearer to it.

He would give the idea some thought. As he tucked the notion away, to the back of his brain, a possible billing came to him: Ghost of The Great Ice Barrier…

Gertie Pyle was floating through life. She was like an ageing bird discovering that the wings that long ago had shed their worn-out feathers had suddenly re-grown stronger and sleeker than they had been before.

Her trips to the Buttercup Dairy were daily now, and sometimes she contrived a reason to walk there, going just because she could.

Her mood was lighter. She had begun teasing Max, as she used to, deflating him when he became pompous.

She wrote lively letters to Tom and showed a keen interest in Maisie, who was now befriending abandoned mothers and steeping herself even deeper in the suffrage cause.

Although Gertie had vowed never to perform again, Maisie believed she should use the soprano voice she'd been blessed with (a voice that now rang round the house in Braid Street whenever she did the washing).

She learned that the Scottish composer, Sir Hugh Robertson, was starting a prestigious choir in Glasgow, and auditions were being held. Sir Hugh's ambition was for the Orpheus Choir to be a world-beater, the perfect fusion of human sound ('No individual voices will be tolerated,' he had announced). Mother, Maisie, decided, would be an ideal recuit.

Gertie had begun to surprise with her new-found adventurousness, but Max was taken aback when, sitting at the window in Braid Street with the sun illuminating the breakfast table, she announced: 'Tell you what Max. One day soon, let's go doon the watter. Just imagine it, on a day like this! And then in summer let's have a trip to Crail.'

Max nodded approvingly, awed at the transformation that had taken place. Here was a woman who weeks ago would have quivered in fear at the very mention of a tram, or a train, and who would not have dared to walk to the road end, planning a boat trip down the Clyde, and talking of going out in the evenings rehearsing with a choir that would be performing here, there and everywhere, even abroad.

He might have said: 'And it's all thanks to Dr Bodie's medical expertise.' But he didn't. And it wasn't, not in his view. It was down to Dr. Bodie fooling Gertie's mind, persuading it that her fears were groundless – a form of confidence trick.

If he were asked now what was his own greatest fear, it would be that the growing clamour over Bodie would destroy Gertie's unquestioning faith in his powers, and that her brain would twig that it been fooled. Then the demons would return triumphant.

There was a limit to the amount of shielding he could provide to save her being confronted with a new avalanche of public claims that Dr. Bodie was simply a handsome, astute, manipulative charlatan.

Max's first step, as he thought about this over his porridge, was to hide that day's Herald.

It was well known that the Medical Defence Union had challenged Bodie over his claim to have earned the initials MD he put after his name, and when he retorted that his only sin was to have failed to add 'USA' after the letters, it was discovered – as the Herald was reporting – that he had bought his 'degree' from a dentist in Bradford.

Even Wilf, a Bodie advocate, had begun to voice doubts, now that the newspapers were digging deeper into Bodie's background.

The day before, when Gertie was out buying morning rolls from the baker's van, Wilf had hurriedly described to Max (before she came back) how medical students in the city were rallying to wage war on Bodie. Hundreds had become involved.

'They're upset because while they have to put four years of work in get a medical degree, he gave himself an MD. You can't blame them. He didn't endear himself to them when he told the papers that it stood for Merry Devil.'

Max resisted the urge to remind Wilf that he had been a Bodie disciple. But Wilf had now recanted, admitting that he, too, was bothered about the effect on the debunking would have on Gertie. She seemed fixated on the man, constantly asking where Bodie was appearing next, saying that she must go to see him perform, and talk with him afterwards to tell him how well she'd been.

Bodie had his defenders. There were those who protested that he was gentle and kind. Yes, he was the biggest earner on the entertainment circuit but he had done healing secretly and for no fee.

What convinced Max that Bodie was more devil than saint was his cynicism. In yesterday's Herald, Bodie was explaining that, like everyone, he had to make a living and he had found that there was not much money in edifying people but lots in terrifying them.

What neither Wilf nor Max knew at that moment was that an Austrian medical student called Philip Figdor had vowed to ruin Bodie, to yank him down from his pedestal. He would show the world that this recipient of the Freedom of London, this idol who was being aped by talented performers like young Charles Chaplin in London, this miracle worker, had feet of clay.

He would persuade his fellow Glasgow University students that Bodie was an enemy of medicine.

It would be war.

They would invade his shows. Their weapons would be rotten food and flying eggs, and their battle cry, which would ring round the halls, would be: 'Bodie, Bodie, Bodie – Quack, Quack, Quack.'

My journal

March 16

Pa is really making an impression on Glasgow. The manager at the Pavilion says he is welcome to go back on the bill any time. Mr Pickard has booked him to do his solo act for a week, saying that with talent his, he would always be welcome, onstage or in the orchestra.

I had met Uncle Wilf by arrangement this morning outside the Arlington from which he emerged pink and damp-haired.

I returned to Braid Street, Pa went out after lunch, and then Uncle Wilf left for the Pots and Pans. Mother asked me to stay for a chat.

She said that Uncle Wilf had just explained that he was willing to help with my bicycling ambitions and was very keen to buy lessons for me and help to set up some sort of part-time bicycling school.

I was embarrassed as I hadn't revealed to Ma or Pa that Uncle Wilf had that morning taken me to an old hall that would be perfect for lady learner riders. I was almost shaking with excitement when I saw the hall with its beautiful floor.

Pa had been most put out, she said, raising objections but Ma had told him that he could hardly stop Uncle Wilf if he wanted to be generous. Who was Pa to tell Uncle Wilf how to spend his own money?

They had fallen out but mother said she would resolve the matter once father had simmered down. My dream teeters on a cliff edge...

Ma seems to have heard some news about Dr Bodie being in bother (not the first time I understand!). He is an enigma, hailed by those he has helped, reviled by the rest of the world.

Her faith is unshaken. She is convinced that the good doctor is indeed good, and in touch with forces that we mortals cannot reach (he is also startlingly handsome, although Ma did not mention this).

You know, Maisie, mother said, it's the same old story – if someone is unique, lesser mortals will do their best to bring them down and destroy them.

'Just look what they did to Jesus,' she said, as serious as you like. I must say, until that moment I had not thought of the famed Electrical Wizard of Macduff in the same terms as God's son!

33

Isa was on Towel Duty at the Arlington and Tina was on Sheets. But as usual, they were having a quick cup of tea in their little side-room before their morning shift in the Turkish Suite.

It was a ritual they both enjoyed greatly, after escaping from their cramped, noisy homes and children for the peace, order and warmth of the swimming baths.

They were chatting about their favourite regular, a comical chap called Wilf. Tina would often enjoy a joke with him when she handed him his sheet, and Isa would have a quick whispered word as she went round collecting towels before putting them down the chute leading to the basement laundry.

In between, one or the other would mop round tiles surrounding the central fountain and would smile Wilf's way if he had his eyes open. As often or not he was lying on his back looking at the colours of the ceiling.

His feet overlapped the bottom of the reclining chair and his long, thin body was encased in the sheet. One day Tina remarked to Isa that Wilf looked like a big, white puddin'.

Isa replied that when the members were all lying there in their white sheets, on their reclining chairs, they reminded her of babies – 'Swaddled weans at the hospital, left there for years and never collected by their mammies,' she said. They threw their heads back and laughed at this and dipped into the biscuit box.

The two Arlington ladies liked Wilf because he was informal and friendly and had asked them to address him as Wilf (the Arlington had its share of West End toffs who expected staff to be servile, as their servants were). They also warmed to him because he was on the stage at the Pots and Pans. Entertainers were glamorous.

'He lost his wife, poor man, so he did. Did you ken, Tina?'

'Aye. Poorly for years. Mind, he looks a bit pasty himself some days. But maybe it's they teeth. Did you see, they're whiter than they bloody tiles.'

Tina took two more ginger biscuits. They nibbled and sipped and watched the clock on the wall. Five minutes more, and they would check the temperature, open up, and drop their voices as if they were in church.

The laundered sheets were already piled up by the door.

'He hails frae Crail, Tina. He told me. Him and his sister.'

'Aye, Crail. Wi' the bonny wee harbour. We once went there. Lovely wee seaside. There's something different aboot Crail. You'll get the odd hoos wi' steps goin' up the roof. My faither used tae say it's a kind of hoos frae somewhere...'

'Frae Holland, Tina. I think Fife people copied it frae Holland.'

'That reminds me, Isa. Did ye hear aboot the man who asked another man if he'd ever been abroad, and he said: "No, I havenae, but I once kent a man who'd been tae Crail." Ma daddy told me that one.'

Isa did not see the joke but smiled anyway.

Wilf was first member in the Turkish Suite that morning and

immediately began teasing Tina, who was pink-cheeked, chubby, and prematurely aged, asking why on earth she wasn't on at the Panopticon as an exotic dancer.

She'd giggled like a girl. 'Och, I would be, Wilf, but I dinna ken what exotic is! And anyway I canna get oot at night because of my six wee jailers!'

She wasn't surprised to know Wilf was in entertainment, he was such a charmer. He talked freely but there was one thing they hadn't asked him: What had happened to his toes? Tina said that one day she'd broach the matter. It was intriguing; they looked as if they'd been nibbled by something while they were sticking out of his sheet.

Wilf settled in his favourite chair alongside the fountain, turned onto on his back and let the heat of the room take all the tension out of his muscles. The process was almost as quick as flicking an electric switch, instant relaxation he had learned to achieve at will.

If only he could do the same with his mind. If anything, lying limp and gazing at the coloured glass lozenges above him seemed to activate rather than damp down his imagination.

This morning it was not long before he was in Antarctica, picturing the little, bad-tempered Scott party scanning the ice for seals to eat, and – back at their beleaguered ship – finding the starving dogs eating each other. He had read about it all at the Mitchell.

He wondered whether, with the right props (surely AE would know where to get ice axes, furs and a couple of penguins?) he could work up this idea of the ghost of young Charles Bonner who'd died as the Discovery sailed from New Zealand. He liked the notion of tragedy putting a curse on the rest of expedition, damning it by causing the bad blood in the crew, and the ship to become iced in.

He simply couldn't get over the irony of it: The boy cheerfully climbing to the top of the mainmast to wave back to people seeing the ship off, and plummeting to his death. Bonnie Charlie's gone 'awa; a poor, doomed innocent, like the Zulu boy.

Having decided that there really was an act to be created from all this, Wilf tried to disengage his mind – and, he thought, to this end what better mental image could there be to invite sleep in this tropical heat than virgin snow and pale ice receding to the blue horizon, and sublime silence?

There was something deeply satisfying, something ancient, about feeling secure and warm when all around you was numbingly cold and frightening. By holding in his head his picture of icy emptiness, Wilf was able to drift into sleep.

He normally spent an hour lying in the Turkish Suite before heading back to Braid Street, and then going on the Panopticon. So when Wilf was still there after an hour and half, Tina went to whisper in his ear that it was nearly noon, and to say that perhaps he ought to be stirring.

She came back immediately to the little side room where Isa was stacking fresh towels.

Isa saw that her mouth was open but no sound was coming out. She believed her friend was having a stroke, and said: 'Tina! Talk to me!'

Tina's eyes widened, and she said very quietly: 'Isa. It's Wilf. His lips are awfie blue. I think he's deid.'

34

Gertie Pyle had never been given to touching. She kept a barrier between her inner feelings and the outer show of them. She had even been sparing with her physical affection with Maisie and Tom when they were babies. She had often wondered whether she was unnatural, not a proper mother.

Of course she would have fought to the death to protect them but somehow fought the urge to cup their faces in her hands, to hug them spontaneously for no other reason than they were delicious, and precious.

But the night the man from the Arlington came with the news was different. The barrier was breached. Max had opened the door and taken the serious-looking stranger facing him to be a policeman asking to see Wilf about the Cecil affair.

Gertie hurried to Max's side, looking over his shoulder.

The man held his hat at his chest at the door, like an apologetic peasant having to explain himself, and a few solemn words came out of the grey face.

It was only after Gertie had fainted and Max had revived her with a damp flannel that she began to take in what the man had said (he had started 'I am very sad to tell you that...' and for a moment or two choked on his words).

Maisie arrived home at very moment of her mother's realisation and, when just yards from the front door, heard a long, unearthly howl coming from a house. She wondered for a moment whether her mother had been scalded, and her paced quickened. Then, seeing the stranger, she was hit by a dizzying fear that something had happened to Tom in Belfast.

Agonising seconds passed before Maisie gathered with a seismic shock that there had been a death, and it was her uncle's and not Tom's. Understanding of what happened was accompanied by her mother's wild and urgent cry – 'Ma puir Wilf!'

Maisie stopped mid-stride and froze. She looked ahead blankly and disbelieving as her mother was hauled to her feet, then, draping herself helplessly over her father's supportive shoulder, was eased away to their bed. Howl following howl.

Gertie threw herself face down in the pillow to muffle her cries, and Maisie, gasping with grief, first stooped to reach out to her mother and then fell on the bed beside her.

Their arms encircled each other and they sobbed together while Max paced about the bedroom, his hands locked in front of him, impotent in the presence of such agony of loss.

Gertie and Maisie clung to each other and when, half an hour later, wails of grief and anger had subsided, and Gertie and Maisie – red-faced and red-eyed – stood up, slowly and heavily, they held hands, wondering what to do next. Even in the pain of grief, Maisie noted with a start that her hand was in her mother's, and wondered when, in childhood, that had last happened.

'I need to see him,' Gertie said, hoarsely. 'And so do I,' Maisie said. Max put out his hands and touched both heads, as if granting a benediction. 'I'll find out where...' he told them in the gentlest tone he could summon.

He tried to put aside his own feelings for the moment, but was surprised to feel the prickling in his eyes. He would have to get a telegram to Tom, and to tell Mr Pickard. There was so much to think about. He wished he could take back words he regretted saying.

Next morning, Mr Pickard called at the house, shaking Max's hand at the door, and then going to his car and returning with a canvas bag.

'His Zulu stuff,' AE said. 'Max. I've met some people, and I've seen a bit. But I've never met another Wilfred. I'm here if there's anything I can do.'

When Max went in with the bag, Maisie – whose tearfulness had been replaced by a dour silence lasting hours – began to weep once more. For a moment, in her head, she was curled up at Wilf's feet and he was weaving a tale of Africa, laughing and waving the knobkerrie.

Gertie emerged in her nightclothes like a white-faced sleepwalker and, seeing the bag at Max's feet, knew immediately what was in it and, without speaking, returned to the purdah of her bedroom.

Later that day, Max made some tea and as Maisie and Gertie sat at the table as still as statues, Tom strode in, smartly-suited and suddenly a man. His face was expectant. His eyes swept the three faces – his mother's, his father's and Maisie's. Who should he comfort first?

He hurried over to Maisie and enclosed her head in his hands. Gertie looked on, hungry to be enfolded but knowing that Tom would not be able to accomplish this simple act of pity without self-consciousness, and that she could not yield to it without embarrassment.

He grasped Max's hand and said: 'Father.'

Max had arranged with the undertaker for Wilf's body to be brought to the house next day and for the funeral to take place two days later.

Maisie was strengthened enough by Tom's presence to help their father make arrangements for the funeral.

She dreaded attending the event, the prospect of all the blackness, the finality, the plumes on the horses, the rattling wheels of the bier, the top hats, the deathly march of the undertaker's men – ceremony that Wilf would have disdained with a wheezy chuckle.

She had been overruled by both her mother and by the undertaker but if she had been allowed her way, she would have been true to Wilf, and there would not have been any of this dry-as-dust pomp, this soulless bit of theatre.

She would have had a jaunty band following the horses, playing Ta-ra-ra-boom-der-ay, instead of the tolling church bells. There would have been big hats, enormous and outrageously florid, and Wilf's Panopticon friends would have come dressed for the stage. The horses would have been brightly beribboned and worn ostrich feather top-knots in the most vivid colours.

The inevitable moment of finality (the moment Maisie was shrinking from, the throwing down into the grave of flowers, the wild ones she would have chosen) would have been followed by a party, a jamboree of joy and laughter, not suffocating, sanctimonious small-talk over tea and ham sandwiches.

In the end, it was as exactly she had dreaded it would be,

and precisely what Wilf would have abhorred – a bleak, barren affair among cold pews and hymn sheets that contained words of comfort that did not do their job. It was a respectable disposal (respectable was the word for it) but it allowed not the faintest glimmer of the man who was Uncle Wilf to light up the proceedings.

My journal

August 26

It is painful to come back to the journal after the many weeks that have passed because the last entry marked the worst moment of my life, one that I can never erase. Dear Uncle Wilf never really leaves my side. The shock is no less shocking even now, and the torment of loss returns each day, at some point, a deep-seated abscess that flares and that lies too deep for surgery.

It's only in the last few weeks that I have realised how Uncle Wilf changed us all, when for years we had been trying to change him!

Mother plunged into self-imposed silence for two weeks after the funeral. She was unreachable, and father grew angry that he was no comfort to her.

I have never seen him cry but one evening he was near it when, as he sat with mother, she rebuffed his rather rough-and-ready attempts at offering solace.

The day after the dreadful funeral I went to the People's Palace where, there is a glass-topped funnel in a wall through which bees pass to and fro to the hive inside the building. I believe is is an educational aid for children.

I took ribbon, and, without revealing my plans, arrived alone as the sun was setting and fixed the ribbons to the funnel, and whispered to the bees that my uncle had passed away, and urged them to carry the news far and wide.

I had a sense of uncle's presence, a smiling approval at my shoulder. Silly? Perhaps. But I do not care a fig.

The sudden blow of Uncle Wilf's death led to other bolts arriving from the blue, for mother, father and myself, when we met Mr Ritchie, his solicitor, at his office in Renfrew Street.

He had asked for tea to be brought for us to his large desk and, with a deep file before him, started by saying that naturally, when Uncle Wilf had been told by the doctor that he was dying, he had sought advice and had made plans.

At this, mother gasped and was steadied by father who reached over to her from his chair. Of course, we had not the faintest idea that Uncle Wilf knew he was dying. Mr Ritchie was appalled that inadvertently he had been cruelly indiscreet with us but knowing it made sense of Uncle Wilf's preoccupations just before died.

I remembered how he had seemed intent on settling an arrangement over the hall for the cycling school, and how he had kept asking about Tom, and inquiring when he might come and visit Glasgow.

Mr Ritchie was mortified that we had been unaware of Uncle Wilf's situation.

'But did he not say? I am ashamed that you have learned of the situation in this way.'

He lowered his face like a penitent schoolboy while I sat there, astonished at my uncle's bravery and touched by his thoughts for my future.

We learned that his consumption was advanced, and complicated by another chest ailment that he might have contracted in Africa.

I'm sure he had decided that mother would suffer less if kept in ignorance.

Then came another shock, and more evidence, if any were needed, of Uncle Wilf's thoughtfulness.

Mr Ritchie, holding up uncle's will, explained that the Braid Street house had been left jointly to mother and father, and not just to his sister.

Mr Ritchie said to mother: 'Your brother was anxious to help you and your husband to stay together, whatever problems might arise, geographical or otherwise. He saw joint ownership not so much as denying you, Mrs Pyle, but a step towards your future security as a couple.'

There were sums of money for Tom and me, with a message for us, lodged with Mr Ritchie, saying enigmatically: 'For a richer life.' I fancy Uncle Wilf was not thinking of monetary wealth.

However, the money is quite enough for me to buy the best bicycle available in Glasgow and to pay rent for a hall for a bicycle school, and perhaps even enough for me to invest in bicycles for the use of paying pupils.

35

Max and Gertie had become less combative and more comfortable as the autumn approached, They had stumbled on the old, worn path of their marriage after being lost in a thicket that made them prickly with each other.

Financial security, Gertie's new-found confidence in travelling and Max's satisfaction in being his own boss as a part-time violin teacher, had combined to give them a feeling of stability and calm.

They rediscovered the ordinary joy of banter; now any conflict between them was jovial, whimsy having replaced the hurtful bluntness that had begun to characterise their daily exchanges.

Whenever Gertie shed a tear about Wilf, Max would offer silent sympathy. All the resentment he had felt about Wilf had ebbed away, to be replaced by a nostalgic fondness, rueful amusement over their silly rivalry.

But just as Max and Gertie Pyle fell into comfortable co-existence, there was a difference of opinion that soured their goodwill for each other, and left Max with a slight feeling of betrayal.

Max and Maisie continued worry that Gertie's improved health might one day be reversed, without warning. Max remained convinced that Dr Bodie's 'cure' was illusory. Maisie agreed that if ever she lost faith in Dr Bodie's integrity, she might relapse. 'Ma believes he can do no wrong. It's almost like worship,' Maisie wrote in a letter to Tom.

'You know,' Max said to Maisie one day, when Gertie was out shopping, 'I picture your Ma as someone believing they can fly, and doing all right at it for a bit until they notice that they've not got any wings.'

They both knew that the Bodie controversy would continue to gain strnth. There had been more revelations about him after the riots that had involved 1,000 students had gone on record as the worst in Scottish history, and there was talk of protests in England.

Few agreed with Bodie's ludicrous claim that he was the most remarkable man on earth but many maintained that he was advancing science. Where else could the public see the insides of an audience member but on Dr Bodie's X-ray machine?

Even the public hangman, who had attended a show before the riots, and subjected himself to the doctor's Electric Chair (albeit at half power), had attested that Bodie had found a far more efficient way of executing people than the rope.

※

With Gertie out of the house, Max read to Maisie from the Herald about a second student riot, this time in London, where Dr Bodie had an outlet dispensing his Electrical Dentrifrice, Electric Liniment, and his Electric Life Pills. An effigy of Bodie had been burned, and police had been assaulted.

Max said: 'It seems the poor Laird of Macduff is now in such a state of shock that he had now decided to retire to the tranquillity of Banffshire and write books.'

In mid-sentence he turned and saw that Gertie was back, and it was clear she had heard what he said.

'Yes, they're still hounding him, Max, and they'll keep at it until he's dead.' Her voice was even, controlled.

Max was flustered. Gertie said: 'It's all right. I know you both think that he's a fraud. The important thing is that I don't, and I am living proof of his power. Well, look at me, am I better?'

Neither answered. Both felt chastened. Gertie made tea. When they were sitting down together, Gertie said: 'I'll admit it now. I had my own doubts. Just a little while ago I had a panic on a tram and got off at the next stop. Couldn't stop shaking. Wondered whether my troubles were back.'

'Why the hell didn't you say, Gert?' Max demanded to know.

'And what could you have done, Max? The only person who could help was Dr Bodie. So I went to see him.'

'You did what?' Max said.

'He was on at the Colosseum so I sent a note in advance and asked if I might have a minute with him when he came off. After choir practice. He didn't reply but I turned up, and he asked them to let me into his dressing room, and he has put me right.'

'You mean you paid for him to talk to you?'

'There was no fee. He isn't as greedy as people say. He said he just needed to refresh what he had done last time, and that I would never need him again.'

'How can he say that? He's failed once!' Max snapped. 'He locked the dressing room and put me in a trance, or whatever, like last time. I was wonky for a while but I was walking on air when I went for the last tram. The fear was gone. Gone completely.'

'But for how long?' Max said. He wanted to protest that Gertie had been devious but did not want to argue in front of Maisie. However, that night, in bed, he said that he was hurt that she could not have mentioned her need to see Bodie.

She replied that he was right but that he was a doubter, and Maisie was a doubter – and that if she herself had lost faith in Dr Bodie she would have fallen once more into the despair that had driven her to him in the first place.

'I understand, I suppose,' Max said guardedly, and put his arm round Gertie.

Gertie decided that she would let matters lie. She would not tell Max that Dr Bodie, who had been kindness itself, had said that she should not hesitate to get in touch if her troubles returned but promised that this would not happen. This time he had managed to eradicate the last traces of her psychic malignancy.

Max eased into sleep, picturing a plump woman rising like a balloon from a park bench, defying gravity but only until the moment when she looked behind and realised, to her horror, that she had no wings.

Gertie dreamed of being in Dr Bodie's big chair in his dressing room and, as he requested, looking into his the piercing black eyes, and losing herself completely until she came round, barely able to stand up, and heard him saying that everything was all right.

My journal

September 3

Tom and I have begun to exchange treasured memories of Uncle Wilf. I let mother read his letters and, inevitably, the tears flow.

In his last note there was a newspaper cutting, from the Belfast Newsletter, a photograph of the notorious union leader Jim Larkin.

He was flanked by his fellow union officers and on the edge of the picture, unnamed in the caption, was a very serious-looking Tom. Uncle Wilf would have teased him about the company he keeps nowadays!

Mother talks of Wilf endlessly but continues to gain in confidence after her little lapse and travels on her own each week to the Orpheus Choir rehearsals.

She has even expressed a preference for trams over horse drawn transport! She has also begun to take Dazzle for morning walks.

I have even persuaded her to join our huge suffrage demonstration in Edinburgh this month.

I laughed when she finally agreed to support this demonstration of women's independence because she had felt it necessary to ask: 'I don't see why not, do you Max?'

Father seems so much more settled and when he is not performing has begun to give violin lessons. Mother is greatly enjoying the visits of his students; they are mothered for a moment or two before tuition begins and as they leave.

I notice father is using the tutor books that he himself learned from as a child.

He paid a brief visit to London, on the pretext that he needed a few items we had stored with Eli. I took this as a welcome indication that he is in Glasgow for the duration.

He found that Haim's fish shop is now a bagel bakery, under new management. Eli, whose mother died, seems less burdened by his responsibilities. Artie is in jail. There is no news of Cecil but the Astoria is showing more moving pictures and providing less live entertainment ('The way of the world, I'm sorry to say,' father grumbled. 'It's all changing.').

When Pa discovered that Houtmann's, where he hoped to buy sausages as souvenirs for us, had shut to make way for another Underground station, I believe he lost all faith in his old stamping ground!

My ambitions have not been dented by all that has happened to us recently but as I told Guillaume in a letter inquiring about their tour venues, I really am anxious now to get on a bicycle and become expert at riding. I will do my good work on two wheels!

Yvette wrote to say that after Edinburgh, Les Bicyclettes are coming to Glasgow. She says that Guillaume would be very happy to visit Saltire Hall with me and advise about the cycling school.

A letter followed from Guillaume. He once more congratulates the family on our part in the strike ('Bravo a tout!') and says that if I would like it, during the week-long Glasgow run, he would set aside time each morning to help me choose a bicycle and to teach me to ride.

As I wait, I re-live that heart-stopping moment, back in London, at the Palace, when Yvette showed me how to ride by holding the back of the saddle as I wobbled along the aisle of the empty theatre.

I recall exactly the sheer exhilaration as Guillaume then scorched me down the slope, shouting encouragement ('Maisie maintenant returnez!').

It is a well-known fact that many women will not even try to ride bicycles because they dread the indignity involved in toppling while in public view.

How considerate that Guillaume has this in mind! He asks me to explore some out-of-the-way local lanes, free of people and traffic, where we might go to practise.

After what I have faced over the past months, including the cruel loss of someone dear, I will not be intimidated by the prospect of a mere tumble from a bicycle. Dear Uncle Wilf's career was a lesson in tenacity and I am learning it.

Guillaume solemnly pledges, in his delightfully formal way, that by the end of the week, and before winter sets in, I shall be expert enough to teach others.

'Maisie – please trust me to launch you safely on your voyage of discovery,' he writes.

He chooses his words well. I feel that this year I have grown up very quickly, and learned who I am and what I want, and that, yes – I am quite ready to embark on a great voyage.

How better to start out than on a bicycle, and with my own tutor?